A Bittersweet Murder

A Bittersweet Murder

A Hart of Texas Murder Mystery

Kaz Delaney

TULE
PUBLISHING

Dedication

For my lovely husband Robert – for your endless patience, love, and support.

Chapter One

I T WAS A funeral for two. One body, one mourner.

Some things are made for two; they're comfortable—even desirable. Things like: tea for two. A tango. A tandem bicycle ride. A cuddle at a drive-in movie.

Funerals aren't one of those things. Funerals are a celebration of life, a time for mutual comfort and support; a time for shared memories.

Generally.

The funeral of Miss Alice Auchinschloss was obviously the exception to that rule. And let me say, being the only graveside mourner leaves a chill inside that would take a whole lot more than a warm spring Texas morning to alleviate. Especially if that wasn't what you were expecting.

I knew because that's what I felt as I stood there alone that Friday morning, bidding my last goodbye to Miss Alice. Shock—and pain for her—had made my prayers for her safe passing more fervent. Well, at least when I wasn't thinking dark thoughts about the people of her hometown. The ones who'd all found something more important to do that morning than giving an elderly lady a respectful send-off.

It was true that Miss Alice hadn't been the most pleasant woman I'd ever met, nor the easiest client I'd cared for, but did that warrant their behavior? I felt I'd gotten to know her in the course of my work as a daily in-home companion, and yes, she was crotchety, but she was eighty-five years old, and I'd actually become quite fond of her. As weeks had turned into months that rapier tongue had lost some of its edge, and I put her initial mood down to the fact she'd just had enough of a life that hadn't been as kind as it could have been.

And in my opinion that was a poor reason to ignore an old lady on her final day on earth.

She was the last of two family lines, and had been for some time. So I hadn't expected any family to come to her funeral, but I'd hoped that some of the townspeople would see it in their hearts to send her off. But they hadn't and so I'd stood alone next to Reverend Peatree, while the grave-diggers lowered her coffin into the family plot under the branches of a sprawling oak tree.

I shivered as the sod hit the hardwood coffin, the sound echoing around a dark cavity that was as cold and empty as the chairs circling the grave.

The morning had challenged every assumption and belief I'd held about small-town life. Even though I was a relative newcomer to Texas having moved from Oklahoma, I thought I had a good idea of what it would be like to live in a small community like Airlie Falls. Blame it on all those cozy mystery stories I'd devoured, but when they'd described neighbors who cared for each other in a place where everybody helped everybody else—I'd fallen for it.

Sure, some of them murdered each other—but for the most part they knew you and you knew them and community trust meant no one locked their doors.

Which, come to think of it, was probably why they were easy to murder—but that was another point completely.

What's more, I'd craved this small-town life. Not the murdering part of course—but that sense of inclusion; of being an integral part of something. And I'd read enough cozy mystery books to consider that I knew these places as well as the people who lived in these magical towns.

Well, so much for believing what you read in books because from what I could see all those authors had got it wrong. Airlie Falls in North Central Texas was nothing like that.

Maybe the good pastor had guessed it would be like this. Miss Alice had, surprisingly—and shockingly in one sense— left instructions that I should organize her funeral. Or more to the point, simply see to it that her wishes were carried out. She'd chosen the readings, prayers, and hymns. She'd not mentioned anything about serving refreshments, and as a love of baking had been one of the things we'd bonded over, I'd offered some options to the pastor. In response, he'd looked at me in an odd way, and then quickly told me not to worry, that his wife, Miz Peatree, would arrange something at the church hall.

Yet that morning when I'd arrived at the manse a few minutes early with two sour cream and peach cakes and a plate of candy bar cookies, Pippa Peatree had been really awkward about it. And as far as I could see, as I peeked over her shoulder, no other preparations had been made. That had surprised me. The Peatrees had seemed like good community people—just as I would have expected from the spiritual leaders of a small rural town. But even they didn't seem to care about Miss Alice's final farewell.

From what I could see it was obvious some kind of celebration was taking place, but that didn't include any platters of food or preparations for a wake.

Of course, the puzzle was solved forty minutes later when I instructed the embarrassed minister to begin the service. A service for two—the deceased and her one mourner. And, I imagined, a whole flurry of family ghosts who held the family secrets. Because—*and maybe I'd just read too many books*—it was starting to appear to me that surely there was more to this situation than an uncaring community.

Afterward I thanked the pastor for the service—an impersonal mash of generic, haltingly delivered words—and taped hymns. And I was sincere. I could hardly blame him for not knowing her when I didn't really know her all that well myself—nor the facts behind the day's strange outcome.

But it still rankled that someone who'd lived such a long life—someone who'd surely left a substantial footprint on this world—should slip out so unnoticed. There must have been family stories. Adventures she'd had? The roles she'd played in the community where she'd lived her whole life? Her interactions in that community before she became too old and unwell to take a further role?

But there'd been none of that; no one to speak for her or tell those stories. And as I walked away, I knew no more about Miss Alice Auchinschloss than I'd known four and a half months ago when I was hired to be her daytime companion and caregiver.

The cemetery was quiet as I headed back to my car—save for the peaceful drone of local bees ransacking a grouping of huckleberry bushes, and the distant chug of a tractor going about its work. It might be early in the season but spring had well and truly rolled into town. Spring blossoms had arrived in an explosion of color and the air was fragrant, and warm against my face and arms. Had I not been swamped in misery and confusion, I would have found such peace in this setting.

That was another thing that made me sad. This pretty little town was a place that I would have happily called home; it had everything I had ever dreamed of. Quaint little stores, a town green, clean air and sunshine, and room to grow your own produce. A place where crafts and *homemade* were appreciated, and to prove it, there was a twice-monthly thriving Craft and Farmer's Market that pulled interest from far and wide. Of course I'd assumed this came wrapped in all the hometown warmth of a Norman Rockwell painting. But now I knew how wrong I'd been.

I was almost at my destination when another vehicle crunched onto the gravel driveway and pulled up right beside mine in the otherwise empty parking lot. An older man— maybe in his mid seventies, balding and a bit paunchy— stepped out and looked over toward me. He was neatly dressed in a pale suit, white shirt, and a bolo tie held by a huge silver and turquoise slide. I paused. Had he come to say goodbye to Alice? My heart lifted a little as he pulled on a white Stetson and took determined strides to reach me.

His right hand reached me first. The left tipped the hat he'd just donned before dropping it back into position. "Miss Hart? Rosie Hart?"

I took his hand, and noted it didn't have the work-roughened feel of a farmer's, despite his well-worn boots. "Yes, that's right. Have you come to pay your respects to Miss Alice? I'm afraid the funeral is over but her resting place is just over near that old oak tree."

"Well," he said pushing that hat further back on his forehead. "That's partly why I'm here. I'd intended to get here earlier but I had a derned flat tire, and it cost me time. I expect it all went to plan? Ol' Alice seemed to have it all laid out as she wanted it to be."

His voice carried that rough cigar rumble and I found it oddly comforting in a grandfatherly way. Nodding, I said, "Yes it did. And you are... I mean are you a relative? Oh no wait, I'm sorry. Miss Alice told me she didn't have any relatives so you must be a friend?"

"'Scuse my manners, young lady. My name is Hank Henderson, and I can't rightly say I was Miss Alice's friend, but I was certainly her lawyer."

My heart sank. "Oh."

His brow morphed into a mock frown. "You look disappointed. We lawyers aren't all that bad you know." There was a twinkle in his eye, and I could see kindness there that sat well with the rest of the image.

I sighed. "I'm sorry. I guess I was just hoping that some friends might have dropped by."

For a moment, he said nothing. Just stared at me. Finally he said, "I can see you didn't know all of Alice's instructions for today. It was in the local paper, and of course the town gossip machine spread it to all corners of Airlie Falls but I guess that news wouldn't have gotten to you. You see," he said, choosing his words carefully, "Alice left a note with me to be delivered to the town paper, to be published when her time came. It was a notification of her death with the categorical instructions that no one from the town or surrounds was welcome at her funeral." He cleared his throat. "I shouldn't be admitting this, but I edited it a mite. She did go on to express her explicit—and unsavory— feelings about several of the townspeople and her general dislike of all of them. I removed that part. It didn't seem to serve any good purpose to hurt people unnecessarily. They're good people; they tried but she shunned them at every turn."

"Oh." It was the second time this man had rocked me off course this morning. Words wouldn't come, which was odd because my head was reeling. Could I owe Airlie Falls an apology? Maybe I'd misjudged them... Perhaps the towns-folk hadn't been as uncaring of one of their elderly members as I'd thought. Had it been the other way around? But she was an old lady. A lonely old lady. Why would she harbor such venom? Why even bother? Why expend that much energy? Unless it was what fueled her? Kept her going? But why? So many questions, but I seemed unable to make any of them into coherent, utterable sentences.

Hank Henderson took my arm and led me to a bench under another sprawling tree that, in its present state, my crazed mind couldn't even identify. "Seems like you've had a bit of a shock. I'm sorry, Miss Hart, I figured you'd worked her out by now. Alice was a troubled lady. I tried to get her help many times, but that ornery old bat—'scuse me—would chase them off with her daddy's rifle. That thing was so old everyone was terrified of it blowing up in her face as much as her being able to actually hit anything."

"I don't understand. I'm not sure why you'd even want to help her if she was so difficult..."

He fiddled with that hat again. "Well, it's no secret and you're bound to hear it sometime, but I was sweet on Miss Alice's younger sister. Marion and I wanted to get married and have a family. Alice was older than Marion and their parents were elderly and needed care. And that derned Alice, she had such a guilt hold over poor Marion. Every time Marion got the courage, Alice'd somehow make her feel guilty for leaving her, and Marion would beg me to be patient a while longer. It should have worked itself out after the old folks passed, but still Alice manipulated Marion with guilt. This time it was for thinking about leaving her while they were still grieving. It always seemed to be something. Some reason… That went on for thirty years. I reckon in the end, Marion died of a broken heart. They called it cancer but I believe it came because she was so broken up. So torn between the people she loved."

"That's so sad! So you looked out for Alice because of Marion?"

He shrugged, his shoulders still powerful beneath his suit. "I might not have liked the old bat, in fact, I think I might have hated her, but I knew Marion would want to know someone was looking out for her. As much as Alice'd allow anyway. I gotta say I was surprised when she chose me to be her lawyer in the end. The family had dealt with some firm over in Dallas for years, but maybe she just figured I was closer, bein' I'm the only lawyer in these parts."

"Still, it's so romantic that you would come today for the woman you loved."

After sharing such a personal story, I wasn't prepared for him to suddenly look embarrassed. "Well not exactly. In part yes. But also in part I'm here in an official capacity. I'm here to hand over the keys of Alice's property and to talk you through a few things." He took a lumpy envelope from his breast pocket and handed it to me. "Miss Hart, Rosie Hart? Miss Alice Auchinschloss has named you her sole heir. You inherited everything. The farm, all her belongings—and a substantial bank balance."

I blinked. And blinked again. My head struggled to comprehend. Surely I'd misheard. Only one thing was certain: Hank Henderson had gone and done it a third time—I was completely speechless.

SOMEHOW HE GOT me to understand. No, not understand, but to at least hear him. And also agree to his suggestion for him to drive me to the property. That was a no-brainer because I was shaking so much there was no way I'd be safe on a road—even in a small farm town like Airlie Falls. I only vaguely remembered the trip. The pretty bluebonnets, so profuse even this early, were for once lost on me. Maybe I waved to Reverend Peatree's wife returning to the vestry. Maybe I wondered about the peach cakes, hoping she could make use of them. Though how my brain even remembered them is a mystery. Everything felt upside down and I had an inkling I knew how the other Alice felt. The one who fell down the rabbit hole...

The events of the morning to that point gathered in my

mind like unrelated ragged fragments; a backdrop to the star attraction filling the rest of my head. Alice Auchinschloss had made me her heir. It made no sense. I hardly knew her, relatively speaking. I probably should have been grateful; excited. But I was numb.

Turning into the driveway of the farmhouse I'd come to know well didn't help. This was Miss Alice's house. It always would be. It was inconceivable that I should be the owner. It felt wrong.

Hank said there were things we had to discuss, things he had to show me. I didn't argue. I'd been practically living there for the best part of five months but my focus had been on Miss Alice. Not on the extent of the house or the land.

Still, I hadn't expected any major surprises when we arrived a few minutes later. But as soon as we pushed open the unlatched kitchen door I knew this was my day, not just for surprises, but for shocks as well.

"Holy mo…"

I could only guess at what Hank was going to say but I suspected I agreed with him. "Wh… what?" My hands flew to my mouth and my first instinct was to jump back; to close the door and run.

Not Hank. Eyes wide, he wordlessly moved into the room, carefully sidestepping the scattered debris that cluttered the entire floor. The silence was eerie. No tick of a clock. No thrum of the old refrigerator. That silence somehow made the mayhem around us even more treacherous;

more terrifying.

Drawers and cupboards had been opened and contents thrown around the room. Dishes, flatware, and utensils joined foodstuffs and papers. The beautiful hand-painted German flour canister that had belonged to Alice's grand-mother lay smashed, its contents forming a thick white carpet that stretched across the vast room. So many times I'd baked for Miss Alice, admired and handled that canister with care. My heart lurched. Like the canister, many of the broken pieces of china had been handed down through generations. Not antiques but representing years of family history. My hands were shaking as I bent to pick up a pretty, flowered pie dish.

Too late I wondered if we should even be in there and the piece almost slipped from my fingers. "What if...?"

Hank turned, and for the first time I realized how pale he'd become. When he spoke I was worried by the tremor in his voice, then quickly comprehended it was anger, not fear or stress. "It's okay. They're gone. Whoever it was—they're not here."

He moved further into the house, and I followed. Every room over two floors of the large house had been vandalized, and yet the levels of destruction weren't uniform; some rooms were worse than others. Weirdly, that calmed me. Something I couldn't quite put my finger on had bothered me from the start, and while it still evaded me, the vague notion it had triggered became clear as I moved through the rooms.

It was a crazy thought, but it seemed that in some rooms, the focus had been more specific; more deliberate. And that's when it hit me—that strange as it seemed—some areas almost looked staged. Like the kitchen.

"Hank, did Alice have anything that someone would need to find?"

"What do you mean? You think someone was looking for something?" He shook his head. "This has been kids, Rosie. Stupid, bored kids! Out-of-towners looking for some cheap fun!"

I didn't agree. "I know this must be hard on you. This was Marion's home... But there's something wrong here, Hank." I paused to let this sink in. "It seems like maybe someone was looking for something specific."

He shook his head. "Ridiculous. What could she have? And why wait until now?" His response made sense, yet as he turned away I saw something in his face. Maybe the shadow of a long-lost memory? Or maybe I was just being fanciful...

I decided I was being fanciful when he spoke again and there was only purpose in his voice. "We need to get the police here. I'll call the Sheriff to warn him to be on the lookout for any strangers in town. Groups of kids who don't belong."

It was pointless to argue, and I also had to accept the fact that he might be right and I could be way off base. He knew this town. Evidence this very day had already proven that I didn't.

"I'm not sure how long this will take," he continued, taking a glance at his watch. "I have another appointment later this morning. Would you be up to drivin' if I get you back to your car? That way I could even drop in to see Sheriff Kinnead in person and get an idea of when he might get out here to take a look at this mess so I can swing back."

I agreed and after he took my cell number, we parted company twenty minutes later.

I THOUGHT I'D been in tense situations in my former career in finance, but this morning proved there was tense—and then there was tense.

That thought brought me up short. *Lordy*—how my life had changed. I'd second-guessed my decision to walk away from that position with the brokerage company so many times. Especially when there was no good reason other than the fact that I'd simply fallen out of love with it—and in truth, questioned whether I'd ever really loved it in the first place.

At times that decision had felt irresponsible and that didn't sit well at all. It hovered too closely to how I viewed my parents and I had never wanted to make the same choices they had. Yet, at other times it felt like I was being true to myself; like I was giving myself time to find what it was that made my heart sing. To do something I loved, and not just settle for something I happened to be good at.

Signing on with the Home Care Agency, which provided companionship and *very general* care for the elderly or infirm, was supposed to fill a gap while I found that magical *thing*. But it had proved to be more.

And now, despite still feeling uncomfortable about Miss Alice's generosity, I couldn't help but think this was where I was meant to be—that there'd been a reason.

More worrying this morning, however, was the prickly little feeling in the pit of my stomach there was more to come. That my true reason for being here wasn't yet fulfilled.

Or perhaps the strange events of this day were playing with my head.

That rationale should have been an easy sell, but for some unfathomable reason, I wasn't buying.

These thoughts had occupied the time I'd taken to get back to the farm, and I'd almost reached the turn into *my* driveway when I slowed. A truck was parked furtively behind an overgrown bush and a guy was darting in and out of some bushes a little further up the road. I placed him as being right in front of Alice's—my—farmhouse. Was it significant? After this morning everything seemed significant.

Taking only a second to consider my options, I pulled in behind the truck. Every instinct told me to get the registration details and get the hell out of Dodge, but a lonely voice argued that if he got away, then any answers I needed would get away right along with him.

Funeral attire, including my now seldom-worn black stilettos, was not the preferred choice for sleuthing. That was something I worked out in less time than it took me to trip for the second time and almost lose my balance on the rough ground. And also that untended bushes and a mass of long, unruly curls don't help either. The only good thing was that the focus required somehow chased away my swirling tummy issues.

Though, by the time I'd sneaked up on the culprit, I figured I resembled a walking scarecrow. Perhaps a scarecrow in mourning.

"You don't need to sneak. It's okay to just come on up and ask what you need to know."

He hadn't even turned around and my shoulders slumped, grieving the wrecked state of my best mourning outfit for nothing. All for nothing. This black pencil skirt had cost me a fortune but now it had the addition of tiny pulled threads that dangled like party decorations. Ruined.

"You knew I was here?"

He turned then and I only just stopped myself from gawking like an impressionable teenager. He was roughly my age, late twenties, early thirties. That deep raspy timbre of his voice had tricked me into thinking he was older but that wasn't the only surprise. His shoulders were broad and he didn't need the cowboy hat to add to his impressive height. Shaggy, sandy-colored hair peeked out from under the hat and fell down over sun-browned skin and skimmed the collar of his denim work shirt. But it was his eyes that held me. Blue-gray. Intense and shrewd. Intelligent.

And at that moment narrowed in on me. "You were making more noise than a herd of buffalo. Why'd you come sneakin' up anyway? I'm just trying to keep this here sign from doing someone an injury."

My head tried to catch up. "Sign?"

He sighed and pointed upward. Until a half hour ago there'd been a rickety sign that arched over the entrance to Alice's driveway. AUCHINSCHLOSS FARM. I'd driven under that sign every day and not given it a thought. Now I saw the rusted metal had worn through and broken away leaving sharp jagged edges that could be fatal in the right circumstance. *Was it significant that it fell this very day?*

"It's been a potential hazard for years and it finally gave way. Lucky I was coming along and saw it fall just before I got here. I've dragged it inside the gate out of harm's way and now I'm just trying to get the rest of it down before it falls, too."

The long-handled implement in his hand was coated in mud and dirt, obviously well used, but neither of those disguised the sharp-tooled edge.

I shuddered to think what damage it could do. "Why are you doing this?"

"Pardon me?" His look was incredulous. Like I'd just asked if it was acceptable to eat beef in Texas. "*Why am I doing this?*" He shook his head. "Not from around here are you?"

"Well," I began, a bit defensive now, "I guess that's obvious."

"No offense meant," he explained. "It's just that this is the way we do things around here. We see a problem—we jump in and help out. It's no big deal. It's just the neighborly thing to do."

Shame filled me. "I'm sorry. That was a stupid question and I need to thank you. If that had come down as I was driving under it, I guess I could be in a mess. What can I do to help?"

I saw so many questions in his eyes, but to his credit he simply glanced over my clothing and smiled, and right then I saw something else—the cheekiness in those eyes. He was one cheeky cowboy. "That's a mighty fine offer, but I think I can take it from here. I'm nearly done." And with that he attacked the remainder of the sign and brought it down with a thundering crash.

Unable to stand and watch him do all the work, I kicked off my heels and grabbed some of the smaller pieces, dragging them away from the driveway and behind the fence and overgrown bushes that lined the property.

He didn't protest or take over. He just worked beside me, his only deference to my smaller stature and female state was that he always managed to grab the big pieces first. I appreciated that respect.

When we were done, I wiped my hands down over my skirt and held out my hand. "I'm Rosie Hart. And again, I need to thank you."

He tipped his hat, just as Hank had done, and smiled. "Jonah Fencott and you're welcome. Are you looking out for this place now that Miss Alice has passed?" A shadow fell over his face as he mentioned her name.

Awkwardness and confusion burned through me. It seemed wrong to somehow say I owned it now—and yet, this was a small town. Probably half of them knew already and the other half would know by sundown. Face burning, I lifted my chin and looked him straight in the eye. "As unlikely as it seems, Miss Alice has bequeathed her property to me. I guess... I guess it's mine now."

To give him his due, he didn't look shocked or suspicious. "So, does that mean you might become a resident of Airlie Falls, Miss Rosie Hart?" The words were pitched low and for no feasible reason my pulse started fluttering faster than the wings of those blue monarch butterflies my gran had been so fascinated with.

I blamed it on the topsy-turvy morning and, again, my face burned—not a frequent occurrence for someone with olive skin. But there he'd gone and done it twice. What was it with Airlie Falls men and their ability to knock me off-center?

"Oh um... well, I'm not sure. It's been such a shock and I've barely had time to comprehend it all... I guess... I mean, I don't know."

Desperate to brush away this awkwardness I hadn't felt since I was a teenager, I grasped on to my inbred southern hospitality like a lifeline. "I'm babbling. I…" I shook my head to clear it. "Please, let me at least give you a cold drink to make up for all that work. I'm not sure what's there but at least we can get water."

He grinned. "Water's fine. Nectar of the gods."

We walked side by side along the long, rutted track that led to the house. Every step making me more aware of just how much maintenance was long overdue on this place. The chat though, was easy; nothing scary or uncomfortable. I learned he was a builder and he owned a building and renovating business; proud of his crew—they were good honest men. I learned he was Airlie Falls born and bred. And proud of that, too. He lived in a farmhouse not far from Alice's and ran a small herd. That he had one brother Ben who was interning at a big Austin hospital. And that, like his brother, he was unattached. I was so absorbed in our conversation that we'd almost reached the kitchen door when I suddenly remembered the state of the house.

I felt the blood drain from my face as I turned to him. "Oh no! I can't offer you anything! How could I have forgotten? Oh my! I'm such an idiot. It was the very reason I was checking up on you!"

Jonah's brows furrowed. "Whoa. Back up there, darlin'. What's happening? Why can't you give me a drink and why were you checking on me?"

They weren't really questions but more of a repetition of my blurted ravings. Like someone trying to make sense of the insensible. But it was more somehow. After the crazy morning his simple concern was almost too much. I hadn't cried all morning. But now a lump rose to fill my throat; cut off my words. In the end it was easier to just show him and I pushed open the door and waved him inside.

He didn't apologize for his expletives and in all honesty, I wasn't sure he even knew he'd uttered them. He was gone mere minutes and then he was back, took one look at me and grasped both my hands in his, rubbing warmth back into them. It was only then I realized how much I was shaking. Yes, it had all caught up to me. All of it. All too much of it.

We might have talked, and I would have loved to hear his opinion, but the roar of another truck moving into the yard caught our attention. A dusty white truck with a faded County Sheriff logo on the driver and passenger doors.

And as the driver stepped out, the set of his chin and wary look in his dark eyes as they zoomed in on me warned me that the surprises—or shocks—for this day hadn't quite finished. Not yet...

Chapter Two

INSTINCTIVELY I MOVED away from Jonah and straightened my back. I returned the other man's steady gaze, ready for whatever was to come. Or so I thought.

He was about retirement age, I figured, and looked like he'd had a good life. Thick gray hair curled around his ears, and his weathered complexion was accentuated by the web of lines that came from advancing years and spending too long in the sun. Interestingly there was no malice in those eyes, just plain speculation. Like every other man in rural Texas, he donned his Stetson as he made his way across the path to reach us. Unlike every other man, he wore the tan uniform of law enforcement, complete with the required leather boots.

He flicked a quick, curious glance to my left and nodded. "Jonah."

"Sheriff Kinnead," Jonah answered. "I guess you've come out because of this mess. Terrible thing. Senseless."

The Sheriff's mouth twisted into an exaggerated kissing pose. "I'll take a look, but I have more unpleasant business first with Miss Hart here."

I stepped forward, my hand outstretched. "Nice to meet you, Sheriff Kinnead. I'm Rosie Hart."

He didn't shake my hand, but his silent perusal of the yard—at least as much as he could see through the overgrowth—somehow took the sting out of his rebuff. I knew he hadn't missed it, but it could seem that he simply hadn't seen my hand waiting to meet his. It was the first time I started to get a prickling feeling that I really wasn't going to like what he had to say.

"My sources tell me you've been takin' care of Miss Alice for the past several months, Miss Hart. Is that correct?"

I nodded. "More than four months. Close to five. I was her companion more than anything. She had cancer and while she was still able to care for herself in most ways, I was employed to be with her to make sure she was okay through the day. Get her meals, ensure she took her medication in the correct doses—old people get confused." I took a breath. "Then I'd read to her, settle her when she was tired. Do her shopping, laundry, ensure the house ran smoothly. All those things."

The Sheriff adjusted the belt over his portly belly and straightened his uniform shirt. "Do you mind tellin' me how you came to get this job?"

I frowned, wondering where this was going. "Through an agency. I was in finance—that's my degree—but I was in need of a change. A friend was doing this work and suggested it as a stopgap. I found I liked it and decided to stick it out for a while until I decided what I wanted to do."

Beside me, Jonah cleared his throat. "Where's all this going, Sheriff?"

It was a question I wanted the answer to as well.

The Sheriff ignored him other than shooting across a warning glance. "Miss Hart, you say Miss Alice had cancer. Did the doctor give her a prognosis? Like did he say how long she was liable to last in her condition?"

Concern prickled up my spine. These questions were really making me uneasy. "We expected her to last a bit longer in truth, but the doctor assured me it happens like that sometimes. She seemed to be doing okay. She had pain but she was handling it. She was still able to keep food down on most days. She had a degree of independence still. That's why I was only employed to be here during the day. I'd often offered to stay over but Miss Alice was adamant that I only stayed for the hours I was contracted." I paused to draw breath. "I suspected it was a money issue and I assured her it was okay, that I didn't mind not being paid. It wasn't like I had anyone to get back home to. And it was a long drive into Dallas every day. It could have served us both, but she wouldn't hear of it." I paused, aware I was babbling again. But yet more words poured forth, like I had no control. "Sheriff, why are you asking all these questions? Is there a problem with the death certificate or something? I called your people as soon as I came in and found her passed."

He forged on, ignoring my question. "Do you have any

medical training, Miss Hart?"

Again Jonah tried to interject. "Sheriff…?"

"I'm just doin' my job, Jonah. I don't like putting people on the spot any more than you do." He turned back to me. "Now, Miss Hart?"

I sighed. "Just a first aid certificate. That's all that's required for this position." Heart thundering, I looked him squarely in the eye. "Maybe Mister Fencott—Jonah—doesn't have the right to know the facts, and I appreciate that, but I think I have full rights to know why you're asking these questions, Sheriff Kinnead. I'm not arguing about answering them, but I have a right to know why you're asking."

His head dropped forward onto his chest, then came back up accompanied by a sigh. "Miss Hart, it grieves me to say this, but the ME was a bit concerned about something in the appearance of Miss Alice and ran some tests. In fact there was a bit of a mix-up in releasing the body so soon because, Miss Hart, it appears that Alice Auchinschloss didn't die from the cancer. She was poisoned."

My hand rose to my throat and I suddenly felt like my legs wouldn't hold me. "Wha… Who…" I shook my head but nothing cleared. Reaching out I groped for the wall and found the solid body of Jonah Fencott instead. He didn't move away, just stood there offering an arm for more support and allowed me to steady myself. "But that's impossible. Nobody ever came to see her and I prepared her meals myself. I always stayed to make sure she ate her dinner. It makes no sense that she was poisoned. It's impossible!"

His silence and steady gaze brought my raving to a halt and it was only after enduring that for a few moments that I realized what I'd done. I'd just implicated myself. I'd just admitted I was the only one who could have poisoned Alice Auchinschloss.

Once more I felt the blood drain from my face. "Sheriff Kinnead, I know how that sounds, but I didn't poison Miss Alice! I had no reason to…"

But even as I uttered those words, I knew that wasn't true either. I had a huge reason to poison my charge. *A house, property—and substantial bank balance.* Only I didn't know about that until this morning. I closed my eyes, hoping to gain some control. "The will. That darned will. Honestly, Sheriff Kinnead, I didn't know about that until this morning. Please, please—ask Mister Henderson."

The Sheriff was still frowning. "Unfortunately, Miss Hart, that doesn't prove the old lady didn't tell you herself."

Jonah inserted himself between the Sheriff and me. "Okay, time out. Look, I know I'm butting right in here, and I have no right. But it seems to me that things aren't going quite as they should. Sheriff, are you charging Rosie? And, Rosie? I don't think you should say anything else until you get yourself a lawyer. That's the sensible advice isn't it, Frank?"

Jonah's eyes burned into the Sheriff's who backed down

from the implied challenge, sighed again, and nodded. "Yes, that's good advice. And no, I'm not charging you, Miss Hart. But it's fair to warn you that you are a person of interest in this case and I can't enforce it, but it would be in your best interest to stay in town and be available for further questions."

"Stay here? But I've told you everything..." Probably *too much* my head was yelling silently. He didn't answer, just stared steadily back at me. And that was my answer. No compromise. This was crazy. It couldn't be happening. My whole life I'd been a rule-follower. I didn't take chances; didn't break laws. I would never have even contemplated this horrid thing. But of course, no one here knew me. No one knew I was that boring little person whose only adventures were in her dreams. I sighed and scrambled for something, anything to help me.

The house. The ransacking. It was the proverbial light-bulb moment.

"Will you at least look at the damage to the house?" I pleaded. "Maybe that will help you to see that someone may have had it in for Miss Alice. It seems like whoever did this was looking for something."

His brows rose. "Hank Henderson seems to think it was wayward kids."

I suddenly knew what it felt like to be hanging over a ledge and feel your fingers start to slip... "I know, but it seemed to me like some of these rooms were staged. Like the person was trying to cover up what was simply a search for something specific."

This time his sigh was one of someone trying to maintain their patience. "And what might Miss Alice have had that someone only now wanted? Seems to me they've had a lot of opportunity to find what they wanted before this."

It was a good argument but I still didn't buy it. "Please would you just look? Maybe take some photos?"

The Sheriff nodded and moved to the house. I stayed outside with Jonah, my stomach churning, my heart thundering—and wondering at the serendipity of this man being here when I needed someone by my side. At the serendipity of that old sign finally giving way when it had. The man didn't know me and yet he'd stood up for me. It was humbling.

I knew it meant nothing more than ensuring the property sign was safe for the community, just as he'd done this morning—it was just what the people of Airlie Falls did—they looked out for each other. I was learning that maybe my ideas about small-town life were right after all. That was comforting. And to think, the dream I'd held for so long to be a part of such a community could possibly have become a reality. Except that I'd probably be in jail instead. And something told me that was an entirely different small community.

His voice—Jonah's voice—reached down through my helpless meanderings. "Buck up now. They'll find this was a big mistake and it'll all be good. Frank Kinnead is professional and I know he can come across like a stubborn ol' bull, but he's a good cop. Fair. He won't let you be charged unless he's got absolute irrefutable proof of your guilt. And he won't find it because it isn't there."

I turned to him, wonder evident in my voice. "How can you sound so sure? And how do you know that about me? You don't even know me. For all you know, I might be guilty."

He shrugged. "Okay. Did you do it?"

"No! Of course I didn't."

Another shrug. "Then there won't be any proof."

I shook my head. "You truly believe me? Just like that?"

At his nod, tears filled my eyes. I couldn't remember a time when someone had had such faith in me; when someone had my back like that. My parents had decided early on that they were destined for far greater things than parenthood—which basically translated to it being too hard—and left me with my grandmother who, while not deliberately unkind, had her own interests. It hadn't been ideal, but watching my parents' nomadic existence from afar convinced me they'd done me a favor.

And this guy was backing me based on... Nothing? My word? It was almost too crazy to contemplate.

Still, I'd need to be careful. Sometimes when something looks too good—it's just that. And of course, I didn't need a psychology degree to see that I was vulnerable right then—or to understand why I was so enthralled with small towns. They represented the family I'd never had. And apart from a few friends—this was the first time I'd ever experienced that kind of blind faith.

His arm curled around my shoulders briefly in a way that didn't make me feel uncomfortable. "It's okay, kiddo. I got a good feeling about you. We'll make it work out."

Sheriff Kinnead chose that moment to reappear, that ever-present frown in place. "I've taken some shots as you asked and I can see why you think it looked staged. But I'm not yet convinced. If you can find me a reason for someone to be searching Miss Alice's house and belongings then maybe that would help." He tipped his hat. "Bye now to both of you."

He turned to make for his truck. "Sheriff?" I called softly. He turned. "Thank you. Thank you for at least giving me the benefit of the doubt."

For long moments he said nothing, just stared at the rough ground. Finally he looked up again and graced me with that steady stare. "You're not out of the woods by a long shot, Miss Hart. I can't lie. It's not looking good and it's probably going to get even worse. I hope not. And if, as we hope, we find that you're innocent, then we as a town will try to make up for this rocky start to joining our community. Stay close for now."

With that he again tipped his hat and left.

There was no way I could stop the tears that rolled down

my cheeks as I watched him drive away. What a day. There probably wasn't a single emotion I hadn't experienced and it was barely midday.

Jonah was moving restlessly beside me. "Rosie, do you have somewhere you can stay? I mean," he said jerking his head toward the house, "I don't suggest you stay in there."

I nodded to show I understood. "No, nowhere. I really don't know anyone around here. Miss Alice didn't have visitors so apart from a bit of shopping, I didn't get to see or meet people. And most times it was easier to shop in Dallas and bring it out with me. I guess I'll find an inn or something. Is there a motel in Airlie Falls?"

He eyed my outfit again. "Do you have a change of clothes?"

Again I nodded and swiped my arm across my eyes. "I always kept a small suitcase packed in case Miss Alice changed her mind and wanted me to stay. I haven't taken it out of the car."

"Good," he said. "Let's close this place up and then you can follow me into town. I've got a place you can stay."

I shook my head, my face burning hotter than ever, my mind shooting back to some of his remarks... "Oh. I mean, I'm grateful and everything—but I couldn...."

He laughed and reached up to drag out some twigs that were caught in my hair, his response cutting off my words. "Don't worry, darlin'. The cowboy code is respect. I wouldn't compromise you like that, I promise. Besides, it seems you could use a friend or two, and there's a B&B that'll look after you in all those respects."

He must have sensed my hesitation. Hesitation I hadn't even expected myself, and all due to weird and convoluted events that had occurred over the morning. Discovering Miss Alice had been murdered was unfathomable. Knowing it had happened while she was in my care was not only shameful and shocking but—I was embarrassed to admit—scary, too.

"It's okay," he continued, "you couldn't be in safer hands. It's run by the scariest woman in town and no one would dare cross her."

"Oh…" I wasn't sure how comforting that was. "Do you, like, know her well?"

"Well enough," he answered with that cheeky grin. "She gave birth to me. And if you're still not sure, she's married to the town's most influential man—the mayor. Who also happens to be my father. You ready to go?"

I DON'T KNOW what I really expected from the *town's scariest woman,* but I *did* know that Jonah's mother didn't even come close to whatever image that description conjured. Fiona Fencott greeted me in a fuzzy haze of hair, perfume, and bone-crushing hugs. When she stood she dwarfed my five feet four and she was sturdy to go with it. And I doubted I had ever seen a more beautiful woman in my life. Everything was in proportion. She was perfect.

Her thick mane of hair was as dark as mine, but accentuated by a few strands of pure silver that added to her
elegance. It was pulled up into a twist, and the loose strands
that fell softly framed her oval face and high cheekbones. It
was her eyes that were the enigma. They sparkled and moved
so quickly it was hard to define their color. Or was it the
warmth shining from them that confused me? She wore the
mid Texas uniform of jeans, shirt—*white, open at the neck,
and with sleeves rolled back exposing smooth, tanned forearms*—
and boots. With only the addition of some chunky gold
bracelets and neck-chains, she looked elegant enough to
grace the cover of any fashion magazine.

Perhaps my face conveyed my surprise because she
looked over my head, a frown settling on that smooth brow.
"Oh, Jonah! Y'all haven't been using that old *scary woman*
chestnut have you? This girl's got enough to worry her
without you frightening the daylights out of her!" To me she
said, "Now, honey, I want you to call me Fiona, none of this
Miz Fencott or Miz Fiona, y'hear?" She directed a mock
glare across my shoulder before turning back to me. "And
don't you worry about me—and for goshsakes, don't listen
to these derned men of mine."

Jonah chuckled behind me but it was drowned out by
the voice of a man coming up behind Fiona. "Don't be
fooled, young lady, and be warned. No one in this town is
game to say 'no' to my wife. She has a knack of getting

people to volunteer for things they never intended to volunteer for."

The words might have been worrying if I hadn't seen the twinkle in his eye as he came closer. "How do you do, Miss Rosie. I'm Clay Fencott. Mayor of his little town, and have been for the past twenty years." He smiled. "We're happy to have you here in our home."

His huge hand engulfed mine, and like Hank Henderson, I didn't sense they were farmer's hands. They were much too soft and possibly the cleanest hands I'd ever encountered. I smiled to try to hide my awe. Clay Fencott was an older version of his son. Big and handsome. If good looks attracted votes, I could see why he'd held his position for so long. As a family, they were a knockout, and I was trying not to stare.

But there was an elephant in the room and someone had to address it. "Thank you, sir. I'm so grateful to you both for finding me a room. You're very gracious, and I'm in awe of you all." I paused, my mouth shuffling positions to find the right way to continue. I sighed and finally moved on. "You see, I'm not sure I'd be so welcoming of someone who's been accused of murder."

Clay rocked back on his boots, and leaned out an arm to rest along the mantel beside him. "Now don't go getting ahead of yourself, Missy. Not that it would make any difference mind you, but Jonah here tells me you haven't actually been accused yet?"

I shrugged. "Close enough." My voiced cracked on the words and Jonah's hand, big and warm, came up to rest on my shoulder.

"No, not close at all," Clay argued, "they're just asking questions. Otherwise you'd be in jail, cooling your heels for a while."

"But more to the point, Rosie," Fiona said, "when Jonah phoned us on his way out here, he said he didn't think you were guilty. And my son might forget to take stuff out of his pockets before he throws his jeans in the wash and his chili is an embarrassment to Texas, but he's as good a judge of character as I've ever seen. He and his father have a knack and I've never seen it lead them astray."

My chest tightened and I prayed the emotion I could feel building wouldn't appear, but my eyes gave me away. They'd filled and try as I might, I couldn't blink the welling tears away.

"Oh, honey," she continued, "a cute little button like you wasn't meant to have tears spoiling that pretty face. Come on out and have some coffee. Or would you prefer iced tea? I've got a pile of fresh sandwiches and salad out here. I wish I had cake or pie to offer, but the good Lord didn't bless me with that gene."

Her men added their good-natured grumblings about that sad state of affairs, but it all rolled off Fiona. Their sparring was obviously natural and her response was to remind Clay she hadn't forgotten his earlier comment. "And by the way, Mayor Fencott, I'd appreciate it if you didn't speak nonsense about my ability to get things done around here. You make it seem like I bully people. I like to think of it as simply offering direction. Folk need direction, otherwise, how would they know what to do?"

That prompted raucous laughter from the men either side of me, and even I smiled. This was what a real family was like and I wondered if they knew how lucky they were.

But then Jonah stepped forward and threw an arm around his mother, and I figured they knew. "You're one of a kind, Mom. And I gotta admit, this town wouldn't be thriving the way it is if it didn't have you." He grinned. "You too, Dad," he added as a deliberately timed afterthought—and which earned him a mock clip around the ear.

While this had been going on I'd barely had time to take in their home, but the vibe it gave off was pure Fiona. My perception was that it was huge, and light, bright, and airy. And spotlessly clean. Any new guests to this B&B wouldn't go home disappointed in the hygiene level they experienced. Most of the soft furnishings I'd seen were in cool yet comforting shades of blues and greens with lemon and ivory accents. Modern mixed with antique in a way that honored the past and welcomed the future. And bowls of fresh flowers had graced every room we'd passed through with their beauty and perfume. Like Fiona, it was breathtaking.

"You have a beautiful home," I offered as we sat at a round table in a sunny glassed-in nook off the kitchen.

Fiona beamed. "Why thank you. It's kind of a hobby. I love decorating houses. Sometimes I help Jonah if he's flipping a house and I just love it."

I thought of the dark old farmhouse I'd inherited. It, too, was huge. But it was cluttered with mismatched furniture from who knew how many generations. The windows were small and heavily covered with dusty brocades. And instead of bright and airy it was gloomy and shadowy. Shame filled me as I realized I was making such an ungrateful comparison. I'd never owned a home and until now couldn't have imagined that happening for years. But as of this morning I did. I was a homeowner, and I would be grateful for the blessing.

Of course that took me straight back to Miss Alice and my problems. The egg sandwich I'd chosen fell from my fingers.

"Want to talk about it?" Jonah's voice was low and close to my ear though I sensed his parents had also stopped eating and were watching.

I shook my head. "I wouldn't know where to start." Bringing my elbows rudely onto the table I dropped my head into my hands. "I've practically confessed to Sheriff Kinnead that I was the only one capable of poisoning Miss Alice. And it's true. No one else came near her. At least not while I was there. We got no friendly—or unfriendly—phone calls. She got occasional mail. Mostly bills. Sometimes legal documents. I gave them all to her unopened as she instructed me.

If there were bills to pay she wrote checks and I mailed them. Naturally she didn't have any online financial setup. She didn't even own a computer."

Clay picked up his glass of iced tea and wiped away some of the condensation with a napkin. "Frank says the poison was ingested, so it was in the food she ate."

I lifted my head. "You've spoken to him?"

"Yes, he called me to talk over some of the facts. I believe Jonah told you that he's a fair policeman and it's true. I've known that man all my life. I know he's not happy about the thought that anyone in this community poisoned Miss Alice, and he'd like to get it cleared away. As hard as it is for you, you're the stranger in town. And in this town, a stranger is always going to look guiltier than a local. It's just the way it is."

I processed those words. I understood the sentiment, but I didn't have to accept them. Because they were wrong. I was that stranger and I didn't do it. Didn't do anything but my job. And for the first time what I was feeling wasn't desperation, but determination. I didn't do this and somehow I had to prove it.

Those thoughts were interrupted by Fiona. "Now, sweetheart, we have to get some practicalities sorted. You are welcome to a room here for as long as you need it—and no we won't be charging you, so please don't worry your head about that."

I thought about Hank's mention of a substantial bank

account. "You're so generous and I can't believe how fortunate I am to have met you. Thank you. But Mister Henderson mentioned some money and if that's the case, as callous as it sounds, I would have the means to pay you."

A look passed between the other three at the table. "Well, about that, Rosie," Jonah began, "the law says that a murderer can't benefit from his—or her—crime so, in this case the benefit will be held in trust until the case is cleared. I'm sorry, honey."

"I'm sorry too, Rosie," Clay added. "I had a talk with Hank as well and he apprised us of the situation."

"Oh…" I felt stupid. Greedy and stupid. "Look please, it's not about the money. I have savings. Not a fortune but…"

"Honey," Fiona said, "don't you worry. Anything you're feeling is natural. And you hang on to those savings for whatever you need personally. Now," she said, back in organizational mode. "Do you have people you need to contact? Family?"

"Just Jess, my roommate—we share an apartment," I answered, shaking my head. "No family to speak of. My—um—parents are not very traditional. I haven't seen them for a while. They… well, they travel the world, trying to right wrongs and set the globe back on its moral axis."

"Oh," Fiona said, admiration underscoring her words, "that sounds very noble. You must be proud."

I looked across at her, unable to continue the spiel I usu-

KAZ DELANEY

ally spit out when asked about my family. These people didn't deserve to be brushed off with the sanitized version. Sighing I said, "Unfortunately it's not like that and I shouldn't have tried to gloss it over. At the moment they're in Australia participating in a naked sit-in to protest about some trees a local council wants to cut down because their roots are tearing up roads and disrupting the town's water supply. Seems it'd be better for everyone to die of thirst than disrupt some nonnative, imported vegetation that has been labeled a national pest in twenty-three Western-world countries. Including the one they're in."

Two sets of eyes watched me—both agog. The third, Jonah's, looked like he was trying not to laugh, which was the best response, really. Way better than sympathy. "And believe me," I continued, "it's not the most ridiculous thing they've done. There have been way worse."

"Oh dear," Fiona managed. "You poor darlin'. Have they always done that? Did they raise you in that lifestyle?"

"Thankfully no. It took me a while to be grateful, but they did me a favor and left me with my, now late, grandmother. She was okay. I didn't ever go without or anything, but she had other interests. Other than me." It was a quick gloss-over of a very lonely childhood, but they didn't need to hear the nitty-gritty.

Fiona though, saw through the cracks in that gloss. Her gasp of dismay was comforting, but unnecessary. I patted her hand. "It's okay, truly. Thousands of kids had it way, way tougher than I did! I was lucky!" I looked around at the three grave faces. I didn't want them to feel sorry for me—not over my family situation—and I forced a smile. "As a matter of fact, some great things came out of it. I learned to be fairly self-sufficient—especially in the kitchen. My love of cooking and baking was born there." I shrugged. "Maybe, I could thank you by baking something for y'all?"

Breaking through the cloud that had descended, Clay rubbed his hands together. "We wouldn't say no to that, would we now?"

Fiona smiled but it didn't hide the tears resting on her lashes. She squeezed my hand. "The kitchen is yours. Whenever and however often you'd like to use it, darlin'. We've got two groups of guests coming in tomorrow. It would be nice to offer them some homemade refreshments when they arrive. That is... I mean I don't want to rush you..."

Smiling, I waved away her awkwardness. "Not too soon at all. Thank you. Baking often helps me to clear my head. Get my thoughts in order."

The smile faded from Clay's face. "And I imagine there are a lot of thoughts to be sorted?"

"Uh-huh." I actually didn't mean to enumerate them but somehow they started to slip out. "First, like why this would happen now? Miss Alice would have been gone by New Year, probably. It's not long to wait. Nine, ten months? Maybe less? Why rush now? And what were the people or person who ransacked the house looking for? Because I'm convinced it was a search. It didn't make sense the way things were left." I traced the outline of an embroidered butterfly on the starched white cloth Fiona had laid out. "It almost seems like time was an issue. But why? And for whom?"

I raised my eyes to three slightly astonished faces and blushed. "Oh dear—I apologize. Sometimes I get carried away." Offering my upturned palms as a way of leading into the explanation didn't really help. "You see, one of my other interests besides baking and crafts and growing vegetables—" I paused again. "I'm complicating this. Let me start again. One of my interests is reading mystery stories and because of my analytical-mathematical side, I like to work things out. Solve puzzles. I'm actually a bit addicted. I'm sorry. I sound like a complete loon. I was just thinking out loud…"

"Sounded fine to me," Jonah said on a shrug. "Cute even. But, you don't, like, go putting yourself in danger do you? I mean, it's fine to think about it and try to work it out, but this was murder, Rosie."

His concern was sweet, but when it all boiled down, it wasn't his life on the line. "I know that, Jonah, and thank you for your concern. But I didn't murder Miss Alice. That means that probably someone in this town did. And they have the advantage. They know all the town secrets. I know nothing. No one is going to come forward and I'm not keen to have any more of my life taken from me." I hauled in a breath. "I respect your faith in Sheriff Kinnead, but I have a feeling that if I'm going to get out of this then it's going to be up to me to make it happen."

The silence lasted only a few seconds. Fiona was the first to recover. "Good for *you!* What can we do to help?"

Jonah, ever practical, or so I was learning, looked to his father. "I think we need to get Rosie a lawyer. Hank would be a conflict of interest and besides he's not a criminal lawyer. So, I was wondering about Monash & Clutes over at Haden."

Jonah had named the closest big town out of the city and I watched Clay process the suggestion. As the mayor he must have had reason to deal with various lawyers. "Had a few dealings with them over the years. My impression is that they're winners but honest. I'll put in a call today, have a chat to them."

I went to argue that I was capable but Fiona waved me down. "Clay knows people, darlin'. And remember not all lawyers are equal—even in the same firm. Better to let him angle for getting you the best—and not the second best."

It made sense but before I could thank them, Clay asked, "Rosie, you probably haven't had time to think about this, but do you remember anything unusual about the last days before Miss Alice died? Her behavior? Visitors?"

"Not really…" I said slowly. "It was pretty quiet, just the two of us." I forced my mind back. "Though," I added frowning, "now that you mention it, there were two things…"

Jonah's gaze sharpened. "Take your time."

"Well, there was a phone call. I know that doesn't seem odd, but Miss Alice didn't get personal calls. Ever. But it was more odd because when I told the woman that Miss Alice was sleeping and asked to take a message, she became all flustered. Then there was some kind of commotion on the other end, like someone was talking to her, and she just hung up!"

"Did she call back?"

"Not while I was there."

Fiona frowned, mulling that over. "And the other?"

"Now I can't quite remember which came first, but these things happened close to each other. The call, and then one day I was driving out of the gate and a woman was parked on the edge of the road. She was out of the car, and peering in through the overgrowth."

Jonah was watching me intently, taking in every word. "Trying to see the house?"

I nodded.

"Did she speak to you?"

"No, that was the weird thing. My first thought was that she was lost, trying to find someone to give her directions, but as soon as she saw me she hobbled to her car and took off!"

"Hobbled?" Fiona asked.

Again I nodded. "She was an older woman. In her seventies, I'd guess. Pretty face but a bit heavy, and I think her legs were troubling her."

Clay steepled those long, pristine fingers. "Could that have been the same woman who called?"

"No," I said thinking it over. "That one was younger by my estimation. I'm guessing, but by her word choices and tone I'd say maybe someone in her forties or early fifties."

Jonah raised his eyebrows. I knew what he was thinking. Slightly strange but not earth-shatteringly unusual. And did either mean anything? Possibly not.

The other two were also quiet, maybe thinking the same thing.

So, again I found myself thanking them—and answering Fiona's query as to the next step. "Well, the way I see it, that house holds the answers. And the secrets."

Jonah's eyebrows rose again fractionally and then dropped. "Unless whoever searched has already beaten us to it."

That was a sobering thought. Very sobering. But it was somehow softened by one little word—*us*. I didn't want to pull these people into my mess, but it was nice to not feel completely alone.

Now I just had to work out how to legally access a house that had been mine for a couple of short hours before it was taken away again.

Chapter Three

"FIONA—IT'S BEAUTIFUL!" WE were standing in the room I'd been allocated in the B&B. It was breathtaking like the rest of the house. "I don't think I've ever slept in a more stunning room." The blue, green, and yellow color scheme had been carried through, and coupled with the white trim, white gauzy curtains, and dark hardwood floors it was both elegant and warm and welcoming. Given the day I'd had, the plush, queen-sized antique bed that looked like I'd need a ladder to climb into was a bit too welcoming.

She squeezed my arm. "I'm thrilled you like it! Now your bathroom is just through that door." I nodded, noting also a set of glass-paneled French doors that opened to a small balcony as Fiona pushed open the set of matching internal doors. "Here's your relaxing area, right here." The small room boasted a creamy yellow sofa topped by a sea of cushions and a cream throw, a bulging bookcase, a desk, and a television set. "And this antique-looking console actually hides a mini icebox. There's a coffeemaker there as well, so everything you need is right here." She closed the cupboard door and turned to face me. "Though, and I want you to listen carefully to this—Rosie, we consider you to be our guest, so please don't confine yourself to these rooms. I'm showing you around, but you're not a random guest here. You're our personal guest. Our home is yours to use as you wish."

If I hadn't been so tired I probably would have cried again. Instead, I simply felt myself go limp with relief and gratitude. It felt natural to turn and hug her. "Thank you so much. For everything."

She smiled and hugged me back. "Welcome to Airlie Falls, sweetheart." She looked at her watch and whistled. "Woo-ee! I have to get moving. Tonight's the first of our spring market weekends and I just know there'll be mayhem across on The Green—that's that grassy park area right here in the middle of town. I know it sounds a bit pretentious to call it a *green* when for most of summer it'll be brown—but I guess it's habit. Anyhow, I'd better get over there and put out the fires." As she reached the door, she turned. "And if you don't mind me sayin', darlin', you look completely done in. Why don't you have a little nap for a while?"

Alone, I stared at the bed. Jonah had brought in my case and then he'd left to check on some work and Clay had returned to his non-mayoral work, which I now knew was as the town dentist. There was an irony there that the man in town who was usually least liked—the dentist—was also the most popular. At least if mayoral votes counted for popularity.

The house was quiet. A couple of women would come in to clean in the morning and prepare breakfast for any guests, but at the moment it was just me. And Fiona was right: The bed was very inviting.

Rolling back the thick, ice-blue satin duvet, I kicked off my shoes and climbed onto the bed. It was heaven and I figured it wouldn't take much for me to drift off. But I was wrong. Now that I was finally alone, everything started pouring back into my head. Every step of the day was revisited, even though I needed to rest.

I wriggled and rolled, trying to find a place that would override those thoughts but nothing worked. The weight of this situation was too much to ignore. Sure the police needed proof, but still, maybe if the circumstantial evidence was strong enough, they'd have enough to charge me. Did that happen? Was innocence ever enough? And then there was poor Miss Alice. Had she suffered? I hoped that whatever she'd taken had acted quickly and while she was asleep. And what had possessed her to leave *me* her entire estate? Possibly there was simply no one else. That was so sad. Or had there been another motive? Finally the signs I knew all too well kicked in. My heart started thundering and heat prickled at my neck and moved up over my face. Anxiety. Adrenaline was running rampant and there was no way I'd be able to sleep.

Action. I needed to do something. Grabbing Hank's card from my jacket pocket I put in a call, only to have it go to voice mail. I figured there had to be an office number, too, but the thought of explaining my situation to get through officious receptionists put me off. Surely he'd get back to me soon. Fully alert and sitting up but with nothing to do, it didn't take long to slip back to Fiona's offer to use the kitchen so I changed into jeans and a T-shirt and headed downstairs.

The kitchen was surprisingly well equipped for someone who claimed not to bake—as was the pantry. But maybe the ladies who prepared breakfast for the B&B guests sometimes served breakfast cakes or muffins?

I knew my own baking choices would be limited to what was available so I started out simple. Canned peaches for a pie was a no-brainer and some chopped pecans and chocolate chips pointed straight to cookies. It was while the pie was baking that I stepped out the back door into the afternoon sunshine. The light directly outside the door was dappled by the sprawling branches of a jacaranda tree that would thicken up in summer and provide welcome shade. The patio area reminded me of pictures I'd seen of Parisian courtyards, with its circled pavers and continental lace ironwork table and chairs made more comfortable by pale gray-and-white striped cushions. Again Fiona's elegance was evident in every corner. There were very few grassed areas as such, just more overhanging trees, shrubs, and low plants that surrounded the meandering paved pathway that led further down the yard. It was like fairyland and eventually led to a well-tended herb garden and a variety of miniature potted fruit trees and a feast for the senses! The colors and heady aromas were rich and sweet and earthy, and I simply stood for a long moment and inhaled all that goodness. The peaches were still only in bud but the orange and lemon trees still clung to the last of their fruit. That gave me another idea and I grabbed a couple of lemons and set off to make a lemon syrup cake.

Maybe it was the strange surroundings but the activity, familiar though it was, didn't help clarify my thoughts as I expected. But then again, maybe it would take more than baking to get my head around the fact that I was suspected of murder.

I cleaned up as the cake baked and the cookies and pie cooled. That done, I paced for a few minutes then stepped outside to the patio table, coffee in hand. For once not even tempted to taste the end results of my baking. Checking for the dozenth time to find no returning call from Hank Henderson made me jittery. My whole body was churning, my head confused and hazy—and so I forced myself to make a practical plan for the immediate future. In truth, that was all I could rely on. A glance at my watch told me Jess would be home now so I put in a quick call. She'd be expecting me home tonight.

There ended up being nothing quick about it and I barely rescued the cake in time. Understandably she was in turn amazed, delighted, and horrified. And demanded details. Reliving it for her was exhausting, and my untouched coffee was stone cold by the time I ended the call. She wanted to come straight down to me, but I managed to calm her. She had shifts at the hospital and with their proposed cutbacks looming I didn't want her putting her job in jeopardy. In three days she was due time off and we agreed she'd bring me some more clothes and maybe stay a day or so.

Jess was more than a roommate. She was the closest friend I had and speaking to her reminded me just how alone I was. If it hadn't been for the Fencotts and their generosity, Lord knows what sort of a bigger mess I'd be in…

It was Jonah I thought of first when I thought of the Fencotts. And not just because he was the one who introduced me to his family. It had been a long time since I'd felt that spark when I met a man, and I couldn't help but wonder if any chance we had of that developing had been stamped out by Alice Auchinschloss's murder. Despite his flirting, though, I didn't know how he felt about me so it was pointless to mourn the loss of something that might never have been. He'd called himself a cowboy and he certainly looked the part. But cowboys were also hard to read. Jonah had said their code was respect—but their modus operandi was flirting. He might flirt with every girl he met for all I knew. I had a lot on my plate and perhaps the best way to proceed with Jonah would be to simply treat him as a friend and be grateful for his help. That way I wouldn't be sending out signals that embarrassed him. Play it cool. That would be *my* modus operandi.

If only everything else in my life could be rationalized so easily.

Hauling in a determined breath I searched the kitchen for a notepad and pen, silently apologizing to Fiona for taking such liberties. Lists. My life had been ruled by lists and I needed one.

First, talk to Hank. Get access to the house.

Second, search the house. For what? Would I recognize the catalyst for Miss Alice's death even if I found it?

Third, talk to people in town. Ask questions. What questions?

Groaning I almost screwed up the paper and tossed it. This was impossible. Just take it one step at a time, I told myself and ran back upstairs for the card Hank had given me that morning. Maybe I'd pressed the wrong numbers earlier? I could only hope.

Thankfully, he seemed genuinely surprised to hear from me though it's fair to say his tone was cautious. That idea crystallized when he seemed relieved after he'd heard my request.

"I can't see why not. As long as Sheriff Kinnead has no objections to you bein' at Miss Alice's, then I certainly don't. I'm figurin' that those kids who ransacked the place probably messed up any evidence there was to find, so I can't see him having an issue with your request."

I sighed at his determination to believe this was *kids* but held my tongue. I needed as many people on my side—

however tenuously—as I could get. I had to focus on getting the proof. That would be the only way to convince him.

"Let me check with Frank—the Sheriff—and I'll get right back to you. Mind you, if he gives his permission I can't do anything today. I have an appointment that's likely to take me right up to market time. And I promised Bobby Don McAuley I'd help out on his chili stand tonight."

I ended the phone in a daze of wonder. *Welcome to small-town life*, a little voice warned. A life could hang in the balance but the chili stand had to be manned. It didn't stress me as much as I'd expected. Though there was certainly frustration and as I packed the baked goodies into airtight containers I'd found in a low cupboard, I wondered how to fill the rest of the afternoon and not go crazy with worry.

I hadn't even completed my task though, when the sound of a door closing, followed by heeled boots clattering across hardwood floors, announced I had company.

"Oh my... This house smells like heaven! It can't be my house!" Fiona's laughter preceded her appearance and when she arrived her eyes were closed, her nose tilted skyward, and her whole face oozing bliss.

It would have been impossible not to respond with a smile. "Don't get too excited," I warned. "There's nothing too elaborate here, just plain baking. I used whatever I could find and that dictated my options."

Her eyes lit up as she lifted lids and looked over the assortment on the bench. "Honey, I don't care if it's baked cardboard. If it tastes half as good as it looks and smells, it'll be wonderful. May I?" she asked, reaching for a cookie.

I laughed. "Fiona, they're yours! Your ingredients, your equipment."

If they were baked properly the chocolate would be oozy and complement the crunch of the nuts. Judging by the look on her face as she chewed, maybe they were okay. "I was right!" she exclaimed with a clap. "These are heaven! *Good grief...* I swear my boys would move back home to Mama if I could bake like this. Rosie Hart, you have a true gift!"

Heat rose up over my neck and crept up my face. "I think you're exaggerating. You haven't even tried the other things yet—but thank you anyway. That's a wonderful response."

She'd grabbed a second cookie and through the mouthful of baked confection, she waved to show she had more to say. "Now, I know you have a lot on your mind, but you and I agree that activity is good for easing your troubles, right? So, I'm wondering if you'd care to help out over at the market this afternoon?" She paused and licked her fingers. "We've had a couple of committee members fall ill, and I could sure use your help."

What could I say? This family had been my life raft. There was no way I could tell her the baking activity hadn't helped, but I owed them. "Sure, just let me grab my boots and a jacket from the car and I'll freshen up and be with you."

Fiona was probably right; getting out and meeting people, being busy and taking in new sights and sounds was bound to be more of a distraction than baking alone in a strange kitchen. But even before I reached my car parked in a small parking bay off the main street, a skittering feeling began in my chest. A piece of paper, secured by the windshield wiper blades fluttered in the mild afternoon breeze. It was ridiculous. I had no reason to be wary of it. Advertising. It'd be some kind of advertising. Had to be. A buy-one-get-one-half-price pizza. But something told me it wasn't.

The print was uneven and scrawled across the page. Like someone disguising their handwriting. The message was clear though: GO BACK TO WHERE YOU CAME FROM. YOR NOT WELCOME IN AIRLIE FALLS. STAY OUTTA WHATS NOT YOR BIZNESS.

I was so intent on reading the words that I didn't hear the footsteps come up beside me. "Rosie? You okay?"

I jumped, clasping my hand to my heart. "Jonah! Oh Lord you frightened me!"

He reached to steady me. "Hey, hey…" he said softly. "I'm so sorry, Rosie, honey. I thought you heard me."

I shook my head. "No, I was—um—kind of distracted." I handed him the note and took his low whistle as a sign of the same surprise I felt. When he raised his eyes back to mine, I felt like the biggest heel but I had to do what I had to do. "Jonah—I hate asking. Truly. But did you mention to anyone that I wanted to poke around? Find some answers?"

At his puzzled stare I explained. "It's just that I'm guessing people know I'm a suspect in Alice's murder—but I only mentioned trying to get my own answers here at lunch."

His arms hadn't moved and they still didn't. If he was offended it didn't show. "Darlin', I've been sitting with a sick heifer since I saw you. And she's the shy type, doesn't talk to anyone."

I grinned. "I'm sorry for asking but…"

He grinned back. "It's okay. Don't worry about it. Let's get back inside though. I think we'd better talk to the folks."

I grabbed my things from the car, and inside we found Clay had returned home as well. After passing over the note, Jonah hit his father with the same question I'd asked him. Clay's brow furrowed as his eyes turned straight to me. "I certainly did not, Rosie. That would have been disrespectful and foolhardy. But…" He turned to his wife who was finishing a small piece of pie.

Instinctively Jonah and I turned to her as well. She at least had the grace to look guilty. "Oh dear… I may have said something…" She wiped her hands, and I noted they weren't as steady as they'd been earlier. "Oh Lordy, what have I done? It was just that people were asking all kinds of questions and I thought I was being careful. But I think I did say that you weren't going to take it lying down; that you'd fight to prove your innocence." Slamming down the cloth she looked to me. "Rosie, I'm so sorry, honey. I thought it was just a general answer. I was trying so hard not to be specific."

I leaned over and took her hand. "It's okay, truly. You may have done me a favor."

Jonah frowned. "How?"

"Well, Sheriff Kinnead might see this as evidence that someone has something to hide. Don't you think? Fiona," I said not really giving anyone time to reply, "I don't suppose you remember who was there when you were talking?"

Her eyes fixed on a spot on the wall as she tried to re-build the afternoon but she eventually had to shake her head. "I'm so sorry. It's been so busy. So many people everywhere. Answering a thousand questions about power supplies and stall numbers and space allocations. It could have been anyone."

"And the market's right across the street. It'd be easy to slip over and leave that note. With all the comings and goings no one would notice," Clay added.

Jonah was close by my side. "Does this mean you'd ra-ther give the market a miss tonight? Despite Mom's claim to need help, we'd get by. We'd understand if it makes you uncomfortable."

"No," I answered on a sigh. "Someone's trying to warn me off. That's more information than I had an hour ago. So, I think it's even more important that I go and help out."

I HAD FOOLISHLY figured Fiona had used the need for help as a distraction. Boy, was I wrong. I ran and lugged and carried and dragged for about three hours until finally everything was ready. It was barely dusk but multiple strings of fairy lights ringed the perimeter of the park area and then wound their way throughout the stalls. The air was filled with music and the mouth-watering aromas from the many food trucks and stalls. Burgers, hot dogs, chili, sloppy joes, tacos, barbeque… You name it, it was there interspersed between the stands of lush local produce, heady-scented candles, handcrafts, and jams and preserves.

Being surrounded by such a feast for the senses, I shouldn't have been surprised to find my appetite had returned. Maybe not in full force but I was ready for something. Despite the early spring chill that was settling over the crowd and layering dew on the stalls, trucks, and tents—to say nothing of the shadows dogging me personally—it felt warm—and fun.

"Ready to eat?" Like me, Jonah had been at his mother's beck and call and by the look of him, I'd gotten off lightly. Now he was beside me and I could feel my determination to remain aloof wavering.

We'd checked out only a few options when Jonah suddenly stopped, and then started dragging me sideways. "Just the man I've been keeping an eye out for…"

Following his line of vision I saw Sheriff Kinnead hovering near the back of a well-lit preserves stall. He was out of uniform—wearing jeans and the traditional long-sleeved pale blue shirt—and Stetson. And I was amazed at how much more approachable he looked. I was introduced to his wife, Brenda, and the other woman buzzing about serving with her. They were both in about the same age bracket as the Sheriff, and I probably could have guessed from the blonde froth of hair, inch-long nails, and wide glossy smile, that the other lady, Merline, as I came to know, ran the town's beauty parlor.

I'd not long had my hair done in Dallas, but? A trim? Everybody knew, no matter what the town, if you wanted to know something chances were the chatty hairdresser was usually the best source.

"Your wife is doing a roaring trade." It was a comment meant to open conversation but in this case it was true.

Sheriff Kinnead nodded, but the furrows in his forehead deepened. "I worry that it's getting too much for her though. She loves it but she struggles to keep up with demand these days. She gets tired. I tell her to just tell 'em to wait, but she won't do that." He shook his head. "Says it's her reputation…"

It was on the tip of my tongue to offer to help her when I remembered my situation and who I was talking to. Probably not such a great idea. I lowered my head to cover the heat that was once more burning a path up my neck and face and let Jonah take over.

Earlier, he'd slid the note we'd taken from my windscreen into a plastic protector sleeve, and handed it over to Frank with a short explanation.

Eyeing the plastic cover Frank shot Jonah a look that I interpreted as *'this isn't exactly CSI New York,'* but he said nothing. Instead his brows rose as he read the words and his mouth slid into that exaggerated kissing pose. His thinking pose? Excitement bubbled through me. This was like my get-out-of-jail-free card. I was waiting for him to admit that I was right; that someone else was involved; someone with a reason to kill Miss Alice. After all, this was the proof we needed, wasn't it?

Those particular words didn't come. His head tipped back and he eyed Jonah carefully. "Did you see this on the car?"

"No," Jonah explained again, "I came along just as Rosie was reading it. She'd just found it."

Those assessing eyes slid to me. "Or maybe she was just about it put it there herself."

That well and truly got my attention. "Wha—??? That's crazy! I didn't write that!"

"Come on, Frank," Jonah urged. "I was there, I saw how shaken she was!"

The older man shrugged. "Seems to me that Miss Hart could have been shaken because you nearly caught her in the act. And you know, it was mighty convenient that you came along right then to be her 'witness'."

"But I didn't know he was coming then! I didn't know

where Jonah was or if he'd even be back!" I argued. "I couldn't have planned that!"

Just like out at the farm, the Sheriff blew out a big sigh and focused on the ground, thinking about his words. When he raised his eyes, I swear I saw regret there. "Miss Hart, I'm just doing what any good prosecutor would do with this story. He or she'd tear it to pieces in seconds. This isn't proof of anything except someone can't spell. Or is pretending they can't spell. It's amateurish and screams *cover-up* to me. Miss Hart—Rosie—this here isn't going to help you make your case, I'm afraid." It was his signal that the conversation was done, so he surprised me by folding the plastic-covered note and slipping it into his pocket. "Still, I'll hang on to this if you don't mind. Now you two go and have a nice evening." He tipped his hat and then turned his attention back to his wife.

Some of my frustration died with his rationale. Seen from that perspective, the Sheriff was right. So what was he saying? Was he telling me to find different proof? Something that would stand up? But what?

As we said our goodbyes to the women, I sensed Jonah hadn't let go of his frustration and after thanking him, I tried to steer him in another direction. Food. But it wasn't as easy as I'd expected and again the wave of gratitude that almost complete strangers would go so far as to help someone, threatened to overwhelm me. And gave me pause. Maybe I'd been too hasty in rejecting the idea of helping Miz Kinnead.

I'd been helped—maybe I should return the favor. If only she wasn't the Sheriff's wife. Still, I'd think about it.

My mind back on the job, I determined to get food into the man beside me. We eventually decided on a bowl of Bobby Don's *famous* chili—if you could believe the signs. Hank served us with a smile, though I wasn't sure how he really felt about me being there. He hadn't gotten back to me and I wasn't sure whether to raise it here.

All evening I'd been catching sly glances from the people of Airlie Falls as I'd worked. In fact I'd gotten pretty good at picking the out-of-town vendors because they paid me no attention. Airlie Falls people were different. Or maybe I was the problem. I admit that while everybody seemed friendly enough, *curious* but friendly, there was also wariness on my side. As I'd looked at every face and shaken every hand, a part of me was wondering if this was the one. The one who'd murdered Miss Alice. The one who wanted me out of town...

Now here with Hank and conscious of what happened with Fiona who'd just let something fairly innocent slip from her mouth, I was reluctant to speak publicly about any of it. Hank didn't share my concern—but then he didn't know about the note. "I heard from Frank Kinnead. He doesn't have any issue with you bein' at the house so I'll meet you there about nine. That suit?"

Frank hadn't mentioned any of that to us just now, but he probably had a whole slew of things on his mind. Hank hadn't bothered to keep his voice low, and I glanced around, feeling like the whole of the town was listening or watching. I nodded briefly, wondering how to change the subject. A mouthful of chili helped find that way. "Oh wow—this really is good. So, Hank, you're not secretly Bobby Don are you?"

"No, ma'am—he isn't. I am." Flustered I turned to see a deputy, not much older than Jonah, not quite as tall but with a really friendly face. His smile was wide and he held out his hand in greeting but his gaze was speculative. He was sizing me up. He'd probably been told to watch me. "I'm Deputy Bobby Don McAuley. Pleased to meet you."

"Hi. I'm Rosie Hart." I pointed back to the chili stand. "This isn't your only business? I mean, I imagined whoever made this did it full time? This chili is good!"

His smile got wider, especially when Jonah told me to stop flattering him or he'd outgrow his hat. "No, ma'am. This is just my hobby. Been the county fair champion three times! I'm grateful to Hank here though, or there wouldn't be a stand tonight. I pulled duty and he usually helps me out when I can't man the truck myself." He sighed. "And seein' how there's only the Sheriff and me and a couple of part-time deputies we share with other counties, that gets to be more often than I'd like."

Jonah asked a question then and somehow within minutes the conversation between the three men had moved to baseball. While they talked I ate and looked around. The crowds were strong and everyone seemed to be doing great business. I hoped so. But as my eyes swept the area, I got the sense of someone watching me. Prickles ran up my spine and I shuffled closer to the group of men around me. I usually prided myself on my independence but I wasn't stupid. Nothing wrong with sending out the illusion that I had friends.

Then I slowly turned. In my peripheral vision I'd seen someone just to my left, someone still, watchful, but as I turned fully they were gone. Only an empty chili bowl carelessly dropped on the grass remained.

Had there really been someone there watching me? Was I just being paranoid? Miss Alice was dead. I'd only been warned off. There was a big difference.

But after we left the stall, I found myself darting glances at everyone we passed, checking down alleys between stands and tents and swinging a look behind me at random times. The problem was that I didn't know who I was looking for; didn't know who I should be wary of…

We ate as we walked, our enjoyment of the food stalling any conversation for a while. It wasn't awkward; in fact if I hadn't been on edge due to my situation, it would have been quite companionable.

I sought out faces I recognized and was surprised at how many were familiar. I'd slipped in and out of Airlie Falls occasionally—sometimes to get a few supplies; sometimes to pick up medication but I wouldn't call myself a regular. It could be weeks or even a month between my visits. Still, I saw Vicki from the general store and the pharmacist—Dan? Was that his name? Another face had me searching again. *Maddie? Amanda? May?* The girl who'd come looking for cleaning work. Miss Alice wouldn't have anyone from town on the property, but as I'd walked her out we'd chatted about her school choices and courses for a while.

The memory faded and I continued my perusal. The Reverend and Miz Peatree were there, and Doc Mitchum as well. There were more faces that were familiar but I couldn't place them, and I looked forward to putting names to them. At the very least, I needed to know if they were faces I could trust.

Playing this silent mix-and-match game, on top of everything else, was taking its toll. After the day I'd had and despite my jangling nerves, it all started to catch up and I was really feeling that lost opportunity to rest earlier. Try as I might, I couldn't cover the yawn that slipped out, and beside me, Jonah tucked my hand under his arm. "Time to get you back to Mom's. You must be wiped out."

I wanted to argue but another yawn beat me to it and diluted any power such an argument would wield.

It was a short stroll to the B&B, which was perfectly placed right on Main Street and adjacent to The Green. Perfect for guests coming to enjoy the markets. It took up a double house plot and I'd learned it had belonged to Fiona's parents and been consistently added to and passed down through each generation. Someone from her family had lived in that house for well over a hundred years. I wondered what that kind of solid family history must feel like.

The door wasn't locked, and by the time I reached the bottom of the stairs, I knew I'd completely run out of steam. Jonah offered to help me but I needed to haul my body up there myself. If I couldn't climb a few stairs how could I hope to do anything else? Like prove my innocence. So, while Jonah made his way to forage in the kitchen, I made my way slowly to my room.

But even after I'd opened the door, my tired brain took several seconds to comprehend what was in front of me. Just like Miss Alice's home, this room had been ransacked. I had very little with me, but all of it had been dumped on the bed and floor and it was evident every piece of clothing and toiletry item had been examined.

Likewise, despite me not having made use of them, every drawer had been pulled out of its cavity and the doors of the empty wardrobes and consoles hung open. Floor rugs had been pushed aside and the bedding hung askew like someone had checked under the mattress.

I'm not a screamer, but I obviously made some kind of shocked sound. And loud enough to bring Jonah to my door.

And then he swore again; just like last time.

Unlike last time, he whipped his cell phone from his pocket and hit one button. Speed dial. "Dad, I'm at the

B&B. Go find Frank or Bobby Don and get them over here. Someone's been through Rosie's belongings."

The excitement should have lifted my exhaustion, but it didn't. All I could do was stare, until finally a lone thought worked its way to the surface: Whoever ransacked Miss Alice's home hadn't found what they wanted.

It was still out there.

But what was *it*?

Chapter Four

BOTH FRANK KINNEAD and Bobby Don arrived; B.D. looking excited and Frank not so. This time my hopes weren't as high as last, but two hits in one evening? Didn't that prove something?

Clay arrived not long after but after checking on us, he left the police to their job. Bobby Don lazily checked over the room while Frank leaned against the doorjamb and watched. In turn, I watched Frank and my heart started sinking.

The questions were similar to last time and I didn't have to be bright to see they were headed to the same place. *How much time elapsed between you parting at the stairs and Rosie crying out? Had you seen the room before you went to the market? Were you in the room with Rosie at any point during the evening?*

The answers Jonah had given were truthful but not helpful—though that wasn't his fault. But the last question really jerked me out of my funk. "No, he was not in my room!" My face burned and I glared at Sheriff Kinnead.

He simply shook his head at me. "You have to get used

to these questions, Rosie."

My arms rose then fell back to slap against my sides. Frustration scorched through me. This was like banging my head against a wall and just as painful. "Do you really think I did this?"

"You have to see it from this side, Rosie. A prosecutor would say your first attempt didn't work and so you tried again."

"Well, from my side it looks like whatever this person is looking for—they haven't yet found it!"

When the Sheriff didn't reply Jonah added his support. "You gotta admit it makes sense, Frank. I mean—for all the suspicion you have that Rosie is doing this herself—there are just as many reasons that someone else did this."

Bobby Don turned toward Jonah. "What reasons?"

His tone was bored and disbelieving, unlike the smiling man I'd met just hours ago.

Jonah balked at answering, and for just a moment he stared at Bobby Don. "I know you have your reasons for being glad Miss Alice is gone and you're feeling justified, but Rosie's future is at stake here, B.D. Some respect wouldn't be out of place."

Bobby Don puffed out his chest. "You're out of line, Jonah. Sure I'm glad Miss Alice is gone—but so is every other family she destroyed!"

The Sheriff stepped in while I tried to process that information. Bobby Don had a reason to want Miss Alice dead? The deputy? And others? The Sheriff cut through my thoughts. "Hold on there! You two act like grown-ups or I'll cuff both of you—even you, Bobby Don! Now, Jonah, could you get on with your explanation? I'm growin' old while you two bicker."

Jonah bit back a word I was sure he wouldn't have wanted me to hear. Sighing, he finally held up his fingers. "First, Mom let slip that Rosie was looking for answers and that made someone nervous. Second, the house wasn't locked—anyone could have come in here. Third," he said holding up his middle finger, "anyone could have slipped across the road to get here. There were people all over going in all directions. And this is a B&B—it's not noteworthy to see someone coming in here. And fourth, anyone who knows us knows Mom would have the entire family over at the market. And Rosie was visible all evening. This person knew where Rosie was—and that wasn't here."

"Point taken, Jonah," the Sheriff said, "except we don't have a motive for this mysterious person. No reason for him or her to do this. Whereas..." He let his voice trail off.

Bobby Don snickered but was put in his place by a dagger glance from his boss.

I managed it, but it was difficult to suppress the anger bubbling within me. What was the use of even calling in these people?

When Kinnead and Bobby Don left shortly after, I knew all the exhaustion I'd felt earlier had long blown away and there would be little sleeping done. Jonah must have realized because when I answered his knock a bit later, he handed me a mug of warm milk. "It's got a slug of bourbon. Dad reckons you can't beat it as a way to wind down when you're buzzed over something. Good luck."

I was grateful for his thoughtfulness and his smile was a bonus. In the back of my mind, I was conscious of the fact that those in crisis make faster connections that were are based on a whole different criterion to the way such things usually happen, but that smile was reassuring, and I needed all the reassurance I could get.

I sipped the milk, savoring the extra warmth of the liquor, thinking about what had been said tonight. I needed to tackle Jonah about his comments to Bobby Don, but I could see he wasn't really in the mood to talk about that man—his friend—just yet.

In the shower, I eventually managed to push those thoughts out of my head and just let the warm water do its job, and afterward I climbed into the big bed. Amazingly I felt myself relaxing and I drifted off to sleep making plans for the next day. Getting answers was a priority. The question pile was growing rapidly.

I WAS SURPRISED the following morning to see Jonah at breakfast. Apparently so were his parents and I tried not to be embarrassed by the smiles and pointed looks that Clay and Fiona swept over us. I didn't want them to get the wrong impression, because I was really beginning to see that Jonah felt responsible for me and that it was his duty to ensure I was okay. Last night had been a case in point. He'd done his duty—and had been the perfect gentleman the entire time.

Naturally the talk had centered on the night before. Both Fiona and Clay had showered apologies on me for not securing the property, which—they added—they'd never had cause to do before. On the other hand, I was conscious of something else. "After all you've done for me, I can't allow this to hurt your business. I was awake early, and I think I need to find somewhere else to stay until this has been cleared up."

The chorus of protests was very comforting but I'd given this some serious thought. "Thank you, but I really think this may be for the best. Your guests have to feel safe and with me around, I don't think you can guarantee that." As I gazed at the three mournful faces staring back at me, I forced a smile. "Look, how about we talk later then. Okay?"

There were still some muttered arguments but I could see the sense of this was starting to sink in. Thankfully Fiona had a mind that wasn't content to dwell on one thing, and I was grateful for her change of direction.

"Rosie, Clay and I had quite a feast when we got in last night. Darlin' you bake like an angel. Now, I've been thinking…"

Clay turned to his son and they both sighed.

"Run, Rosie. Run fast," Jonah warned good-naturedly. "We've seen this look before. She's got a plan and you feature in it."

I grinned. Couldn't be too bad, right? "Okay…"

Fiona ignored them. "Now you saw the great array of food we offered last night, but did you notice there's no dedicated dessert truck or tent?"

I hadn't.

"Of course we have all those homemade jams and pre-serves and breads and muffins. But no proper desserts. Mary Blakely used to do it until her arthritis got too bad, and then her daughter May Belle was going to take over but then she discovered she's having triplets to go with the three little ones she's got at home." She paused and leaned closer. "I've heard her ankles are the size of Texas, poor darlin'—and so she's bowed out too. So I was wondering…"

"You want Rosie to run a dessert stand?" Jonah's tone was incredulous. "Mom! Have you been on another planet? You don't think she's got enough on her mind right now?"

Fiona waved him down. "I know all that. Don't make me out to be heartless because you know I'm not. But it'll help her get to know the town. Let them get to know her before this all gets bigger than it is already." She shrugged. "Then once this whole mess has been cleared up she won't be facing that battle of getting Airlie Falls to accept her."

"Fiona…"

She rolled over Clay's interjection. "These stands are profitable enterprises! She could build a little business and work her way into the community. For the most part these are good folk and it's an opportunity for them to get to know her."

I agreed that most of the people in Airlie Falls were probably decent people. Except for the one who was a murderer.

Clay cleared his throat and wiped his fingers on his napkin. I noted that the lemon syrup cake had been added to the breakfast fare and he was enjoying his second slice. "If you'd allowed me to finish," he said patiently, "I was about to say I agree with you."

"Oh. Thank you." Fiona leaned over and squeezed his hand, her smile full of the love she obviously had for this man.

My own heart swelled as I watched them, and so before I started blubbering again, I needed to voice my own thoughts. "So do I." I paused to make sure they understood. "That is, I agree with Fiona and Clay."

I wasn't sure whose surprise was the greatest. Fiona's or Jonah's. But it was Jonah who spoke first and I could see he wasn't happy. "Rosie, you don't have to do this…"

"Jonah, it makes sense. They can get to know me—but more importantly, I'll get to know them! It gives me a valid reason to ask questions without seeming too obvious."

"Perfect," Fiona said, shooting her son a meaningful glance, and not even trying to hide her own delight. "It'll take a bit of time to set up so I'll get started on the arrangements as soon as I can."

I stood. "And I'm going to meet Hank."

Shaking his head, Jonah stood as well. "I'm coming with you."

That pulled me up short and I understood why he'd turned up for breakfast. "I'm grateful for the offer, Jonah, but I can't let you do that. You have your business and your farm. Please… I've taken enough of your time."

"Hmnn…" For a moment that's all he said. He simply stood, eyebrows raised, and contemplated my response. Finally he said, "Did I ever tell you about the other cowboy code?"

I sensed his parents' eyes shifting from one of us to the other. Like at a tennis match.

"There's more than one?" I asked.

He shrugged. "There's possibly one for every occasion." At that I heard his father snort. "But the one for this occasion is that we finish what we start."

Fiona seemed to agree. "That's kinda true, honey. And I know I'd feel better if you weren't alone out at that place."

I looked across the three faces. Did I need to remind them that they barely knew me? That they weren't responsible for me? I said none of this. Instead I sighed. "Okay, just this once. But you have to understand I can't go on disrupting your lives."

The one thing I insisted upon was taking separate cars. That way he could leave and I had my own independence as well.

⤿

HANK WAS ALREADY at the farm when we arrived. Since the break-in he'd securely locked the place and this morning he'd opened up and was surveying the mess. Surprisingly there was little damage—which I thought was another point for my argument.

While I dealt with business, Jonah went for a trek around the farm. A corner of it adjoined his property, making him a neighbor. Maybe he was thinking of putting in an offer if it came up for sale? And if it came up for sale that would mean I'd been found guilty of murder. Not surprisingly my hand was shaking when I reached out to take Hank's.

"Just what is it you're looking for, Rosie?" His smoker's voice was even more crackly this morning.

"I wish I knew, Hank—Mister Henderson. It's just a feeling." I paused, forcing myself to calm down. That and standing almost exactly where we'd stood yesterday brought back the question I was about to repeat. "Are you sure there's nothing Miss Alice might have had that someone might want to find?"

"Call me Hank," he said matter-of-factly. "Well, you

know I've been thinkin' about that." He paused and scratched his chin. "I don't see how it helps, but I know she's been mad with some people in town from time to time. I remember Marion told me she was keeping some kind of journal about them. But as I said, that was years ago—some of it going back sixty years. Maybe more."

I agreed that a sixty-year-old squabble didn't seem to have any relevance to now. But it was better than nothing—and somewhere to start.

Jonah appeared just as Hank's cell phone rang. When he'd finished the call he looked stressed. "Saturday! You'd think a man could get some peace!" To me he said, "I apologize, Miss Rosie, but it seems I'm urgently needed somewhere else. Or so my sister insists. Now, I'm gonna give you this here key, but you understand that until this business is settled, this place is not legally yours." He cleared his throat. "But I'm going to use my discretion and allow you access as you need or want it. And I wish you luck."

To Jonah he said, "I'm not sure Rosie's seen the 'little house'." He dug in his pocket for yet more keys. "I'd hoped to show her myself but perhaps you'd take over?"

Jonah nodded and as the men chatted for a few minutes longer, I moved into the main house and again looked over the mess. It was probably pointless to sift through all this hoping to find a hidden secret, but I also couldn't leave the house in such a state. I pushed around some of the food-stained papers with the toe of my sneaker, my mind weighing up my options: Search now and clean later? Clean now and search as I go? Not major decisions in the grand scale of life, but timewise the wrong decision could cost me.

And then on a sudden surge of determination I reached for a trash bag and some gloves. The mess was overwhelming and distracting me from my primary purpose. It had to go. I'd start here in the kitchen and work my way through. I'd examine every piece of paper as I went. And hope.

I'd barely begun when I felt Jonah crouch down beside me, watching me study every piece of paper before either discarding or stacking for a second look. "So, do we have a plan here?" I started to protest but he cut me off. "How about I take care of the basic trash—the food and broken china, things like that. I'll stack all the paper and mail and notes as I go. Deal?"

Of course it was a deal. It was a dream deal. What was the point of arguing? I put all my guilt aside and set down to work with Jonah just a few feet away, working with me.

A piece of purple ribbon caught my eye in the debris sea of brown and white. I picked it up, running my fingers down over its satin-smooth finish. Such a pretty color. A memory itched somewhere in my head; trying to come forward. For a second or two I stared at it, sure I'd never seen it here before and yet... Why did it seem vaguely familiar?

Shrugging I tossed it toward Jonah who immediately picked it up. "You offering me first prize, honey? Might be a bit premature."

I grinned. That whiskey voice got me every time; seeming to reverberate through me. And making me remember that purple wasn't the color of first prize—but the color of passion. That was enough for me to turn away to hide the color of embarrassment surging through me.

Thankfully he was unaware of my thoughts and continued chatting as we worked. It was nice easy conversation, making me laugh sometimes and wonder the next, and each of us taking moments to stand and stretch cramped muscles. But nearly four hours later when the lower floor looked almost livable and despite the box of papers I still had to go through, I wasn't feeling hopeful.

"Everything I've looked at is an old sales receipt, birthday or Christmas cards from years ago or medical appointment reminders. Since Miss Alice shut herself off from the town and especially after Marion died, there's been no life!"

"But if you're right about someone searching for something then there *was* something at one time. Something big."

It didn't take as long to straighten the upstairs area because the search had been so much more methodical up there. And I didn't hold out hope for any clues from the pile of papers I'd accrued. I'd glanced at each one and I was pretty sure they were simply basic household accumulation.

One pleasant surprise was opening back the thick dusty curtains and window coverings and seeing how the light changed the rooms into something that had the potential to be quite pleasant. At the moment the heavy furniture, mud-colored walls and dark brown, almost black woodwork trim wasn't doing it any favors.

It was evident the house had been continually added to over the years and despite the rambling haphazard layout, it had a quirky appeal. And I wondered how it would look if Fiona waved her magic over the interior.

Jonah trudged up the stairs after dumping another bag of trash onto the back of his truck. "Any luck?"

I shook my head. "I didn't expect it to be easy or the other person would have found it. But now I'm here, I'm even more worried. All the obvious places—drawers, wardrobes, under the bed—have been searched already. I don't know where else to look!"

"Yep, I'm hearin' you…" he said glancing around. Eyes narrowed he wandered around the upper floor, banging on various walls, and stomping on the floor listening for a change in depth that might indicate a cavity. Shrugging he returned to the landing. "There's got to be somewhere but for now I'm not seeing it either. Maybe we need a break? That might clear our heads."

We'd sustained ourselves on coffee, water, crackers and a pack of sweet, store-bought cookies I'd just purchased at Miss Alice's request last week. I'd imagined he meant more of the same, but when we got back downstairs he kept on going right out the front door.

"Where are we going?"

His grin was as mysterious as his tone. "It's a surprise."

I'd never really been further than the immediate yard around the farmhouse. I didn't ever like to be too far from Miss Alice, even when she was resting. And besides, it was pretty overgrown and I'm a bit cowardly about things that creep and crawl. But Jonah found the entrance to a track about two hundred feet from the house just where the trees and vines were most dense. Amazingly once you got past the entrance, the track wasn't quite as overgrown, and with his heavy boots tramping down the rest, I happily followed.

Focused as I was on closely following his footsteps, I almost collided with him when he suddenly stopped. But as I looked up, my apology died on my lips.

Before me stood the prettiest house I'd ever seen. This was obviously the "little house" but *little* was only used in the relative sense. It was a regular-sized house, in fact bigger than most, surrounded by a wide clearing save for some mature pecan trees, and a couple of peach trees that shaded the front and side. The wood siding was painted a light gray with bright white trim and highlights of red in the door color and window boxes. If I'd been asked to choose exterior house colors, I'd never have chosen these, yet they worked so well.

It was just two levels and an attic, with a deep porch around the front and side and dormer windows upstairs. Garden beds that hosted tired weeds had been thoughtfully placed at one time and a paved path led to deep, wide front steps to the entrance.

"It's breathtaking. Who owns this place?"

Jonah shrugged. "Well, as soon as we get this legal mess settled—*you do*."

"Wh… What? How?"

Jonah pulled a set of keys from his pocket, jingling them as he spoke. "It's part of the estate. It's on Miss Alice's land."

"Another whole house? Crazy! Why?"

"Well"—Jonah began settling his Stetson more comfortably—"I only got the brief version from Hank, but it seems this was built sixty something years ago, for Miss Alice and her beau. That relationship apparently fell apart and Miss Alice didn't take up with anybody else, so the house was then promised to her sister, Marion, and Hank. It was the last project the girls' father ever undertook."

"Are you telling me no one has ever lived here? No! That can't be true. Surely…"

"Completely true according to Hank," he answered as he scooped an arm around behind my back. "Want to take a peek inside?"

"Absolutely!"

Inside was enchanting. The airy foyer was lined in wide boards that were kind of funky and modern despite their age. A fireplace dominated the living area, and there was a large dining room as well as a good-sized kitchen complete with a walk-in pantry and separate preserves larder and a cozy eating area. This was a proper farmhouse! Apart from the mudroom, a couple of other rooms downstairs were undefined, but the possibilities were endless. The walls were painted in pale, welcoming colors and the trim was fresh white. And there were so many windows! But it was the high ceilings and quirky little built-in cabinets and nooks that gave it such unique character.

As I made my way up the slightly curved white staircase, I let my fingers brush the balustrade. "Why is there no dust? If this place has never been used—there surely should be dust? And cobwebs?"

"That's an easy one," Jonah said from behind me. "When she was alive, Marion regularly cleaned this place. When she got sick, Hank brought in a crew to take care of it to save her fretting, and apparently he's paid them to clean it once a month since. There's no furniture, or movement to make dust so it doesn't really need more. It was done just last week."

My heart was full. How could an empty building exude such warmth? Especially when it held such a sad history. "Amazing. I've probably said it before, but that word just keeps going around in my head."

Four spacious bedrooms, one of them surprised me as a fully fitted master, as well as a family bathroom—which matched the half bath downstairs—all filled the upper floor. And it was as delightful as the lower floor.

Jonah nodded toward the master bedroom. "Hank was still hopeful right up to the end. With Marion's permission, he renovated to create a proper master suite and updated all the plumbing."

Breathlessly I flitted from room to room flicking on light switches and taps to check utilities. "I could so easily live here. It's so much cozier than the other house. So light and airy! It's perfect." As the words left my mouth an idea hit. "Oh, Jonah! This could be the answer I need! Do you think Hank would let me stay here?"

His answering look was both incredulous and wary. "You do realize there's no furniture here, right? And I know you want to protect my parents' business, but no one there is arguing that you leave. And besides, you'd be completely alone out here! If someone wanted to hurt you—you'd be a sitting duck!"

I lifted my hand to count off his objections. "One, I could choose some pieces from the old house and haul them over. Two, I won't be alone. My friend Jess is coming down day after tomorrow with some things I need. She's about to start a week's leave so she'll stay here with me!"

He was shaking his head. "Seems like a lot of trouble..."

I didn't want to really get into it with him. As cruel as it sounded after all he'd done for me, this had nothing to do with Jonah. It would be between me and Hank. Changing the subject, I spun and laughed. "Well, one thing is for sure, I doubt Miss Alice hid anything over here! This place is completely empty."

He took the cue, smiling along with me. "Who knows? Don't they say what you're looking for is always in the last place you look?"

I stopped mid spin and stared hard at him. "What did you say?"

He frowned. "I said—"

"I know. I heard what you said. Miss Alice used to say that all the time. I remember because she always added a weird little laugh as though there was a joke and I didn't get it."

I cast my mind back. This conversation had triggered another memory. Or a sensation—like something I should know. I saw myself standing in the den, dusting the crammed bookshelves. Miss Alice on the sofa propped up on pillows, watching me. She'd never let me take the books off the shelf to clean them, just dust their spines. She claimed there were some valuable tomes there but I never saw any evidence of that, just well-known authors collected as any reader would collect titles. Miss Alice liked mysteries—just like I did. It gave us something to talk about and share and there were plenty of those. Why was I remembering this in relation to finding things? Had Alice uttered that saying when I'd been dusting?

Then it hit me! "Jonah! I've been a fool! She was teasing me all the time and I missed it. She must have always distracted me when I got close... Quick, we have to get back to the main house!"

He didn't argue, but as soon as we stepped outside he was on full alert. "Smoke! It's coming from the farmhouse." He pulled his phone from his pocket and tossed it to me.

"The local volunteer brigade chief is listed under 'Fire.' Find it and call him! I'm going to race ahead and try to fight it off."

Chapter Five

H E WAS GONE before I had a chance to even open his phone. It took seconds to find the number and contact was pretty much immediate. Obviously it was a dedicated line. Once I'd passed on the information I took off after Jonah.

I found him at the back of the kitchen, with a garden hose trained on a smoking pile of rags and papers as flames licked skyward. I recognized some of the smoldering papers as some that we'd discarded as trash and dumped in Jonah's truck, even as the combined gasoline fumes and smoke burned my eyes. "They're on their way. What can I do?" I called as soon as I'd cleared the trees.

"Thankfully there's water in the well and it's pretty full," he shouted back. "Come and take this hose. Keep moving around the perimeter. Get it good and soaked. I think this is the main point but I can see some sparks up further," he said pointing to where smaller red flames licked at the aged clapboard. "I'll grab some buckets and try to get them out before they pick up the scent of that gas!"

I ran to take the hose, only taking the spray off the side

of the house long enough to fill the buckets. While the first filled, Jonah pulled a clean bandana from his pocket and dampened it before tying it to cover my mouth and nose. Then, a filled bucket in each hand, he sprinted to each spot, disappearing into the smoke and returning over and over to refill and take off again. As more flashes appeared in the dry grasses close the house, I was just beginning to fear we couldn't keep it controlled when I heard the distinctive whine of the sirens close by. My heart released some of the stress it was storing when the old truck rumbled into the yard and made its way to the farmhouse.

Three men jumped from the fire truck and then truck after farm truck raced into the yard and farmers and Airlie Falls residents—men and women—emerged, each wearing a hard hat and carrying shovels and picks. *Fiona would have her hands full at the markets getting help to man empty stalls.* Someone tossed a hard hat to Jonah and I realized he, too, was one of these volunteers, while another scooped me out of the way and yet others attached the wide heavy fire hoses to the in-ground well mechanism.

Everyone was there. I saw Clay over the far side and was reminded again—not that I needed it—that I was in a small town. Where else would the mayor be part of the volunteer fire service? Others came into view—the woman who ran the café where I'd had some delicious soup a few months ago. Reverend Peatree was there and also his wife. And a girl I'd seen the night before; Jonah had identified her as the editor of the local newspaper. She was petite and dark-haired and her elfin face seemed swamped by the hard hat. I'd put her at only about my age, which impressed me; she'd obviously achieved a great deal to be awarded the editorial post. According to Jonah she hadn't been in town long. Like everybody else, she was streaked with soot and grime—some more than others, I mused as I struggled for clear identification of a few. This wasn't easy work.

I was embarrassed that all I could do was speculate on volunteers and worry about my own concerns. I felt useless, but I understood they'd all shared some sort of training and that I could be a hindrance. Yet, at the same time I was so grateful for these people, I was also angry that there'd been a clue right under my nose and now I could be too late to get to it. I couldn't get that out of my head. But as the swarm of volunteers set to work amid the curtain of smoke, burying flames and spraying chemicals to eliminate the threat of the gasoline, I began to relax a bit more.

So far the damage to the house was minimal—at least as far as I could see—and limited to the kitchen. And with each passing minute the volunteers were taking the lead over the crackling fire. Just as with each passing minute I was becoming more and more aware that someone was playing a deadly game. Both my car and Jonah's truck were in the yard. Did this person realize we weren't inside? Or didn't that matter? Were we to be two more casualties? And for what? What was so important?

I itched to get into the house and it took an age but finally the fire chief declared the fire beaten and everybody began tidying the yard and packing up. Before I could head inside there were things to do; things I needed and wanted to do. I made my way around the crew, thanking them individually. They were a good bunch and the camaraderie couldn't hide the level of trust that bound them together and I found myself fighting a pang of envy.

One guy, who was introduced to me as Chuck, pumped my hand enthusiastically. He was probably in his late fifties, maybe sixties, and his gray hair was cut short, marine style. His skin was browned and weathered from years unprotected in the Texas sun. "So you're the gal who's gonna take over this old place? Lotta work but it could be worth it. Used to be good grazing land here and I remember my granddaddy talking about old Mother Auchinschloss's produce plots. Good growin' land here, he always said. My old Paw, he was always tryin' to win the county fair prizes but she had the gift. Cleaned up every year, she did. Took out every major prize."

There was so much to answer there, but I was caught on the bit about growing fruits and vegetables. It had always been a dream of mine, and one that potted herbs on our windowsill in Dallas hadn't even begun to realize. But before I could begin to dig further into that he moved on. "Funny that we're out here; at ol' Miss Alice's place. My daddy got a letter from her, you know. Right outta the blue. Just last week—just before she died, really."

That stopped me cold. "A letter? Are you sure?"

He nodded, again enthusiastically. "Oh yeah! Saw it myself!"

"You saw the letter?" Excitement rippled through me but I knew I had to proceed carefully. "Chuck, I know this seems like a rude question, but I don't suppose you know what that letter was about?"

His head dropped and he scuffed a clump of weed with the tip of his boot. "Well, it's not that I'd mind tellin' you now, Miss Rosie, but when I said I *saw* it, I really meant I saw the envelope. My daddy's getting on in age and I know he gets a bit impatient, but all I remember is that he just said it was a bit of nonsense and the past should be left in the past. He screwed it up and put it in the trash."

The building excitement left me like air leaving a burst balloon. In a rush. And that space was filled with questions. How did Miss Alice mail that letter? I thought I was the only person who saw her; that was the message I'd always gotten from her. There was no way she could manage that task on her own. So, who helped? She hated the people in the town. And what was in the letter?

"Chuck, are you sure your father didn't say anything more? About the contents of the letter?"

By the apologetic look on his face, I knew what I was going to hear, but before he was able to say a word a woman joined us. Smoke and grit smeared her jowly face. She was

short and round and her graying hair perched upon her head
like a cap. In fairness the unflattering style was most probably a good case of *helmet hair* because she'd also been
fighting the fire. And I was ashamed to admit my own
unflattering assessment of her was solely based on the sour
expression aimed at me. I'd found most folk here were polite
to my face, irrespective of what they were otherwise thinking.
But this woman was letting it all hang out on show and I
could almost have written her opinion of me. She was hiding
nothing. And it hurt.

"That's enough, Chuck. We don't need to be talking
about family business to strangers."

The man flushed under his tan. "Miss Rosie here's a
friend of Jonah's, Chrystal, and I don't think we should be
branding her a stranger." To me he said, "'Scuse my manners, Miss Rosie. This here's my wife Chrystal. She's gets a
bit protective over family; she didn't mean any disrespect."

Dragging at his arm to indicate it was time to go, Chrystal glared at him and I was under no delusion at all that she
meant every bit of that disrespect. Nor that poor old Chuck
was in trouble. I figured he'd get an earful once they were
out of my sight. He knew that too, if his reluctance to obey
her silent command was any indication.

I watched them walk away—him half a body taller, but it
was she who was obviously in charge. She was all but dragging him, not once loosening her grip even when they
slowed to speak to someone.

It had been an interesting conversation though and I wondered if Chrystal knew more than Chuck did. I believed him, and perhaps her distrust of me was purely based on the fact that I'd practically been accused of murder. If so, I couldn't honestly say I'd act any different in the same circumstance. What I *could* honestly say was that I was more confused than ever.

I needed to talk to Hank. And though I hated being yet another encroachment on his Saturday, I didn't think this could wait. But first I needed to get inside.

Jonah appeared beside me. His face blackened from smoke and his expression grim. "I know you want to go inside, but I have to get permission from our fire chief first." He nodded to one of the men securing the fire hoses.

No, no, no... I wasn't going to be stalled any longer. I'm not sure if I nodded. I hoped I hadn't because that would seem to be deceitful given the plan that was forming in my head. And as Jonah walked away, I glanced back toward the house, knowing I had minutes. Maybe seconds.

Trying not to draw attention and yet move quickly was the hardest part. For everyone else, the excitement was over and they were caught in that post-urgency letdown. They were wandering; the rush was over.

The kitchen door was the only one that offered access and I had to be careful. I reached it and hovered close, waiting for that precise moment when everyone was momentarily looking another way. Then I slipped inside, squinting in the gloom and trying not to slip in puddles. The gloom deepened as I made my way further into the house, the smoke-blackened windows not helping as I stumbled over furniture that we'd moved in our search and cleanup. Finally I made it to the den and went straight to the bookcase. It was almost impossible to read the titles but suddenly I remembered my phone and hit the flashlight app. As the light sprayed across the books there was just one title I longed to see.

And there it was.

I almost laughed out loud but I was aware that trouble in the form of the fire chief and Jonah was about to descend upon me. So, I snatched it up, shoved it up under my sweater and quickly made my way outside, this time letting my phone flashlight lead the way.

Heart thundering I'd just stepped out when Jonah's voice was right there close to my ear. "You went inside, didn't you?"

I wanted to lie, but I couldn't. Lying had never come easily, and apparently I had so many tells, it was futile to try. "Yes."

He moved to stand in front of me, and at the same time handed me a hard hat that he pressed against my stomach. "You know how dangerous that was? And do you know that any fire officer—volunteer or not—has the right to arrest you for entering a building deemed unsafe?"

This was getting really uncomfortable. "No... but—"

He cut me off. "So, I've got a deal for you. I won't arrest you if you have dinner with me tonight and tell me what was so important that you risked your life. Deal?"

Like I had a choice... I nodded.

The fire chief, a.k.a. Dan Casey the local pharmacist, came across then. "I 'spose Jonah told you that we think the building is safe?" Narrowing my eyes I shot Jonah a glance that told him there'd be more later, and smiled back at Dan who had more to say. "Of course I'll get the city investigating team down here as soon as possible and they'll check it out, but most of the fire was contained to the outer perimeter and I can't see how any major structural areas were compromised."

"I can't thank you enough. You've all been amazing."

He shrugged. "It helped that Jonah was on the spot. Who knows what would have happened if that fire had been left unattended for much longer? Could have been a whole lot worse. 'Specially with the amount of gasoline that was used. We were mighty lucky with this one."

I nodded. "There's no question then that this was deliberately lit?"

"None at all. My guess is that the lighter knew what he was doin' too. But that's just my take on it. It's pretty straightforward and those investigators will fill in any gaps. Now, what I will warn is that you limit your treks into the house to the bare essentials. Like, if you have a bag to collect, get it and get out. We could be wrong about the safety issue—though I'm pretty sure we're not—but who knows? Maybe they'll get lucky with some fingerprints or clues as to who did this." He glanced at us both. "So, you folks all right if we pack up?"

We nodded, and Jonah added, "Hey, record time getting here today, Dan! I didn't get a chance to say earlier but I was mighty grateful today was the day that record was broken!"

He slapped his friend on the back as he said it, but I noted the fire chief shuffling from foot to foot, like he needed a fast escape. He glanced over his shoulder to where his wife was hauling hoses. "No problem, Jonah. Just good luck. I'd just gotten back from deliveries out Greensville way and was passing the fire truck shed when the call came in."

Jonah grinned and slapped Dan on the back again. "Well, we appreciate it. Thanks, buddy. We'll let you get going and get out of here. I'll be checking in with you later."

Dan nodded and moved away. I stood and stared thoughtfully after him. That man had just blatantly lied. Greensville was geographically located in the opposite direction to the farmhouse. Dan claimed he'd been out there, yet, his truck had been parked at the side of the road not far from where we stood right that very minute. I'd noted it as I passed it on the way to the farm. He hadn't been delivering supplies out Greensville way. Had Jonah noticed it?

I turned to ask but was immediately distracted by his guilty grin. I narrowed my gaze. "You tricked me! You knew this place was safe! I call that dinner deal off because it was made under dishonest circumstances."

That cheeky grin held as though he was waiting for this moment—which of course he had to be. "Not the way I see it. You see, honey, that firefighter privilege is to be used at our discretion, and for all you know, I may not agree with Dan that the building is safe to return to. So, I was just doing my civic duty."

"By blackmailing me?"

Slightly moving the hard hat I'd subconsciously continued to clutch, he poked the package that was shoved up inside my sweater and his smiled deepened. "I'm grieved that you see it that way, ma'am. Perhaps you'll see it as protecting you." His voice lowered to not much more than a whisper. "Because while I've been here talking to you, I've also been shielding you from the crowd at large. And trying to hide that package that's about clear as possibly could be. Maybe if you were carrying a few pounds you'd get away with it, but as it is, it literally sticks out."

"Oh…" Instinctively I tried to hide it and almost dropped the hat in the process. The last thing I needed was anyone guessing I'd taken anything from the house.

"It's okay, the hat's doing the job I hoped it would, but it's not exactly subtle." He looked around. "Stay here a moment." When he returned he was carrying a heavy firefighting jacket that was about five sizes too large for me. At least. I pulled myself into it, winding it tightly against my body. It was bulky and thickly padded and I was pretty sure I could have hidden another person under there with me and no one would have noticed. So hiding a mere novel was no problem.

"But won't people wonder why I need it now? After everything's basically over?"

"Got it covered. Literally you might say," he replied with a grin. "I told them you were having a bit of delayed shock and I needed to warm you. I think someone's headed your way with a thermos of coffee, so if you have any acting skills, now would be a good time to employ them."

He'd barely got the words out when the girl I'd been told was the newspaper editor was beside me handing over a thermal mug. "You're Rosie, right? Pleased to meet you. I'm Midge Moylan. I've got some coffee—it might help warm you. It's hot and sweet. And I have a candy bar here as well. The sugar will help with the shock."

Heat flooded my face. This was like lying, right? Taking the mug and candy bar I muttered my thanks and tried to focus on something other than the deceit I was sure people could see a mile off.

Surprisingly, my embarrassed state helped because when my shaking hands fumbled with trying to juggle the mug, hold the book in place and open the candy bar it was indeed interpreted as shock. "Hey, it's okay," Midge soothed, patting my shoulder. To Jonah she said, "Maybe you should just get her home. A warm bath would help." Her eyes appraised me. "I hear she's been through a lot in just a day or so..."

Forever the newspaperwoman, I thought. Up close, without her oversized hard hat, she was as pretty as I'd thought earlier. Petite, fine-boned. That aside, I recognized that we shared the same elfin-type build and coloring. Even our hair was similar. It was a weird sensation, and made me wonder how people saw me, because behind those big brown eyes was a hard edge that I assumed had been honed as part of her profession. I figured nothing much would get past her. But then again, maybe something just had. Maybe we'd fooled her.

Or maybe we hadn't.

It put me on alert, and I didn't have to act when I felt my limbs start to shake and warm coffee spilled down over the outsized jacket. Noting this was for real, Jonah looped his arm around me. "I think that's a good idea," he told Midge. "I'll just get her to the car." As we passed through the stragglers, Jonah was eyeing them all carefully. In moments I knew why. He was working out who hadn't driven his or her own vehicle. The fire chief's wife had obviously arrived in the fire truck. He tossed her his own keys. "Hey, Vicki? Can you get this back to the B&B? I'll drive Rosie's car."

When he'd helped me into the passenger seat, he whispered that he was going back for my bag and the keys to the house so he could lock it up again. "And by the way," he added, "the deal is solid. I saved your sweet..."

I pushed at his shoulder. "All right… All right. I get the picture."

Smiling, I watched as he made his way back, stopping for the occasional word—and one hug. Midge Moylan was the one receiving the hug and I pushed back the little twinge of discomfort that aroused.

That fact was forgotten minutes later as we made to leave the property. We were in a line to enter the roadway, behind a couple of farm trucks awaiting passing traffic so they could move. The obstacle was just one car. A battered, pale green Chevrolet, and as it passed, my heart leapt. "Jonah! That's the car that was stopped in front of Miss Alice's house that day! Look!"

I hung my head out the window, trying to get a better view but when the driver saw me, she accelerated faster, speeding away.

Jonah blew out a gust of exasperation. "I can't follow! There's no room to overtake these trucks." He was right. By the time the trucks had lumbered back onto the road, the car was long gone.

DINNER WASN'T QUITE the romantic promise made out at Miss Alice's old farmhouse, which was fine by me. Fiona was, of course, over at the markets but she dropped back to the B&B just as we arrived from the farm, took one look at me, and suggested a quiet night. Her argument was strong. "You'll get no peace. Everyone will want to know every detail and you'll barely get a chance to eat."

She made sense, but proving we were still playing by his rules, Jonah insisted on doing the cooking. It had been an eventful few days and I didn't argue. We had the private quarters to ourselves. The two groups of guests were either at the market or in their rooms and Fiona and Clay, once he was presentable again, would be busy with the market till late in the evening.

More surprises were in store when Jonah served the meal. He'd created a chicken pesto pasta dish that tasted as good as anything I'd had at our local Italian back in Dallas.

"I'm impressed," I said taking a break to sip the icy beer he'd opened. He'd claimed it was the best thing for cutting through the smoke we'd inhaled, and I'd found no reason to argue so far.

I was on the sofa, feet up as per suggestion, which felt weird because there was nothing wrong with me. But in truth, the cosseting felt kind of felt nice. I couldn't handle it all the time, but I could cope with a bit of fuss occasionally. Like now.

From his position on the floor beside me, Jonah took my praise in his stride. "We have Chef Clay to thank for this."

"Pardon? I watched you prepare this yourself."

He nodded. "Neither of my parents bakes or cooks—they were being fully truthful when they told you that, but my dad is king of the grill. He's a barbeque machine. As a result he keeps his freezer and pantry pretty well stocked." He shrugged. "When I moved out I taught myself some basics and so I just used what I could find."

I held up my icy cold Shiner. "Well, cheers to Clay's freezer. And to you for taking those ingredients and turning them into something amazing."

Jonah was always so self-contained that it was strange to see him suddenly uneasy with the praise. It was kind of sweet actually. To hide his discomfort he pointed to the book I'd mysteriously covered with a scarf. "So, what was worth potentially risking your life for?"

Chapter Six

I HELD UP both hands with crossed fingers. "I'm not sure it's anything yet. I thought it was only fair to do this together, so I haven't looked yet."

"Well, thank you for that, but what makes you even think it might hold something we need?"

There it was again. That little word *we*. Stifling a smile I said, "It was something you said about finding something in the last place you look."

He nodded. "I remember—and you said something about Miss Alice laughing as she said it?"

"Uh-huh. And then I remembered this book. I always dusted the books on the shelf and we'd discuss her favorites. She'd choose which one she wanted me to read to her. I got to be fairly familiar with the titles on that shelf. This one," I explained holding up the scarf-wrapped parcel, "wasn't on those shelves, so I never paid that much attention to it. It was with the information books and she always rushed me through that section. And now—I think—I know why. But I must have subconsciously remembered the titles anyway."

He was still frowning when I handed over the parcel for

him to unwrap. The scarf fell away leaving the back cover facing him. He raised one eyebrow. "Hard cover. It's not an information book though, it looks like a novel."

I nodded. "It is. Turn it over to the front."

The next thing I heard was his laughter. "I don't believe it. That's its title? *The Last Place?*"

I grinned along with him. "If I'm right, she was clever."

"Time to see then," he said passing the book back over.

Gingerly I opened the cover but nothing awaited me. Anxious, I gently shook out the pages, hoping something was tucked in there, but again nothing appeared.

Disappointment surged through me. I'd been hoping this was it.

Jonah reached out to take it from me, examining the inner lining of the front and back covers. Then running his hands over the same area. Then repeating that action twice more. "Could be something here…" He pulled out a pocketknife and opened it to expose a sharp blade. Holding the book close he slid the knife down the inner lining of the cover and then gently pulled it back.

And out fell a photo.

My gasp conveyed as much disbelief as it did surprise.

He held the photo out to me. "I don't suppose you know anyone in this shot?"

"Hardly!" I answered after I'd studied the six young people lounging and picnicking on the bank of a river or stream. They were so relaxed. So happy. They probably would have looked happier if they didn't have pen marks slashed through them. "This is weird. Really weird. And it must be—what? Fifty years old?"

His eyes narrowed. "Sixty-three years and nine months. Give me a minute and I'll tell you how many days. I might be a bit stumped on hours and minutes."

"What? How can you know that?"

Winking he turned the photo in my fingers. And I saw the date printed neatly in the left corner. What was missing was any indication of the names of the subjects.

"Oh." If I hadn't been aware of being in Fiona's elegant home I would have aimed a cushion at him. "And here I thought you had some kind of psychic ability." He grinned and I turned back to the photo. "What does it mean, though? Why did she hide it? It's not like it's incriminating. At least as far we know." I shrugged. "It actually looks fairly innocent."

He didn't answer and I looked up to see him staring speculatively at me. "What?"

"Rosie, you've wondered several times why Miss Alice left everything to you. And yes, I know there's no one else and you were obviously genuinely kind to her. But—and maybe I'm crazy—but maybe she wanted you to find *this*. Maybe it's a bit of a puzzle."

"What? That's insane! Why would she do that! And what kind of puzzle? She surely couldn't have known she'd be murdered so it's not a puzzle that leads to the identity of her killer."

"I'm not sure," he said slowly, "but you said one of the things you shared was a love of mystery novels. Maybe it's a mystery she wants you to solve?"

My head was reeling. This was all too incredible to be true. There were way too many variables. The big one being that if Miss Alice hadn't been murdered, I wouldn't be searching for anything! And therefore I wouldn't have found this.

I said as much to Jonah. "And maybe there's an answer right there," he said. "Maybe she intended to give you more hints. But then of course, she—"

"Was murdered," I finished quietly.

"And maybe she has given you hints and you didn't realize?"

Those trailing words hung heavily and I groaned. Forcing my brain to recall every conversation was an impossible task and I felt exhausted at the prospect of even trying.

We were both silent for a while, and then he asked, "What are you going to do now?"

I shrugged. "First? Find out who these people are…"

THE NEXT MORNING was another lesson on the vagaries of small-town life. Despite the gathering crowds, who waited patiently, the market didn't begin on Sundays until after church. Though, because the markets were such an important part of the town's success and well-being, church times were adjusted to allow for that on market weekends and so by ten-thirty everyone was back at their stands.

I'd missed Fiona and Clay earlier so I wandered across in search of them and maybe a muffin and coffee. Thankfully I'd managed the latter two before I tracked down Fiona. She looked as gorgeous as ever, despite her claims of being completely harassed.

Because of that I almost backed down and didn't show her the photo but a rare spurt of selfishness took over. She perused it slowly, then passed it to Clay who'd come across to join us. "I recognize this guy on the end," Clay said. He looked skyward and then clicked his fingers. "John Thatcher Jones."

My head snapped up. "Why does that name seem familiar to me?"

"Well, his name was in the paper a couple of weeks ago, darlin'," Fiona offered. "Maybe you saw it then?"

Clay nodded. "Very tricky situation that. He was a local guy who died recently, but he wasn't well known. He was something of a hermit. Seems he'd lost his brother some years back and that's when he shut himself away. When John Thatcher died he left the proceeds of his house to have a park area created on the land and named after the brother."

"Yes, I do remember!" Alice had been really bad that day. We'd started off okay. We had breakfast and read the paper together, me reading aloud to her. Then, as sometimes happened, she went downhill very quickly. She'd become really anxious and needed extra medication and while she eventually rested I'd continued to read the paper. "And council rejected the idea?"

Clay sighed. "It wasn't an easy decision, Rosie. We have some protocols in place that we're guided by in situations like this. We have to be. Any council that doesn't is just invitin' a whole lotta headaches." He pushed his sunglasses further up over his nose. "Basically we're limited when naming public areas. There's a certain criteria that has to be met before we can even begin to discuss the possibility— things like how the person contributed to the betterment, growth, or establishment of the town, et cetera—and this time there was just nothing to go on."

I understood but I could see it must have been difficult. Such a delicate situation. But there was something else niggling me. "Jones…" I repeated. A common name. Very common. And yet. I snapped my fingers! "I've got it! Do you remember when I told you about that phone call? The one from the woman who hung up on me?"

Clay nodded.

"Well, there was some kind of commotion in the back-ground—like she was being served or something, and I heard someone say something to her. Now I'm sure those words were: '*Are you ready, Miss Jones?*'" I paused. "Sure of it…" It sounded like I was trying to convince myself and I prayed my memory wasn't playing tricks and making the dots all line up.

Clay rubbed his jaw with a long finger. "Jones is a very common name, Rosie," repeating what I'd silently been telling myself. "It may not have anything to do with this."

It was a long shot. I knew that, but still? To have that name come up twice? I appreciated Clay's caution but I'd hold on to my own hope on this one. I pointed back to the photo. "And you don't recognize anybody else?"

"Not offhand, but Fiona and I weren't even born at the time this was taken."

At the mention of her name she stepped back into the conversation after being needed by a vendor. "But, honey, I know who will know. After we've closed up this afternoon, I'll take you to meet the Fab Four."

I remembered that term from when my parents were around in my childhood. "You're going to take me to meet *The Beatles?*"

She laughed. "Better, honey. Better. Now, you meet me back at the B&B at four. We should be done by then. Sunday is a short day when we have an extended weekend like the first of a season."

Considering I was about to become a part of this market setup, this was interesting to me and it was nice to focus on something pleasant that might be in my future, instead of wondering how I'd look in orange or whatever color the Texas Corrections Board had chosen as this season's new black. "The Farmer's Market isn't always this long and hectic?"

Dramatically she wiped her hand across her brow. "Darlin', that would completely do me in! No, this here is one of our four big market weekends. We do them to celebrate the beginning of each season. The rest are just Saturday and Sunday, no night markets, and they happen every second weekend. We have a month break after Christmas and if the weather's real bad in winter, we sometimes—not often—just open on a Saturday. Winter crowds are much smaller."

I nodded, my mind momentarily flirting with things I could create for my own stall, and the pretty ways I could present them. Shivers of excitement fluttered through me. Was it possible to really live your dream? Or was I just being teased by the possibility, only to have it taken away?

The belief that the direction of my future was all up to me reinforced itself and I made my goodbyes and excused myself to try and find Hank. As it turned out he was hanging out over near Bobby Don's chili stand.

First, I hit him with the possibility of living in the erroneously named *little house*. He chewed on that for a moment, along with the fat cigar he also chewed on. I hadn't seen him with it before, but on Hank, it made sense.

As he pondered he was shaking his head. "I just can't see how that would work, Miss Rosie. There's no furniture there and…"

He was cut off by Fiona who was obviously passing. And

listening. "Now I'm not even going to apologize for what I just heard, but as welcome as Rosie is with us, this seems like a mighty good idea!"

Hank's frown deepened. "How do you see that?"

"Well, I see it as a win-win situation. Now if the worst happens—which it won't," she assured in a quick aside, "then it's your moral and legal responsibility to sell that property for the most you can get, right?"

He nodded, confusion still wreathing his face.

"And that means," she continued, "presenting it in the best way possible. Now bear with me here: That little house is the jewel in the crown out there. The big house has amazing possibilities, but with dual occupancy, the little one will clinch the sale. So why not let Rosie move in while we wait out this mess? She can decorate and modernize to bring it up to this century, which will only add to the value, right?"

Hank chewed furiously for a moment. "And just who's gonna pay for this update?"

"The estate of course! You release the funds to a responsible third person—"

"And that would be someone like you, I take it?" he answered in the knowing tone born of long acquaintance.

"If you insist," she shot back breezily. "Hank, the estate can't lose. Whatever is spent can be gained back double-fold. And if it doesn't need to be sold, then Rosie has a beautiful home."

"Hmmn, I guess it would be good to have someone on

the property to save any more nonsense like we've had the past few days. Though, I'm not sure I like the idea of it bein' just a slip of a gal like you, Miss Rosie."

The *slip of a gal* tried not to take offense. "Hank, an eighty-five-year-old woman lived out there alone and she was okay. So, I think a fit, almost thirty-year-old could cope."

This last comment seemed to cause the old lawyer some embarrassment and he dropped his gaze to his worn boots. "Well maybe that was before all this business."

My heart picked up its pace. "Hank? What are you saying? Does this mean you finally agree with me? That you believe that someone out there may have an agenda?"

His gaze now swept the area. "Well, I had a talk to young Jonah and Dan Casey. Dan says that fire was deliberately set and Jonah swears you were with him the entire time and not even near the house when it was lit. And I may as well tell you that Sheriff Kinnead now has his doubts about your involvement as well." Perhaps it was reading the hope and relief that swept through me that prompted him to remove the cigar and hold up a warning hand. "Now, mind you understand this doesn't mean everything has changed where you're concerned, but it's fair to say it's cast some doubt. And another thing you should know is that it was Jonah who spoke to us and convinced us to open our minds a bit. Not that it took much. I can accept one random act but not a whole passel of them."

While this long speech had been delivered, Fiona's hand

had crept in to squeeze mine. It was an even tighter squeeze when her son was named as the one who'd gone to bat for me. Again. She was a proud mama and she had reason to be. Whereas I didn't want to get my hopes dashed by any of it—not the legal part and not Jonah's intentions—so I tried to maintain some calm. Though I had no hope of controlling the grin that split my face when Hank added that he agreed with Fiona about the house and would get the paperwork rolling the next day.

This of all days was sizing up to be the best day I'd had, so far, in Airlie Falls.

High-fiving me, Fiona made her way back to her voluntary duties as Market Manager, promising we'd talk later. I moved on as well, promising myself a little bit of time out to look around the market in bright sunshine and get a feel for it. Maybe it was in part the news I'd gotten from Hank, but the more I wandered, the more excited I got. Plans were racing and building in my mind faster than I could keep track.

I'd source my supplies—or as many as I could—from the local producers. I made a mental note of egg suppliers, fruit, honey, molasses, goat's milk, cow's milk, pecans… Vegetables. Cheese. So many more as I passed their stalls. My mind whirled. I'd have to get Fiona to introduce me. Maybe if things worked out, I'd eventually be able to grow some of my own, but for now, I'd proudly make use of local produce and ensure customers knew that.

Of course, I thought adding to my mental list, I'd have to build a relationship with the general store operator for the other staples and maybe the unusual ingredients I needed.

The only downer during my reconnaissance mission was when passing the Kinneads' jam and preserves stall. Today she and the Sheriff hustled behind the loaded tables, but Miz Kinnead looked exhausted. In fact, taking in her pale complexion and the sheen of perspiration giving her a less than healthy glow, I would have guessed her to be quite unwell. Life was unfair in putting her husband up as a barrier to me offering her some help. Or was it my own cowardice? I needed to think about that.

I'd made a complete pass around the entire market, amazed at the size and scope and therefore not surprised it had gained so much fame and interest. At the far northern end the offerings were both artistic and practical and they excited me as well. Miniature sheds that offered an idea of what the real thing would look like, and other woodwork items like swings and rocking chairs. Beehives as well—with all the gear. There were even some small livestock stalls offering farm stock like goats and chickens to small-time farmers or those with bigger urban yards. Just as I'd like to be, if I was able to beat this situation. I sent up a small prayer. The yearning in me intensified when I came across chicken coops and fabulous ironwork, and I could immediately see that coop out at the little house and a new arched sign hanging out over the gateway to replace the rusted old one.

I was getting away from myself. Letting my dreams and hopes cloud my purpose. Yes, that dream was so close I could almost reach out and touch it. But that small distance between me and fulfillment of that dream housed a big ugly mean alligator, ready to chomp me up. And barely a moment went by when I didn't remember that fact.

Unsure of how to pass the next couple of hours I headed back to the B&B, and only when I reached into my jeans pocket for the key I'd been given, and my fingers touched the photo, did I remember Hank. I'd forgotten to ask him about the photo! And also if he'd posted the letter to Chuck's dad!

Charging back across The Green proved to be futile. He'd gone. Or if he hadn't, I couldn't find him. Guilt tempered my decision to call him. It was Sunday. Besides, the Fab Four might be able to answer everything.

The house was empty again and I made for the kitchen. Clay and Fiona would be exhausted when they got back. I didn't know what their regular routine entailed, but even if I prepared dinner and they had other plans, it could keep, right?

Scouring the freezer and pantry I came up with a simple but warming menu. Racing back across to the market I picked up some fresh ingredients and then headed back to the kitchen.

Potato, leek, and bacon soup was safe. The salad could be

made at the last minute. A biscuit-topped beef and vegetable casserole would keep if not needed, and an old English dessert my friend Jess's grandmother had taught me, would finish it off. Queen of Puddings, as it was called, was light and sweet. Perfect after a heavy meal. Custard base, then berry jam, and topped with light fluffy meringue and baked. It would have time to cool to serve at room temperature.

Delicious aromas filled the house and while the last element baked, I made some coffee and started listing some of the ideas I'd come up with for my own stall.

The timing was perfect as I'd just taken the casserole from the oven when I heard Fiona and Clay traipse through. For a moment concern filled me that I'd again taken such liberties but the looks of pleasure on their faces replaced it with relief. Still, I had to ask, "You don't mind?"

"Oh, darlin'," Fiona said launching herself at me for a huge hug. "This is divine! I can tell you the last thing we want to do when we get back is to face preparing food—and maybe we're getting old, but we're also too tired to go out! This is a dream come true and we can't thank you enough!"

"I have a complaint though," Clay was quick to add. "And that is that I have to wait! This smells wonderful, Rosie."

After Fiona sent him packing with a hunk of leftover peach pie to tide him over she grabbed her truck keys. Funny how everyone in Airlie Falls drove a truck. I guessed it was practical and maybe that would be me one day.

THE FAB FOUR lived in a retirement village compound just at the edge of town. *Riverbend* had been purpose built and was surrounded by mature magnolias, shade trees and magnificent gardens. We found the four we'd come to visit sitting at a table in a gauzed porch, each wearing a visor and each holding a hand of cards.

"Poker," Fiona whispered as we drew near. "It's their obsession. Just don't get tricked into playing with them. They're unapologetic cheats."

All four ladies were well into their eighties, two with white fluffy hair, one with blue tinges, and one pink but their eyes were bright and alert and I figured not much would get by without them knowing about it.

I was quickly introduced: Lori Sue, Betsy, Martha, and Ethel Therese. Lori Sue pointed to the last woman introduced. "Just call her E.T. We do!"

They all beamed, proud of their cleverness. I learned that Lori Sue, one of the two fluffy white heads, was Clay's aunt, and she was as petite and delicate as he was tall and broad.

"We haven't interrupted your afternoon snack have we?" Fiona asked, looking about and searching for evidence of just that.

"All done," E.T. answered. "But you're a great excuse for us to order some coffee. They don't usually let us have it after lunchtime. But they can't deny our guests can they?"

"Good idea, E.T.," Betsy chirped. "And get cookies too. And not those oatmeal, fiber ones—they taste like cardboard."

"Now, dear," Lori Sue said looking shrewdly at Fiona, "what brings you out here? Sunday isn't one of your usual visiting days." As though she'd premised bad news, the old woman's hand suddenly gripped the table, alarm now tingeing her words. "It's not the boys is it? Or Clay?"

Fiona hugged her aunt-in-law. "No, darlin', the boys are doing well and Clay's fine and fit. Well, he will be after he's had a little nap. I swear these markets are getting busier and busier."

Betsy nodded. "But you're doin' such a good job for this town, dear, you and Clay. To think eighteen years ago this place was ready to turn up its toes and now look at it? It's thrivin'. All thanks to you."

Fiona smiled, her fondness for these women obvious in her tone as she answered. "I need to come out here every day and get a dose of this. You gals are good for my soul."

Lori Sue was still watching her niece-in-law carefully, though she shuffled around to make room when E.T. returned leaning heavily on her walking stick and followed by someone in uniform pushing a trolley laden with a coffee pot and all the trimmings, cookies and even some cake.

When the attendant left and the others looked at E.T. expectantly she shrugged. "I told them the mayor's wife was here visiting with a mysterious special guest and we should take this opportunity to make a good impression with good Texas hospitality." She cleared her throat. "I may have mentioned something about newspapers and publicity, but you know how confused I get sometimes…"

I could barely suppress my shocked grin. Blatant manipulation! And they looked so sweet and innocent! It was easy to see how these women were good card sharks. And it was obviously their modus operandi because the other three took it in their stride, offering their polite congratulations on a job well done before diving in to chow down like they hadn't eaten in a month.

Fiona was laughing to the point of tears rolling down her cheeks but I began to worry. Was hunger an issue? Did they get enough to eat here? All worries, though, disappeared when one said through a mouthful of cake, "Try this, Rosie. It's good. I had three pieces this morning."

Once they'd had their fill, Lori Sue turned back to Fiona. "So what's the problem?"

This time Fiona answered instantly. "First I need to give you a bit more information about Rosie, here." I cringed but Fiona marched on. "As ridiculous as it seems Rosie is a 'person of interest' in Miss Alice Auchinschloss's murder."

Of course they didn't know me at all; knew even less about me than the Fencott family did, so I was uncomfortable with Fiona's declaration that my current situation was ridiculous. They had no way of discerning that, and I certainly didn't expect it to gain me support. But wonders kept happening here in Airlie Falls.

"Well that *is* ridiculous," Lori Sue agreed immediately.

E.T. nodded vigorously. "I agree. Whoever murdered that old bat should be given a commendation—not hounded by the police!" And while the other two added their indignant agreement that it was all totally unfair and that Sheriff Kinnead needed a stern talking-to, all four were looking at me with something akin to awe and pride.

My heart sank. Really? *Really?*

"So, what can we do?" asked Betsy, her pink hair moving gently in the breeze like a freshly whipped stick of cotton candy. "Hide her out? My room's at the end. I could push her out the window when they come to do the beds and clean."

"Thank you, Betsy," Fiona answered—and amazingly with a straight face. "Nothing so extreme for the moment but we'll keep that in mind for the future. No," she continued, "what we need is some information about this town and the past."

Lori Sue nodded briskly. "Well, you've come to the right place. The past is what we're best at."

"Well, it is where we spend most of our time," E.T. added quietly.

I pulled out the photo and Lori Sue whistled before passing it over to the others who huddled around it, pointing and muttering among themselves.

Martha eyed her friends. "You think this was taken that

very day?"

Lori Sue shrugged. "Could well have been. That day or just before. I think they picnicked there often."

A prickly sensation was building in my stomach. "You recognize these people? There was a special day?"

Chapter Seven

"OH YES, DEAR, this was a tight group," Lori Sue explained. "Spent all their free time together. Well except for the younger Jones boy. What was his name?"

"John Thatcher's brother?" Fiona asked. At Lori Sue's nod she continued. "Jethro—but they called him Jed." To the others she said by way of explanation, "It came up in council business recently."

"He wasn't quite right," E.T. said, tapping her head, "if my memory serves."

The others agreed but Lori Sue as the seemingly appointed spokesperson explained further. "Beautiful boy to look at; breathtaking. And sweet-natured as you'd ever get. But he'd have never been able to work or take care of himself. Such a tragedy. And then when he died... Oh Lordy, what a commotion. Some said it was a blessing but no heavenly favors were enjoyed by that family. It was more like a curse. It destroyed them."

She stared at the photo for several more moments then pointed at the strikes through each figure. "I take it this is Alice's handiwork?"

I shrugged. "I assume so, but why would you immediately assume she did it?"

Four faces rose to meet mine. "She didn't tell you?" E.T. asked, but it was a rhetorical question and she didn't wait for a reply. "John Thatcher Jones was her beau. They were betrothed. And then young Jed died and John blamed himself and cut himself off from not just Alice—but the world really. Like a ghost he was. He died recently you know? And the biggest surprise was that folk thought he'd died years ago. That's how long it'd been since anyone'd seen him."

A silence settled over the group as we all retreated into our own thoughts. Mine were chaotic but perhaps I spied a glimmer of an idea within all those swirling questions. I opened my mouth to voice one but was drowned out by a loud gong.

"Dinner," Fiona whispered.

Given all they'd consumed I was sure they'd be happy to sit and chat a bit longer but I had fiercely underestimated the needs (or desires) of healthy octogenarians. They were out of their chairs like shots and heading off in the direction of the dining room before even saying proper goodbyes.

"Roast beef and gravy," E.T. called back by way of explanation. "And pineapple upside-down cake with ice-cream."

I looked across at Fiona and read the same futility there that I knew must be on my own face. "Can't compete with that," she said on a shrug.

JONAH CAME BY for dinner and I tried to ignore the pointed but good-natured remarks from his parents about suddenly seeing him so frequently. He'd spent a catch-up day out at his own farm and though his eyes reflected the hard work he'd put in and he was freshly showered, I felt I could almost smell the vitality and sunshine on his golden skin from where he sat beside me at the table.

He wasn't a man who had to be heard all the time; he calmly took things in his stride—so his carefree silence in the face of this ribbing was to be expected. But when he inhaled appreciatively and winked as he passed the biscuit-topped casserole I knew he'd added fuel to their fire.

Thankfully oblivious, Clay was tucking in. "So, how'd you go this afternoon?"

"We were doing great up until the dinner gong rang," Fiona answered.

Both men laughed, and Jonah shook his head in wonder. "You were flirting with danger to even *try* to visit them a mere hour or so out from a meal. Brave women. You could have been crushed in the stampede."

After the resultant chuckle died down, I said, "It was fascinating learning more about Miss Alice. Such a tragic past…"

We were all quiet, letting that thought swirl around us, and when Fiona excused herself to answer the phone, I let more of the day's conversations roll over in my head. How were they all connected? And more importantly, how was I going to connect them? But just as Jonah raised an enquiring eyebrow, a warning knock pounded on the main door before boots clapped against the hardwood floor.

Was it because this was a B&B or because it was the mayor's home—or just because it was Airlie Falls that people seem to think they could walk in? And did. And no one questioned it.

All eyes were turned to the hallway when Deputy Bobby Don appeared. Removing his hat, he nodded. "Evenin'. I apologize for interrupting your dinner, Mayor."

Clay waved him in and Jonah pulled out a chair. Apparently the sharp words they'd exchanged the other night were on some kind of backburner. "You had dinner, Bobby Don? We've got plenty. And don't start stressing, Rosie did the cooking, not Mom. And it's as good as it gets."

"You're livin' dangerously, son," Clay chuckled. To B.D. he said, "But he's right and we have plenty. Let me grab you a plate."

Bobby Don's eyes darted from the food to my face and back and I had a feeling he was tempted, but something was holding him back. Something that was making him uncomfortable. Me?

He held up a restraining hand. "It's okay, Mayor. I won't

be stayin'." His eyes had held mine during his little speech. "Miss Rosie? Sheriff Kinnead would like you to come down to have a chat with him in the morning. He suggested nine o'clock."

"But I thought..." Or was that it? Was this meeting so that he could apologize to me for assuming I'd murdered Miss Alice? But if that was it, Bobby Don would be a whole lot more relaxed.

"You can tell Sheriff Kinnead that Rosie already has a previous appointment at eight-thirty that's likely to take all morning," Fiona said as she strode back into the room. Taking her chair she continued. "So, unless he has another meeting, twelve-thirty would suit her well."

Bobby Don shifted from foot to foot, his hat twisting in his fingers. "I'll pass that on, Miz Fiona. And, Rosie? Sheriff also said that if you have a lawyer then maybe he better be present as well."

My fork slipped from my fingers, its clatter ominous in the sudden silence. Not an apology then...

"What's this about, B.D.?"

"Well, I can't rightly say, Jonah," the deputy answered. Then he tapped the side of his nose. "We've been doin' a bit of investigating and we've turned up something we think is 'very interesting.'" He made quotation marks with his fingers, but he needn't have. We got the emphasis.

I didn't think I was the only one to get that maybe B.D. was the one who'd discovered this *information*. It was in the way he puffed out his chest when he passed on his news. And in the covert glance he shot me right at the end.

It left me feeling a bit sick imagining that man—any person actually—raking through my life to reveal something *very interesting*.

After he'd left, dinner was a much quieter affair. I'm not sure if anyone ate much. I didn't and my thoughts were so tangled that I didn't even look at what anyone else did. I excused myself before dessert, unable to cope with the weight of exhaustion that had come over me with Bobby Don's words.

But as weary as I felt, sleep still eluded me until the early hours and I found myself having to rush to make it to my *previous appointment*. The call Fiona had taken had been from Lori Sue, and that's where I was headed. Fiona had suggested we meet straight after a meal because they seemed to get distracted as it got closer to mealtimes.

Fiona was traveling with me, and despite being grateful, I knew I was horrid company. Even the thought of Jess's arrival that evening wasn't enough to lift my spirits, and that had been the one thing that had kept me going.

Fiona kept up a one-sided conversation as I drove, appearing not to mind that I found it too difficult to contribute. She was clever—she focused on something fun to take my mind off Sheriff Kinnead and the reason for his visit by chatting about the little house.

"Let's meet there this afternoon," she suggested. "That

could give us time to look over Miss Alice's house to see what we can move across and what we need to buy. All we need are the essentials first. It can be decorated slowly. It's always good if you can live in a space first to see how you'll use it. Then we can decorate."

Even in my misery it was hard not to be caught up in her enthusiasm. Hard not to hope...

And that was a good thing because there was more of a spring to my step as we greeted the Fab Four.

Lori Sue got straight down to business. "We realized we didn't tell you everything yesterday, dear."

"No," added E.T. "We need to fill in a few gaps. We chatted last night after dinner, getting our memories straight."

We walked through to the back gardens. The sunny courtyard they chose was welcoming and peaceful, and the air crisp and refreshing. As the sun rose higher it would burn through and despite only being spring, by noon it could be too warm to sit here for long. We settled into a grouping of cane furniture padded with cheerful, tropical-patterned cushions and I held my breath hoping one of my companions wouldn't decide to order food.

I didn't want to waste a moment—just in case. "You mentioned a particular day when we spoke yesterday?" My eyes roved from one to the other.

Martha nodded. Her soft blue hair blended perfectly with the baby-blue knit jacket she wore over her cotton print dress. The contradiction of fluffy exterior and razor-sharp mind was awesome—in the literal sense. And it applied to all of them. In their pastel colors, with their gentle demeanors, sweet smiles, walking aids, and orthopedic shoes but it was the eyes that gave them away. Shrewd and intelligent. They'd experienced a lot of life and they'd survived to tell the story.

"That day," Martha continued, "was the day young Jed died."

Betsy shrugged. "Or as some say—"

"Was murdered," E.T. finished.

Lori Sue sighed. "We're just speculating and you all know it." To me she said, "It was never proved. They ruled it an accident. But there were some folk—Alice for example— who vehemently believed that Jed was murdered."

I shook my head. "But Jed was the intellectually challenged one, wasn't he? So how would anyone benefit from his murder? Why would they murder him?"

"Alice had a theory. She was always reading those mystery books of hers, and she claimed she was gonna prove it. 'Course she never did," Lori Sue said.

"Okay..." I was trying to make any kind of sense out of what they'd said. "Did Miss Alice ever give you any hints?"

Four heads moved in negative response. "Not that we know of or remember," Betsy added.

Fiona had been sitting quietly, seemingly perusing the lush garden. "What about that day? What do you know about it? Who was there?"

The ladies tumbled over themselves to speak but Lori Sue held up a hand and the other three settled in silence. "You girls can correct me if I'm wrong or fill in blanks but Rosie won't hear anything if we all talk over each other."

Settling back she began her tale. "They were all there, out by the river where it runs through Alice's place—your place now—having a picnic. All the people in that photo, plus Alice. Seven of them. Alice must have taken the photo. They were always together, that group. Sometimes Jed was with them and sometimes he wasn't. You have to remember that we didn't have a lot to do with them because we were a little bit older and I guess we had our own things to do. Four or five years makes a difference. At that stage, we were probably chasing babies or making a living. Anyway, moving on, there was a lot of confusion over what happened that day, if I recall—and where everyone was at the time."

She stopped to draw breath and I was reminded that these were elderly ladies. Very elderly.

E.T. sat forward, leaning heavily on her stick with both hands. "Lori Sue's right. There was a lot of confusion. Alice always said she and John Thatcher didn't see what happened to Jed. They were away from the group—canoodling apparently. Of course their papas weren't happy about that, but she admitted it proudly."

"Do we know what happened to Jed?"

"Apparently he fell," Martha put in. "The back of his head was pure caved in. Cracked his whole skull to pieces.

Like he'd smashed it against rocks or something just as hard."

My mind recalled the property I'd sort of inherited. It was reasonably vast and I'd barely seen a fraction of it, but I didn't recall any hills or high spots. "How far did he fall? For an injury like that it would have needed to be a substantial distance…"

I could see Fiona frowning, and I was sure her mind was traveling in the same direction as mine.

"Well, that's just the thing. There isn't a high spot out there. Sure there's the dip where the land rolls down to the river, and the natural rises of the land, but nothin' he could have climbed up on and fallen from." Lori Sue shrugged. "They said he must have tripped backward over a rock and whacked his head. And the others supported that. And in fairness there are some big rocks out there by the river."

Fiona fixed her glare on her aunt. "They saw him do it?"

"Well, one saw it apparently, that girl… What's her name? Ivory? Ivory Sternuk as she was then… Maybe she still is… Anyway, the others claimed to have been looking away for that moment but when they heard the scream they all concurred that was what must have happened."

None of it made sense. "And you say no one benefited from his death?"

Again the combined negative response. Betsy shuffled back in her chair and I could see pain in her eyes as she moved her legs. "The way I see it, there were only losers. Of course poor young Jed lost his life; the Joneses were just devastated; John Thatcher Jones cut himself off from the world; and Alice Auchinschloss's life and future crumpled before her eyes—and that began a lifetime of hatred with the town. Not only did she lose her love and chance of a life with him, Alice was also genuinely devoted to Jed so she was just riddled with grief."

"And don't forget the other loser. Ivory Sternuk! She never got her chance with John Thatcher," E.T. chuckled.

"Oh surely she got over that silly crush!" Lori Sue exclaimed.

"Not according to her sister! Brenda Kinnead claimed it took years for her sister to stop pining over John Thatcher."

The name Kinnead sent a pang of misery through me, but that wasn't why my head snapped up. "Sheriff Kinnead's sister-in-law was involved in this? The one who had a crush on John Thatcher and was the only one who saw Jed fall is related to the Kinneads? The same girl?" I shook my head. "Well, hardly a 'girl.' She hasn't been a girl for a long time; not if she's about the same age as everyone else."

Martha was nodding. "Early eighties if she's a day."

"My, my... Ivory Sternuk. Wonders will never cease," Fiona muttered seemingly lost in her own thoughts.

Martha shrugged, aiming her comment at Fiona. "'Course, Frank wasn't married to Brenda at the time. He wasn't even in the force then. Too young. He and Brenda were just little kids. Probably not even in high school."

"What about the others? Who are they?"

Eyeglasses were adjusted or cleaned as they leaned forward. Martha pointed a knobbly finger at one of the two unidentified men. "I think that's Forster Jacobz. What do you think, girls?"

As the photo was pulled ever closer to their eyes in turn, assent echoed along the line. Fiona looked impressed. "His granddaughter, Delvene, runs the café," she whispered to me. "Have you met her?"

I shrugged. "I've eaten in her café occasionally."

Fiona smiled. "Nice girl, you'll like her." The intent in her eyes was unmistakable. Apparently I was going to formally meet her. And soon. Although I wondered at any reciprocal feeling. I may well like her—she'd always seemed pleasant, so I didn't doubt that. But if she discovered I might be about to cause trouble for her family by asking questions—would *she* like me?

The 'girls' were still looking at the photo and muttering. While I was waiting I looked around, turning to a movement at one of the windows of the long hall that looked out over the gardens. A woman was walking through the corridor and I leaned forward to ensure I was seeing correctly. And suddenly everything froze. It was the mystery woman! The one outside Miss Alice's and then at the house on the day of the fire!

I took off, running along the pathway, curving through the gardens to reach the door that led back inside. Turning right, I walked as quickly as was safe, taking care around the elderly and their various walking aids. I slowed as I met each one, aware that my movements could confuse or alarm them, but despite my attempts at speed, the woman had disappeared. Again.

Defeated, I trudged back to the group, expecting a barrage of questions and knowing they'd all be watching for me. I cut them off by diving in with my explanations first, unable to keep the frustration from my tone.

"Describe her," Martha ordered.

I did, but I held no hope they'd really be able to identify someone from such a general description. But as I'd found many times on this recent journey, I was wrong.

"Hmmn, sounds like Haven Jones," Lori Sue replied. "I saw her here the other day as well. I'm not sure who she's visiting, but I can tell you it was like seeing a ghost! We haven't seen her for years!"

"No, but she *has* been in and out of Airlie Falls lately, apparently," E.T. supplied. "One of the ladies in the east wing was telling me that her daughter had seen Haven driving around in that beat-up car of hers. Seems she's visiting people from her past."

I held up a hand. "I hate interrupting this—but did you say 'Jones'? Surely we're not talking about the same Jones family?"

"Of course, sweetie," Lori Sue explained. "That's John Thatcher and Jed's sister. Younger. Her life wasn't fun after

Jed died, with her brother locking himself away and her parents grieving."

"They had a sister?" This was getting to be too much to cope with. Surely if anyone had revenge on their minds it would be their sister? What had brought her back to Airlie Falls, especially if the girls were correct and she hadn't been around for years? And why was she avoiding me? She didn't even know me—nor I her!

Martha nodded. "Yes, dear! Just the one sister. Two boys and Haven. She eventually got away and married—and you wouldn't believe it but she married someone named Jones! Didn't even have to change her name! Some thought she should have been Haven Jones Jones—but she decided against it apparently."

I curbed my impatience and waited for the story that would eventually come. E.T. took up the narration. "Of course by the time she was old enough to marry, her family had all but been destroyed by then. The older Joneses had money once. Real money. But they died paupers. In fact Haven supported them in the end."

Betsy wasn't going to be left out. "Apparently her only daughter—Haven's daughter Barbara—blamed Airlie Falls for the fact that her inheritance was lost. She's quite bitter about it."

It was a stretch but was it possible the woman who phoned Miss Alice around the same time I started seeing Haven, was Haven's daughter? The daughter who had a grudge against the residents of Airlie Falls and—if my instincts were correct—probably and especially against the five people who'd been with her uncles that fateful day.

Well, another mystery solved but it seemed the more I discovered the more questions it raised.

"Now this photo," Fiona prompted bringing the girls back to task.

I frowned as I watched them. They were tiring and I was beginning to worry. But like the troupers they were, they dived right back in.

"Right." E.T. patted her white cotton-ball wispy hair as she turned to me. "Now the girl on the far right is Charlene Madison. She lives out here at Riverbend, too. Over in the other wing." She leaned closer—eyes twinkling. "Her younger sister Merline has the beauty parlor in town and comes out here to make sure we're still beautiful in our golden years."

I smiled back. "And an amazing job she does."

The old ladies twittered for a moment and as it died away I noted Martha's face fold into a frown. She looked at her friends, eyeing each meaningfully before she spoke. "Of course there is that other business concerning Charlene..."

The other three seemed to suddenly find their shoes interesting. Again it was Lori Sue who took charge. "In for a dime, in for a dollar, girls. We said we'd help, so we may as well spill. Though, Rosie? We've never said a word of this to anyone else."

"Goodness; sounds intriguing!" Fiona murmured.

"Private is a better word," Lori continued on a sigh. "You see, we were just sitting in one of the courtyards one day a few weeks back. We were trying to find some sun, and we accidentally overheard a conversation."

"Charlene?" I asked. "Was she speaking or was she the subject?"

Lori Sue shook her head. "No, she was speaking. Yelling more like. We know we should have moved but I think we were all mesmerized. Besides moving isn't a quick and easy exercise for us, and we were embarrassed that we'd heard it at all—and I guess we didn't want to get caught. So we just stayed where we were."

Betsy's turn to shake her head, though in disapproval or shame, I wasn't sure. "She was talking about a child—a babe—she'd given up for adoption when she was a girl."

Almost bursting now, Martha jumped in, "And that kid was right here!"

Lori shushed her. "That's not right, you silly old goat! Her *grandchild*, not her child. And someone was begging her to meet with him. Or her."

Martha had taken no offense so I let this new information roll down through my logic filters. Was this important? Relevant? Maybe. "Did she meet up?"

"We're not sure," E.T. answered. "There was also mention of the father—or grandfather as he'd be—but the voices dropped and we couldn't make out the name."

I tapped my fingernail against my phone. "So, there's a grandchild somewhere out there who's keen to meet his or her grandparents?"

"Oh, not somewhere, dear. Right here in Airlie Falls."

I stared at them all. Being given this information was like finding an extra piece of a jigsaw puzzle. You think it fits, because it matches the rest of the picture—but there are no more spaces. And so, you have no idea what to do with it.

While I tried to process it all, the ladies had drifted into another conversation until an exclamation from Betsy silenced them and snapped me back to the present. "Oh, I just remembered! I feel like a silly old fool!"

"Nothing you haven't felt before, Betsy," E.T. told her. "Just spit it out."

Ignoring the slight, Betsy drew her hand up to her chest. "It's just come to me! It was something Merline said a couple of days ago. When was she last here?" Betsy didn't wait for a reply. "Oh it doesn't matter... The thing is that she said something about Charlene getting a letter. Now I admit I was drifting off at the time—*Merline gives the most amazing head massages, don't you know*—and that's why I almost forgot about it. Probably would have completely forgotten if we hadn't been talking about her and Charlene right now..."

"Betsy!" Lori Sue demanded. "The point?"

Betsy's hands were fluttering and I reached over to take one in mine; calming her. "Well, it's just that I'm sure she said the letter Charlene received was from Alice!"

There was a chorus of *oohs* and *aahs* but I ignored them. My mind was racing ahead prompting a chill that rattled through me, finding every bump and crevice, startling my every nerve end.

Another letter? "Tell me," I said, only barely remembering not to squeeze too tight on Betsy's hand. "Would one of the people in this photo be related to someone called Chuck? His wife's name is Chrystal."

The older four faces were momentarily blank until Fiona said, "Chuck and Chrystal? You mean the Kings?"

Then all four faces were animated. "The Kings? Oh yes, dear! Yes!"

"Chavez King! That's him! Chuck's father," Lori Sue said pointing at the dashing young man in the photo. "We should have remembered earlier."

"His maternal grandfather was Spanish…"

"Very good-looking man if I remember correctly…"

Amazingly I managed to hear it all and absorb it all. Two of the four living people in the photo had gotten letters from Miss Alice. I couldn't help but wonder if it had been all four.

Unfortunately I also heard and absorbed the repercussions of a trolley being wheeled along linoleum floors, then an obvious bump followed by the hum of wheels rolled along carpet. Cups and dishes rattled and one look at my informants' faces told a story. Sure they were hungry and thirsty as usual, but they were also drained. And more than one was ready for some pills and a rest. After caring for Miss Alice, I recognized the signs. And while I was grateful for their time and interest, I was also speared with guilt. Catching Fiona's eye, I rose.

"I'm so very, very grateful to you all, but I don't want to overstay my welcome. I think we'll go and leave you to enjoy your morning snack and maybe have a rest?"

Gratitude, regret, and fondness shone back at me from the beautiful old faces before me. "My dear, we're loving bein' useful to someone again," Lori Sue said quietly. "And we'd love it if you came back again."

I smiled and hugged each in turn. "I'd like that very much, and I know I'll still need your help."

Back in the car Fiona checked the time. "We have the best part of two hours before you meet with Sheriff Kinnead. I say we calm your nerves with some herbal tea. What do you think?"

I doubted anything would calm those nerves but I'd rather be with someone as I waited out the time, than alone with my thoughts. "I assume you mean at the town's café and not at the B&B?"

Her smile said it all and she settled back into the seat. For a moment she watched the passing scenery, and I wondered if she still saw the gorgeous wild flowers—like the cheerful bluebonnets—or whether she was just used to them now. Her mind wasn't on wild flowers though. "Well, what a productive morning. Do you agree?"

I sighed because I'd been thinking the same thing. "Yes,"

I said, drawing out the word, "but confusing too. I feel we learned a lot, gleaned a lot of information. But is it all helpful to my situation or not? I wish I could pull everything out of my head and lay it all out and study it from a different angle."

"That sure would make it easy. By the way, what did you make of Charlene's baby story?"

"I don't know. I can't see how it's relevant to our case. If it was a secret Miss Alice was planning on exposing then why wait sixty-four years? And who could it hurt now?"

"The father? Grandfather?"

"No, it doesn't make sense, but then again, neither does poisoning Miss Alice! The answers must be there. I just have to work out where!"

She chuckled at my frustration; the deep husky sound fading away when I groaned out loud. "What am I doing? *What am I saying???* I'm feeling like an arrogant fool, Fiona. Why would I think that I could solve a real-life mystery? Those stories I read are manipulated by the author! They're created to be solved. They're not real! And this is my life I'm playing with—and it's very real!"

I sensed her frown and then felt her hand against my arm. "Honey, don't you go beating yourself up. You're resilient and brave. And you're not alone. You remember that."

The words were nice, but my frustration ran deep. "I know, I know... And I'm grateful, I truly am. I just wish I knew where to go next; what to *do* next..." I shook my head trying to clear away the confusion. "I keep thinking that I'm missing something obvious. Jonah suggested Miss Alice had left me a message. But if she did, what is it? Where is it? And what if she didn't? Then I'm just wasting more time."

"You're letting this stress get to you, darlin'. We've just started. There are a lot of rocks that we haven't turned over yet, don't you worry."

My thoughts fully hitched themselves to Miss Alice as I drove on. I saw her face, her scowl, her smile—though more rare. The woman had made me her heir. Whether it was out of some self-serving reason or just pure kindness, I didn't know. But I still felt guilty that I was only hearing negatives and I hadn't done anything to defend her. "Was she as bad as everyone says, Fiona? Miss Alice, I mean. Was she really that horrible? Sure, she was as miserable as a cat without a tail a lot of the time, but she had her better days, too."

Fiona sighed. "You gotta remember, as Clay said earlier, he and I weren't even born when all this played out more than sixty years ago, so obviously we didn't know her then. So, I guess my opinion is based on what I've seen as an adult and town scuttlebutt."

"Like what?"

"Well, from what I've heard, she was always difficult. Selfish, I guess. But then a lot of people are selfish and it doesn't make them all bad. Her sister, Marion, was the opposite, but Miss Alice made it so that Marion was ashamed to show her face here much. The townsfolk didn't care, they'd have welcomed Marion any way she chose, but I suspect that Miss Alice was putting so much pressure on her sister that it was easier to just stay away."

"Is that a reason to hate her though?"

"Oh, it was way more than that. Old Alice tried every way she could to cause trouble. Here's an example: This is rural Texas; we're surrounded by ranches and farms, so animals get out. It's an accepted fact here. But Miss Alice would report it to the authorities and then inspectors would descend in droves and people would find themselves getting unfairly fined. And of course while they were here..."

Her trailing words let me fill in the gaps. "Oh... I see. They started poking around other properties?"

She nodded. "In a community like this, if animals get out—or any other drama happens—we all just pitch in and help out. We don't go running off with tales. And if there's damage done, likewise we patch it up. These are good people, Rosie. Salt of the earth. Every farmer, rancher, and town person knows it could happen to any of us—not just those on big properties." She waved her arm. "Myrtle Szykov lives right on the edge of town and she's only got a couple of goats and a sheep, but I swear those rascals have caused more damage than any herd. It proves it could happen to anyone! And we just all help out."

She paused for breath. "Over the years, Miss Alice was responsible for more than one farmer losing an entire crop season because some bogus complaint she made meant that unnecessary investigations held up planting time. It was so sad. And wrong!"

My mind went back to the accusation Jonah had aimed at the deputy. "Fiona, was Bobby Don's family one of those affected?"

She nodded. "There were a few families like that. Dan Casey—the pharmacist and fire chief—was another. His and Bobby Don's were the worst hit but there were others."

The fire at the farm was started by someone who knew what they were doing... Fire chiefs understood fire. And Dan prepared some of Alice's medications. Could he have poisoned her? Retribution?

But why now? It always came back to that one question.

I made a mental note to try to find out where each of those men were the afternoon and evening of Miss Alice's death.

Fiona was on a roll, and not ready to wind down yet. I sensed her frustration building. "This is a hard life out here. Sure we love it, but it's tough for the farmers and ranchers. A bad season can send them to the wall. That's how our dance nights started."

We'd arrived at the B&B and I flicked my head toward her as I parked the car. We'd walk the short distance to the café from here. "Dance nights?"

Everything in Airlie Falls was slower than in Dallas, including the pace we walked. As we strolled I felt the change in Fiona. The topic soothed her; her voice softened and a smile played around her mouth. "After one of Miss Alice's meaner episodes, one of our farmers was in big trouble. We'd devoted our Farmer's Market profits, but we needed more, so dance nights were born. It was a way of keeping the city folk here longer, getting them to part with a bit more cash. And they were such a success that we continued them. Randomly and always in summer. We've got a good system. We set up a dance stage, string pretty lights—and a few of the good ol' boys turn up with their guitars and fiddles, even a small electric piano... We provide refreshments—for sale of course—and there you have it! We all love those nights!" She chuckled. "Come to think of it, maybe we should be thanking old Alice!"

Dance nights... A misty image materialized and I was momentarily powerless to pull away from it. Warm summer Texan nights. Music, pretty lights, and a certain sandy-haired cowboy with soulful eyes and a smile to melt chocolate. His arms around me...

Suddenly I remembered that certain cowboy's mother was right beside me, and I'd have been mortified if she'd somehow read my thoughts. Unbidden, a squeaky little gasp escaped my lips, and I kept my face low to hide the embarrassment that was spreading through me.

My worst fears were realized when I heard the words, "Oh dear... that's not good."

How could she have done that? How could she have read my

thoughts? Despite my shame, my head jerked up only to find Fiona's focus on something in front of us.

Following her gaze, my own reaction was more of curiosity—and a fair chunk of foolish relief. "What th—"

Chapter Eight

A GIRL I recognized as a teenaged waitress at Delvene's café was draping black ribbon across the closed doors under a black wreath that hung front and center.

Fiona's pace picked up to almost a run. "Emmy Kaye? Honey? What's wrong? What's happened?"

The concern in Fiona's voice was so real, reminding me of my fascination with all things small town. These people genuinely cared for each other.

The girl's normally pretty face was blotched and swollen and even as we approached I could see fat teardrops glistening on her long lashes. Turning to be enveloped by one of Fiona's hugs seemed natural.

Pulling back she swiped her hand across her face, catching her hair, leaving the rich brown strands stuck to her wet cheek. I leaned in to lift them away. "Are you okay?"

She nodded and hauled in a deep breath before saying, "It's Mister Jacobz. Delvene's granddaddy. He's gone, Miz Fiona. Passed real quick. Delvene's taken off to be with her Mama and Mawmaw."

"Oh that's so sad, dear," Fiona soothed again. "I didn't

realize he was unwell."

"Well, I guess that's the thing. Delvene's madder than a skillet full of rattlesnakes right now. Seems her granddaddy was fine, and then he got some letter and then just after that, he had some kind of turn or attack or something. Doc said it was his heart and probably had nothing to do with the letter, but Delvene's on the warpath." Eyes wide, she shook her head. "I'm tellin' ya, I wouldn't like to be the one who sent that letter!"

My skin prickled the way it had out with the Fab Four. "Delvene blames the letter?"

Those eyes somehow appeared to grow even wider. "Yes, ma'am! Says her granddaddy would've been around for years more if that letter hadn't turned up!"

I didn't have to ask, guess, or wonder who'd sent that letter.

It took a little while before we could move on; it didn't seem polite or right to rush off, but as others gathered to hear the news, we made our way back to the B&B.

"I have to call Clay," Fiona said as soon as we moved into the cool of her entry. Once more the order, color, and beautiful fragrance permeating the home immediately calmed me and I headed toward the kitchen as she made her way to the study.

I imagined that as members of the community, she and Clay would pay their respects, but being mayor and first lady of Airlie Falls probably brought additional responsibilities in these situations.

There was still quite a bit of time before I was due to see Sheriff Kinnead and with suddenly nothing to do I felt the stress begin to build again. What could all this mean? Why did he want to see me? I knew only one thing—it was more likely to be bad news than good.

My hands were shaking as I boiled water for tea and once more I turned to the distraction that would help calm me. Having perused the pantry and cupboards I knew what was available. The Fencotts would no doubt want to take offerings to Delvene's family and I set to work. Date and pecan bars would keep well and freeze if not needed immediately, as would a ginger cake with a zingy lemon frosting. I was well into the task by the time Fiona walked into the kitchen.

"I hope… I mean I thought you might want to take food with you? To help the family? They'll probably have a lot of friends and relatives call…"

Perhaps Fiona saw the uncertainty in my eyes because her smile was instant and warm, crushing my doubts. "Oh, darlin'! You're a blessing. That's so generous of you, especially when you have so much else on your mind." She gave me a quick hug. "And I'll be making sure they know who did the baking. Don't you worry!"

"Oh please. That's not necessary. I just want to hel—"

"Help schmelp!" she scoffed. "Honey, I'm thinkin' of the success of your future baked goods stand at the markets! The more people who learn about your magic, the better!" She grinned. "Don't be shocked now. I may not agree with my sons that I'm the scariest woman in town, but I will admit I never let an opportunity pass by."

I wasn't shocked but I was scared to give in to the spear of hope that shot through me when she mentioned the market stall. Could dreams really come true? And so thoroughly and rapidly? I'd never have imagined becoming such an integral part of the community so quickly.

Returning her cheeky grin I had a sudden thought. Fiona was either an angel or the devil incarnate. Either she could help me make those dreams come true, or she was just torturing me with a tantalizing glimpse of a future that would never happen. But then she hugged me and I figured no hellion could be filled with such love. So I just had to accept she really believed it could all happen. I just wished I could do the same.

With an airy wave she then excused herself to do some work in her office, while I finished up. But not before she claimed the last bar that didn't quite fit into the airtight container I'd found in the corner cupboard.

Before scooting upstairs I ensured the kitchen was spotless, then checked the time. I'd decided to walk to see the Sheriff, and was glad to still have time for a quick freshen-up first.

I didn't call goodbye as I slipped from the house. I knew Fiona would insist on accompanying me, and I just couldn't take more of her time. In my mind I was proving to be a big enough burden.

The day was perfect. It had blossomed into its early promise of a warm spring day. The sky was endless and blue, the flowers bold and proud and fragrant in their matching boxes along the sidewalk down Main Street. Store awnings offered shade and I appreciated it. The "warm" spring sunshine had started to burn through the sheer sleeveless blouse with its fluted armholes that I'd teamed with my jeans. I'd chosen it because it was light and cool—and was a favorite, hoping it would give me confidence—but I could see where sleeves might have helped.

It shouldn't have surprised me to be greeted by so many as I passed by. And greeted warmly. Despite my stomach churning faster than a 747 engine, I dug deep to return their smiles, trying to enjoy what could be the last time I walked this street without this shadow of an official murder charge hanging over me.

There were fewer people down the end of the street that housed the police station. Set back in a quiet corner, the low, flat-roofed building with its adobe walls was painted a muddy color and tipped a nod to Spanish architecture. The paint was flaking in the parts visible through the lush magenta bougainvillea that clung determinedly. I figured that bold, rich vine was probably the reason no one had attempted to paint. And cutting it down would be criminal.

I almost smiled at my accidental pun. Almost. A loose-limbed shade tree provided relief off to one side, and I focused on the rustic hardwood benches at its base. Maybe I should try to gather myself there before heading inside; give my shaking legs a break?

I was almost there, just ready to collapse onto that seating when someone popped out from around the other side of the tree.

"Oh Lord!" One hand flailed wildly, the other went to my heart.

Someone reached to steady me, and as they made contact my vision cleared. "Jonah?"

"Hey... You okay?" He indicated another bench behind the tree, hidden from the street. "Sorry, darlin'... I was just here waiting for you. You don't need to go through this alone." His smooth whiskey voice was like a magic balm. It rolled over me, calming me.

Managing a smile I nodded that I understood and appreciated the thought. "Thank you so much. But I think your dad organized that lawyer—"

My voice was shaking and he reached to warm both my hands. "I was thinking more in a personal capacity than a legal one."

Whatever I might have answered was cut off by a shout from another voice I recognized. Turning we saw Hank lumbering toward us, his hand raised in some kind of silent message.

"I'm sorry, folks," he began right after greeting us. "Seems that lawyer Clay contacted has had an automobile accident on the way down here and he's not gonna make it."

My heart jerked a second time. "He's dead?"

Hank frowned, thinking over his words. "Oh... Poor choice of words. Sorry again for that." He paused, pulling the ever-present cigar from his mouth. "No, he's not gonna make this meeting. He's fine as it turns out, but the hospital has advised him to rest up. He's pretty bruised and sore."

Try as I might, I simply couldn't control the tears that welled in my eyes. I was truly sorry for the man, and managed to say so, but I also knew I was probably sunk.

Hank waved away my concern, and while Jonah moved in closer to slip a comforting arm around my waist, Hank ignored my distress, slight though it was. "Now the reason I know all this," Hank continued, "is that he called me to ask me to fill in for him."

My eyes widened.

Jonah's low-whistled response complemented my own. "Is that a good option for Rosie? Isn't there a conflict of interest?"

Hank shrugged. "Miss Rosie, whatever else I am or whoever else I've represented, I'm an honest lawyer. An honest man. You need someone to listen and look out for your best interests, and if you trust me, I can do that today."

It was a no-brainer really. I'd sensed I could trust Hank from the beginning. I didn't even need to think; I immediately nodded. And then my little procession filed in to face the ogre in his den.

The woman who greeted us sat behind a makeshift desk that was really just a kitchen table incongruously covered by a lace tablecloth that appeared to be hand crafted. A computer screen sat in the center. On one side of the desk sat a dish of sweet caramel candy and on the other a dish of Warheads. One for the good and one for the bad? Which would I be offered?

Beside the desk stood a water cooler and beside that a side table also covered in lace. However, instead of the usual paper cups, the table boasted sparkling drinking glasses and a jar of store-bought cookies.

I'd absorbed all this in one quick glance. Now looking at the woman herself my first impression was that she obviously went to Merline's beauty parlor. Her hair was big and tizzy but her smile made you forget that in an instant. She introduced herself as Janet Falkes, Frank's—not much—younger sister and leaned over to claim a kiss from both Hank and Jonah.

My head was already reeling at the surprise of the police department interior looking like your granny's parlor when she said, "Now you go on back there to Frank's office and he'll be with you in a moment. He's just slipped off to the little boys' room."

I choked back a nervous giggle. Sheriff Kinnead would not be happy to hear her sharing that information with a potential criminal. Jonah's hand rested on my shoulder and I felt him squeeze, but I dared not peek at him lest I laughed out loud. I did start to wonder if Janet added that to make me feel more at ease. That thought solidified when she whispered, "Now don't you let that man bully you, you hear? His bark is way worse than his bite…"

I'd sobered completely by the time we settled ourselves in the office. Hank and I sat side by side and Jonah propped up against a wall just to my right. I liked that I barely had to turn to see his face. Just as Sheriff Kinnead walked in Jonah winked and gave me a thumbs-up sign. Ridiculously, it helped.

The Sheriff greeted us and thanked us for coming, then set his confused gaze on Hank. He nodded after receiving the explanation and then started fiddling with some papers on the desk before him. If it was a ploy to make me nervous, I needed to congratulate him. It worked.

Finally clearing his throat, he focused on one sheet of paper and then raised his eyes to mine. "Miss Hart, Rosie?" I leaned forward. "Do you recognize these words?"

It took me a moment to bring the printed page I'd been handed into context. Then it fell into place. "Oh my blog! Yes, this is my blog." Well it was part of my blog. "I haven't actually been very active lately. It was something I was doing to pass the time between jobs."

He nodded. "A blog. That's like an opinion piece you publish on the internet and anyone can read it, right?" At my nod his whole face did a funny squiggle that I interpreted as him questioning the sanity of doing such a thing. Too nervous to say more I simply waited for him to settle and continue. "And so, as I understand, you're admitting you wrote this?"

"Of course I do. It would be there on the internet for anybody to read, so why would I deny it?"

"Did you consider denying it?"

I looked from Hank to Jonah and then back to Sheriff Kinnead. "I don't get that question. Why would I consider denying it?"

The Sheriff rubbed his nose, and his mouth did that exaggerated kiss thing. "You don't think there's any correlation between this"—he tapped the page—"and your current situation? That it might make you look guilty?"

"Guilty?" Was the man crazy? "No, none."

He shook his head. "Would you mind listening to this paragraph then?" He didn't wait for a reply. "*It's cruel to watch her suffer. She's old and she's in pain. She's paid her dues and it's her time. I believe that her caregiver not only has the right—but also the responsibility—to end it now.*"

I sensed rather than saw both the other men shift back away from me. But why? This was ridiculous.

"Frank," Hank said quickly, "if you're gonna charge Rosie with something this isn't the way. She hasn't even been mirandized!"

Sheriff Kinnead held up a hand. "Don't go getting ahead of yourself, Hank. At this stage we're just talking." To me he said, "Rosie, do you have objections to answering these questions?"

I shook my head. "No, but they're not making any sense! What on earth could my blog have to do with Miss Alice's death?"

He wasn't giving up. "Rosie, you wrote this about someone called *Belle*—is that correct?"

"*Someone* is a funny way to identify her, but, yes I wrote it about Belle."

He wrote something down. "Hmmn… Would you agree that you felt the same way about Miss Alice as you did about this Belle? That she'd suffered enough?"

"Rosie," Hank growled, "as your current counsel, I'm advising you not to answer that question."

I shrugged. "But why? Thank you, Hank, but this is ridiculous. I'll answer and hopefully we can clear this up." To the Sheriff I said, "Of course I didn't! To start with Miss Alice wasn't on her last legs and anyway, she had options. Not like poor Belle. I felt very passionately about Belle. Okay I admit she was a dog, but she deserved to be treated humanely."

In front and to my left I heard shocked gasps. To my right I heard a slow chuckle and when I glanced across, I saw dawning comprehension, though I didn't quite understand what he'd comprehended.

"Miss Hart, I warn you that speaking about an old lady like that isn't doing you any favors. You're talking about humanity in one breath and then calling the poor woman a dog!"

"But she was! What do you want me to call her? A bitch? Sheriff, you're not the only one getting hot under the collar here. What has any of this got to do with Miss Alice? Belle was one hundred and nineteen years old! Well at least if you believe that every year is equivalent to…"

The look on the Sheriff's face stopped me. Not that he'd have heard me anyway. Jonah's chuckle grew into a full-blown laugh, uncontrolled and free, drowning out everything. It was a wonderful sound. On the other side of me, Hank also began to snicker, quietly but still a snicker.

Sheriff Kinnead's face, however, was suddenly so red I feared for his health. When he warned them both to regain control or he'd ask them to leave, the laughter grew louder.

"Put him out of his misery, Rosie," Jonah managed. "Tell him who Belle is."

Again confusion swamped me, leaving me feeling I like I was missing something huge. And obvious. "Why? He's got the blog right there. He knows Belle was a dog my neighbor had taken in and was caring for."

Veins expanded dangerously on the Sheriff's temple. "Miss Hart!"

"Frank!" Hank yelled, trying to be heard over his friend's bluster. "Listen to what she's saying! Unless I'm completely mistaken Belle was a dog! A real dog! A four-legged, tail-wagging animal!"

The Sheriff hesitated.

Hank filled the breach. "Let me make it easier. Rosie, what breed was Belle?"

"A dachshund. A rescue dog. My neighbor had been beating herself up over whether to put her down or not, and it was breaking my heart. Belle was suffering so and crying all the time. The vet said there was nothing they could do; that it was cruel to keep her suffering like that. I was thinking about it a lot, and so I wrote about it. It was a popular blog, a lot of people commented…"

Sheriff Kinnead's color faded. His eyes narrowed and for a moment his mouth was moving but no sound came out. Finally he said, "Let me get this straight. This really is about a dog? The kind that barks and—" Any more words failed him.

"A sausage dog!" Hank inserted on a gasping chuckle.

Outside the door I heard dishes crash to the floor, and laughter that someone was trying unsuccessfully to mute.

Indignation rushed me into speech and I ignored whatever was happening outside. But at least I finally got what I'd been missing. "Of course it is! You didn't really think I was talking about a human being? Wasn't her age a giveaway? Who lives to be one hundred and nineteen? It's all right there…" Frowning, I turned the page over and then leaned in to look at the other pages the Sheriff had been shuffling. "You don't have the other page? The beginning of the blog? The photograph?"

Through gritted teeth he said, "It appears I do not." I

heard his knuckles crack and then his breathing became so erratic I feared he'd pass out. "Would you all please leave. Now." It was an order, quietly given and forced through tight lips, but an order just the same.

We were barely in the reception area when we heard the roar. One word. "McAuley!"

This prompted both men with me to let fly with their own roars—but of laughter. Janet, sitting at her desk blatantly crocheting a fine lace item, joined them. "Poor Bobby Don," she said between chortles. "Maybe he should just stick to his chili…"

Outside, Hank had to support himself against the wall of the building until he could stand unassisted. "That was the most fun I've had in a long time," he muttered as he wiped tears from his eyes.

Jonah had casually thrown an arm across my shoulder. "Can't argue with you there, Hank. We'll have to keep on our toes though. Ol' Frank isn't going to forget that we watched him being made the fool. He'll want payback."

Hank shook his head. "He'll be okay. He'll go out and shoot a few targets and get it all out of his system. There's only one person needs to be on his toes."

"Bobby Don." It was uttered in unison and like a match to dry tinder, ignited more gales of laughter.

When they'd calmed down, Hank fixed his eyes on me. "Now, Rosie, I don't want you to go thinking this gets you off the hook, but it does prove to me that they're scratching to find anything substantial to use against you. Still, you need to stay alert and don't go doin' anything to make yourself look bad."

I wasn't sure what that meant, but it gave me the opportunity to bring up the other things on my mind. I told them about the letters and the information we'd gotten from Lori Sue and the girls. Perhaps I shouldn't have been so free with Hank, but he'd never hinted that he wanted to see me charged or that he thought I'd been guilty. Apart from that I'd felt a shift in our relationship during this short experience. It felt like we'd bonded somehow...

Jonah had listened intently and his questions about whether I'd spoken to any of the oldies who'd gotten letters held more of a worried tone, whereas Hank's query about how Alice mailed the letters was pure curiosity.

We parted on a flurry of hugs with me promising to catch up with Jonah at his folks' place later. Whatever happened there, I consoled myself with the thought that I'd end up with a good friend.

When I got back to the B&B I left a note for Fiona telling her I'd finished earlier than expected and was going out to the house and for her to meet me whenever she was free.

Thirty minutes later, it was no easier going into the farmhouse this time than it had been since Miss Alice died. As always the silence was eerie, but now too, the whole place was permeated with the distinctive aroma of wet ash. Actually it was worse than the actual damage.

Shivers trickled up my spine and at first I jumped at every creak and groan the old building offered. Upstairs was brighter; not as overwhelming. No flames or hoses had affected the upper level, but as I wandered through the rooms I saw little that I thought would be suitable to take over to the other house. I didn't want the old beds, though maybe the bedheads could be refinished. Maybe side tables...

My phone rang as I composed my mental list.

"Rosie? Hank here. Listen, I'm out here at Riverbend." As usual, his big voice boomed down the line, making me think he barely needed a phone. He could have just yelled to me from there! More importantly, I wondered if he ever considered that other people might be listening? He'd be difficult to ignore, and I knew from experience that there were many curious minds and loose tongues out at Riverbend. His words filtered back through my thoughts. "I just wanted to check your whereabouts because I've got some information I think you'll find real helpful."

"Information? Please tell me it's not some other blog that someone misinterpreted."

He chuckled. "No, this came from Merline's sister, Charlene. She's agreed that I should tell you, but I think we'd better meet and discuss it face to face. Are you free this afternoon?"

We agreed to meet at the farm as soon as he could get out there. In the meantime, too many questions reeled around in my head. Hank had sounded serious, and he'd intimated that it would be beneficial to me. Excitement buzzed through me. I looked at my watch, knowing I'd have to keep busy while I waited or go crazy.

I headed back upstairs. Miss Alice didn't have a vast or elaborate wardrobe but it would have to be sorted at some stage so maybe I could begin that job. One wardrobe in particular was interesting. The clothes were old, but barely worn. Wispy chiffons and lace, silky numbers so fine and thin they weighed almost nothing. She would have worn these for John Thatcher. My heart clenched. Dust, bugs, and time had taken their toll, seeping into the grain of the fabrics, making some of them so fragile my fingers slipped right through. It was eerie. I felt like the clothes had crumbled, just as her life had. So, so sad...

I'd been so engrossed that time had disappeared, and just as I thought I should look out for Hank, I heard a noise downstairs. I didn't even consider being afraid, I simply added one more garment to the discard pile and headed down to meet him.

I'd just stepped off the last stair when I saw him. He was in the living room and at first my brain couldn't comprehend what he was doing on the floor.

Until I saw the blood. It was everywhere. Seeping out of Hank way too quickly...

I think I called out; later I wasn't sure. The last thing I remembered was his gray face as I ran to him.

And that's when I felt the pain...

Chapter Nine

IT WAS THE smell I noticed first. That eye-watering antiseptic smell that you only ever associate with hospitals. That was followed by maybe a full minute of confusion before everything came tumbling back. "Hank!" Jack-knifing into a full upright sitting position had been instinctive. And stupid.

"Hey... Easy. Take it easy." I knew that voice, even if the room was spinning too quickly for me to actually make out the person speaking.

"Jonah?"

"Sure is, honey." Gently he guided me back onto the pillows. "I'm just gonna call the nurse now. Okay?"

I wanted him to wait, to tell me what was going on, but he was insistent. The nurse bustled in, took my vitals, checked my pain levels, asked me a pile of questions, and then after my assurances that I felt fine—warned me to rest.

I tried to be patient. She was just doing her job, but by the time she left I thought I was going to burst. So many questions buzzed around my head, one of which probably wouldn't be asked: *What was Jonah doing here?*

The room was bright and before the first question could leave my lips something else occurred to me. "Is it still Monday?"

He shook his head. "Tuesday, darlin'. You've had a nice long snooze."

"For real? And Hank? Is he okay?"

His smile slid away. "Mom's sitting with him and his sister right now. He took a bad whack and he's in a coma. They haven't given up hope but he's gonna need a lot of attention and prayers."

My hand came up to my mouth, effectively capturing the gasp I had no chance of controlling. "This is terrible!" Shaking away the images that suddenly appeared in my head, I reached across to him. "Jonah, what happened out there? Do you know?"

His eyebrows slid up under the shaggy hair that fell across his forehead. "Sheriff Kinnead is probably on his way here as we speak, but I know we were depending on you to fill in some of the gaps."

I shrugged. "There's not much to remember. I saw Hank on the floor and as I went to him, someone hit me. At least that's what it felt like. Who found us?"

"Mom and Frank arrived at the same time pretty much. Mom was there to meet up with you and the Sheriff was acting on a tip that you'd hit Hank with a heavy frying pan."

"What? That's insane! Jonah, I didn't hit anyone! I got hit myself!"

He nodded. "I believe you, honey. I gotta say it didn't look good. Mom and Frank found you draped across Hank, and the frying pan was lying there right by your side."

My chest was suddenly doing strange things. "Is Frank—um the Sheriff... Is he coming to arrest me?"

The smile reappeared and I was never so grateful for its presence. "Don't go worrying until you have to. Both Frank and the doc agreed that there was no way you could've hit yourself hard enough on the back of the head to knock yourself out. Especially with that frying pan. And at that angle. Impossible in fact. And as it had your blood on it as well as Hank's—well..."

I nodded, hoping I'd start to feel relief but when a slight knock tapped on the door I almost jumped out of bed. Jonah was quick. He was on his feet and his arms enfolded me as Fiona's face peered into the opening.

"The nurse told me you were awake? Are you okay, honey?"

I nodded. "Hank?"

She shook her head. "Just the same."

Her face was lined, and dark shadows under her eyes told of her exhaustion. "Have you been here all night?"

She looked over at her son and winked. "We're a tough bunch, aren't we, darlin'?"

Heat burned through my body. Had Jonah stayed here all night as well? It seemed he had. But before I had time to bluster my gratitude, Fiona said, "Do you remember anything, Rosie?"

"Only seeing Hank and getting hit. I didn't see anyone. I didn't know anyone else was there."

"Just what I was going to ask."

We all turned to see Sheriff Kinnead pushing through the now open door. I hated having such a violent reaction but I immediately began to shake, and Jonah tightened his hold, whispering soothing words as the other man removed his hat and approached the bed.

"It's okay, Rosie. I'm not here to harass you. But I do need some answers. Like, what Hank was doing out at the farm."

"Well," I began, looking at each of them in turn, "he called me because he had some information he thought I might find useful, but he felt it would be better to tell me face to face." I shrugged. "I was already at the farm waiting for Fiona, so he came on out."

The Sheriff shuffled his hat from hand to hand. "I see. And did he say where he got this information?"

"Yes, actually he did. He said it came from Miss Charlene—Merline's sister. He was out at the retirement village and called me from there."

"Well that's easy," Fiona put in quickly. "We'll just go out there to Riverbend and ask her ourselves."

The Sheriff's mouth went straight into its kissy mode. I was beginning to recognize that habit as one that preceded something he didn't really want to have to say. "Might not be that easy, I'm afraid." He sighed and looked at Fiona. "I've just come from the retirement village. I'm sorry to say that Miss Charlene passed away through the night."

"What?" Fiona spluttered. "But she wasn't even sick! I saw her at church just last week! Merline brought her out from the village and she said she felt marvelous!"

Ignoring Fiona, the Sheriff chewed on his cheek for a moment. "And, Rosie, you say Hank gave no indication about what he was going to tell you?"

I was still reeling from the news that another member of that group from the photo had died in not much more than a week! "No! Nothing. Other than the fact that Charlene had agreed he could share it with me."

Jonah straightened and settled his butt on the edge of the bed. "Surely there has to be some kind of connection here, Frank? I'm not much into conspiracy theories, but this seems way more than a coincidence to me."

"Careful what you're saying there, young man," Frank warned. "Because what you're intimating here is murder and I'm not prepared to let that notion get out into the community before I've checked everything out. You hear me?"

Jonah nodded. "I won't go sharing my opinions, but others won't be so respectful and you know it."

The older man's shoulders slumped. "I know, which is why I'd appreciate any help I could get. Now I got jobs to do, so I'll bid y'all goodbye." He tipped his hat. "You get well now, Rosie."

As he left, Fiona's phone sprang to life and she excused herself to answer it, only to come back looking even more distressed. "Oh, honey, I can't believe I have to deliver even more bad news. Your friend Jess can't get down here. Seems she tripped at work and broke her ankle. Her mom has taken her back home for a few weeks. Such a lovely girl—she's just so upset about you. She was sobbing!"

Fiona looked like she was going to join Jess in the sobbing and I wouldn't be far behind her. This was the last thing Jess needed.

"Oh poor Jess! You called her?"

"Oh I hope you don't mind! I knew she was due to arrive so I found her number in your phone to give her the news. It actually suited her to take one more shift, then come down. I gave her my number in case you… Well you know, in case it took longer than we expected."

"I don't mind at all. I think it was very thoughtful."

"Well, I think it was meant to be—not that I want to see your friend hurt," Jonah growled from his place at my side. "Moving out there to the little house hasn't been sitting real easy with me, and since all these things have happened, I'm even more convinced it's not a great idea. Rosie, I'm hoping you'll stay at the B&B until this mess is cleared up."

I wanted to protest but Fiona cut me off. "Well, I don't think she has a choice, Jonah. The doctor will only release her if she's got someone to watch over her for a few days. Concussion is a serious condition!"

I'd never really had people take over my life before. I was used to making all my own decisions, but then again, I'd never been accused of murder or attacked before either. Somehow in light of all that it seemed easier to agree. At least for now. Besides, I was tired.

As though reading my mind, the nurse reappeared, took all my vitals again and suggested it was time I had some rest. I didn't want to seem ungrateful to my visitors but I could have kissed her.

What I didn't expect was to receive one instead. From Jonah. It was light and quick and happened after Fiona left.

No words, just a wink and a little salute. And the kiss.

And then he left.

But even that couldn't block out all the questions filling my head.

THE NEXT MORNING brought good news. I could leave the hospital, though just as per Fiona's warning, only into someone's care. That someone being her. Of course.

I was still worried about her until I also heard that Clay and Jonah had organized a roster of people to sit with Hank, who had only his sister and her family. Hopefully Fiona would get some rest, and I certainly didn't intend to be any more of a burden.

Due to all that had happened, Fiona still hadn't made it

out to Delvene's grandmother's house to pay her respects and I was uncertain when she asked me to tag along. And now of course, there was Merline's family to be considered as well. Was it ghoulish to meet people for the first time when they were grieving? Particularly when I also had an ulterior motive?

My bang on the head had left me tired and more than a bit jumpy. In truth I'd have been happy to hide out in Fiona's house, but that wouldn't help this situation. I'd gone over and over everything I knew—and none of it made any sense or answered any questions.

The only thing I was sure of was that Miss Alice's death was somehow connected to the day Jed Jones died. More than sixty years ago. So, what prompted Miss Alice to act now? What was in those letters? And who was frightened enough to be pushed into committing murder? And if Jonah's guess was counted, that person had possibly murdered twice.

In the end, my decision to accompany Fiona was prompted by the lady herself. Clay was busy with prior commitments, and he'd already paid his respects earlier. And looking at Fiona's face still bearing the residue of her exhaustion, I just didn't want her to go alone.

Delvene's grandmother, Joy, was a sweet lady who, in her eighties, still worked her own garden and canned her own fruit and vegetables. Her farmhouse was very similar to the little house in design, just smaller. It was cozy and homely and the predominantly floral décor suited the owner. Pot-pourri scented the air, and every flat surface including the walls, was cluttered with the memories of a long, full life. Photographs, souvenirs, hobbies, heirlooms, and trophies. If ever I got to live in the little house it would be bare by comparison. It was a sobering thought.

The town of Airlie Falls continually surprised me, though by now it really shouldn't. The family was so wel-coming and grateful for our visit. They saw nothing odd about a stranger appearing to offer condolences and were most appreciative of the desserts we'd brought to help out during this time.

As Delvene's mother and various aunts cleared away it was obvious the days had been spent in an endless round of tea, coffee and cake. And stories. There were already guests there when we arrived and the stories were flowing. As much as I would have loved to share this insight into family life, when Delvene headed to the kitchen for fresh cups and to refill platters, I followed.

"Thank you for being so gracious," I began.

"Not at all," she replied, though I saw the strain on her face. She was grieving and playing hostess. As comforting as the guests must be, it would also take its toll.

"Here let me help," I said, leaning over to take the china and fresh napkins. "You look exhausted. The last two days must have been very difficult."

She was a pretty girl, and about my age. Despite her

grief, her short dark hair framed a face that was lively and interesting. Now though, she was frowning. "I really loved him. He was the most amazing grandfather. We had such a beautiful bond." A tear slipped down over her pale cheeks. "I'm going to miss him so much."

I reached out to pat her arm. "I'm so sorry. And even more sorry if I'm making it worse." When she managed a weak smile and shook her head, I crossed my fingers and prayed I wasn't about to go too far. "Delvene, Emmy Kaye hinted that you were angry over a letter?"

The pale cheeks were suddenly suffused with color. Turning away, her movements as she refilled dessert platters were controlled but the haste gave her away.

"I've made you angry. I'm so sorry."

Her head dropped to her chest and the movements ceased. When her shoulders started heaving I realized she was quietly sobbing. Unsure of whether my comfort would be welcome now, I tentatively rubbed her back. Finally she raised her face and turned back to me. "I'm sorry. No, you haven't made me angry," she said between the gulps of air she was drawing in. "But the letter made me very angry."

"Delvene, did you know your grandfather wasn't the only one to receive a letter from Miss Alice?" I took the frown as a negative. Pursing my lips I wondered how to proceed, but she was staring at me so I just dived in. "Look, I can solemnly promise and assure you I'm not asking for superficial reasons, but do you have any idea what the letter said?"

Her fist hit the counter. "That's the thing I'm most mad about. Until now, I didn't even know who'd sent it! He screwed it up and burned it before we got a chance to look at it!"

"But it upset him?"

She took a moment to compose herself. "I will believe until the day I die that the letter killed him. He was old, I get that, but he was in good health! He helped me in the café—washing dishes—just the day before he got that letter!"

I nodded. Even with my minuscule medical knowledge her argument didn't hold water. If it was his heart, as Emmy Kaye had intimated, then that could happen with no warning. Not that I was going to mention that to her now. Or ever.

Calmer now she said, "Why would Alice Auchinschloss write to my grandfather?" Without pause she rushed on, "You said others got letters as well? Who? Maybe they'd tell me what their letters were about? At least I'd know what upset him so."

Shame filled me as I hesitated to share the names I knew. I'd been asking her personal questions and encouraging her to share, and now? "I'm not sure..." As her eyes widened in disbelief, I sucked in a deep breath and gave the answer that would cause the least grief. "Well, Charlene Madison—"

Now her face had morphed into shock. "Miss Charlene who just passed? She got one?"

"Got what?" We both turned, surprised to find we had

company. Her eyes, warm, smiling, switched from one to the other of us. "Oh forgive me. Have I interrupted?"

I recovered first. "Hi, Miz Peatree. Would you like me to take that plate?"

"Hi again, Rosie. And I wish you'd call me Pippa." The pastor's wife handed over the plate of cookies covered in plastic wrap, honest concern now shadowing her blue eyes. "How are you? I'm so embarrassed that I haven't been to visit with you since..." True to her word, her face suffused with blotchy color, but I was pretty sure her embarrassment wasn't because she'd fallen down on her visiting schedule.

I helped her out. "It's okay, Pippa." My eyebrows flipped up under the curls I was never able to contain. "I *have* been kind of busy lately. It's not your fault."

"Well, thank you. That *busy-ness* is all the more reason I should have called—this nonsense with Miss Alice and the fire and then yesterday..." She shook her head as though unable to comprehend it all. That made two of us. "But I'll be checking in with you real soon."

Turning to Delvene she added, "The Rev—Peter—mentioned you were seeing a lot of visitors so I figured I'd bring over some more food. Now, I want you to promise to holler if you need more, you hear?"

Delvene thanked her. "Have you been to see Merline? She visited yesterday—before Miss Charlene... Her sister... Before she passed." The weight of all this death was taking its toll and she looked weary. Dragging in a long breath, she paused, her face echoing the confusion on Pippa's face. "It's just so hard to believe. I feel so bad for her and her family. I'll try and visit as soon as I can."

Pippa gave her a hug. "Oh bless you. She'll fully understand you have your hands full here. I was there earlier and Peter's still over there now. He'll get back here later to finalize arrangements for the funeral. He also can't believe how things have panned out. Your poor grandfather and Miss Charlene and then he's been trying to check in on Hank Henderson as well. It's like the community has fallen on its head and doesn't know which way is up."

An involuntary shudder rippled through me at the mention of Hank. Pippa saw it and her hand went to her mouth. "Oh, Rosie! How thoughtless of me! Are you okay? Peter called to see you as well, but you'd already checked out of the hospital."

I could only nod.

Delvene, however, was still stuck on the letters. "Pippa, has Peter said anything about anyone getting strange letters from Alice Auchinschloss?"

"I'm not sure if Pete has, but Charlene told me she got one. Why?"

Delvene's eyes shone. "Did she tell you what it said?"

Pippa frowned. "I don't think it was too scary. I was on one of my regular visits to the folks at the retirement village and I still had a lot of people to see, so maybe I didn't listen as well as I should have done. But I think she said it was something about letting the past go? Or letting go of the past?" Her eyes once more flipped from one of us to the other. "Oh dear. Is it important? Should I have listened more carefully?"

I reached out to pat her arm; to reassure her. "It's okay, Pippa. Though, I wonder—did you actually see the letter?"

She frowned. "No, but I'm pretty sure that's what she told me."

It didn't make sense to me, but right then Fiona came through and I knew without her saying that it was time to move on. The shadows under her eyes had deepened and I knew how she felt. I was struggling as well.

THE TRIP HOME was predictably quiet. Fiona excused herself to rest up before she had to do it all over again with Merline's family. But I was in that unique and weird state of nervous exhaustion. Tired but wired. So, I did what I do best. I headed to the kitchen. Merline's family would need sustenance for themselves and their visitors as well.

Boring as it seemed I made the same offerings because one: I knew we had these ingredients—even if this effort would require a trip to the store to fill empty canisters. And two: I was too tired to be creative and I knew I could switch to automatic pilot with these recipes if that exhaustion kicked up a notch.

The house quickly filled with that sweet sugary aroma once more and I made a cup of tea and nibbled on a warm date and pecan bar. It was one of those treats I never tired of.

Unlike this investigation. No, not true. I wasn't tired of it, I was just flummoxed. I felt like I was getting nowhere and worse—that I was wasting precious time.

Taking showers or a having a swim or bath always helped when I was mulling over a problem. Something about the soothing effect of water freeing parts of the brain that activity stifled. I hoped it would help today, and so after finishing up, I headed upstairs.

Afterward, I couldn't claim an amazing epiphany but I did formulate a plan. Lying on the bed, refreshed and wrapped in a light robe, I decided to start making lists, trying to see how people connected. I didn't want to ask Fiona for a whiteboard but I'd get a load of cardboard later and stand my lists around the room on various flat surfaces.

But before I could make lists I needed information. Lots of it. Because the one thing I was short of was motive. And without motive I'd be doing nothing more than throwing hypothetical darts at a list of names. While blindfolded.

Obviously another trip out to see the Fab Four was in order, as well as a conversation with Merline and then Chavez King—as long as I could get past Chrystal, that is. And of course I needed to talk to Ivory Sternuk—if that was still her name, and maybe even Brenda, the Sheriff's wife and Ivory's sister.

I'd been focused on Miss Alice being murdered by one of the seven people who were at the picnic the day Jed died. The only fly in that ointment was that only two of them were still alive. Five of the seven had passed away—Jed, John Thatcher, Alice, Charlene and Delvene's grandfather, Forster. Of course that didn't mean that one of the remaining two wasn't guilty, but it's not terribly clever to commit a crime and then end up as the only suspect left standing. And this situation was a bit like that.

Of course, it also didn't mean that the two who had recently passed hadn't murdered Miss Alice before they passed over themselves. Maybe the burden of guilt was too heavy and one of them basically willed himself or herself to sleep.

And if one of those two hadn't done it? Again, the problem I found was that most of the survivors were infirm. Their age and health status hadn't allowed for them to be flitting around killing people. Nor starting fires or conking people on the head. Did it? But then again I was still to meet the last two picnickers. Perhaps that would change my perspective completely.

I didn't remember dropping off to sleep, but when I woke a couple of hours later it was midafternoon and a note was propped up on my bedside lamp. From Fiona—she hadn't wanted to wake me. She thanked me profusely for the baking and said she and Clay would be back by dinner—and that Clay would grill, so I was to do nothing. The last was underlined. Twice.

I smiled. Part of me was a bit sad I'd missed the opportunity to see Merline, but inflicting myself on one grieving family today was probably enough.

There were still a couple of hours before I'd be needed back here for dinner. I went over my options. I wasn't supposed to drive for a couple more days and even though I was feeling rested and had no headache or dizziness, I'd be disrespecting Fiona if I ignored that order. Adding that factor to the equation seriously reduced my options.

Living in the center of town had its advantages though, and a stroll to the grocery store cum general store added another option. I'd met the owners Dan and Vicki briefly before—most recently out at Miss Alice's after the fire—and they'd seemed like regular hardworking folk. But still, I was nervous as I walked into the large area that seemed to be divided quite neatly into groceries, hardware, pharmacy, and refreshments bar. Of course with Dan Casey being the town's pharmacist—as well as volunteer fire chief—that made perfect sense. It was a bright cheerful space and I was sure the retro soda fountain bar with its lime green and hot pink padded booths and outrageous selection of shakes and sundaes must be a huge hit with the people who came to the market days.

I couldn't walk in there though and not remember that Dan Casey's family had been ruined by Miss Alice's interference. And of course he had access to poison. *Easy access.* The man himself was serving a customer on the far counter and he'd glanced up when the bell tinkled above the door to announce my arrival. Was it my imagination that his eyes narrowed fractionally? It was probably no secret I was collecting information. Did that bother him?

Every time I'd been there in the past it had been busy with customers and gossip. And not quiet, whispered kind of gossip. Here, customers called to each other across sections and aisles, carried out conversations the same way and not only was nothing sacred, it seemed anyone could join in. As I drew near I wondered how many of those recent conversations had featured myself as the chief subject.

I headed straight to groceries, nabbing one of the dozen carts as I passed by.

Despite my list, it took no time until I was back at the checkout counter where Vicki herself was on duty. It was an opportunity to thank her again for helping out with the fire.

"Oh heck, honey, that was just a baby fire, thank goodness," she said as she finished running my groceries through. "But if you're gonna hang around here in Airlie Falls for a while, you might want to join us! We're a ragtag bunch but we're friendly and we can always use another set of hands."

I was assuring her I'd certainly be interested if indeed I was going to *hang around* when one of those disembodied conversations started up deeper into the store. It was the name *Ivory* that caught my attention, and she was being asked if she'd received one of those weird letters everyone was talking about. Trying not to appear to be eavesdropping while pretending to focus on Vicki was hard work, and faking a dropped coin purse might have been corny but it solved my problem.

While I supposedly rummaged for scattered coins, the voices carried to me. The woman I assumed was Ivory answered, "Of course I did not! Why would you assume I'd get one of those things?"

Person 2: "Well it seemed they were going out to folk about your age."

Person 3: "I heard every person at Riverbend got one and that they were death threats."

Ivory: "Well that's just ridiculous then, isn't it! I don't even reside at Riverbend as well you know, so naturally I didn't get one. And that settles it."

Person 4: "Chavez King got one and he don't reside out at Riverbend neither."

Vicki: "Well you've all got it wrong. My boy Dan Junior plays soccer with one of the interns over at Lake Family Lawyers in Dallas. The ones that used to look after the Auchinschloss family? And he said that Miss Alice called them up and asked them to collect the letters and mail them for her. He said there were four. Just four. And he oughta know because he's the one who collected and mailed them. And got *a quarter* as his tip for his trouble!" Her raucous laughter drowned any other responses, but it didn't matter: Two important pieces of a puzzle had just been found.

Wow. I wasn't sure I'd ever really believed in kismet before but this moment had made me a convert. Right place. Right time.

This new information rolled around in my head. Without asking a single question I knew the number of letters mailed, who mailed them, and how Alice managed that.

And via deductive reasoning, I was certain I knew who'd received them. So that actually cleared three questions.

I straightened before my calves cramped, wishing I'd done so a bit more leisurely when the room began a slow spin. I grabbed the counter until it settled, focusing on a display of gift-boxed candy elaborately wrapped and bound with rich purple ribbon flecked with gold.

Thankfully, Vicki was busy with the next customer and had missed my dizzy turn. But still, there was something about the candy that held my attention even after the dizziness had passed and I'd reached out to pick up a box when I realized my former luck hadn't yet run out. Mid reach, one last sentence floated over to me.

Ivory: "Oh all this letter talk! You've gone and made me forget what I came here for!"

And as a sturdy, indignant octogenarian bustled past toward the door in blue sweat pants, a matching blue-and-white sweater, and with a walking stick she wielded more like a weapon than an aid, I was right on her heels. Chocolate forgotten.

Chapter Ten

"MISS IVORY?"

She'd taken off at a speed consistent with a gallop and as I struggled to follow I realized that my head still had a way to go before healing was complete.

After the second call she slowed, curiosity evident as she turned to glance behind and then finally stop. I waved and continued the few steps to meet her. "Miss Ivory? My name is Rosie Hart, I used to work for Alice Auchinschloss and I wondered if I could talk to you for a moment?"

I swear her face paled at the mention of Miss Alice, but she straightened her back and gave no other appearance of being afraid or concerned. "I haven't seen that woman for years so I've got nothing to say about her!" She paused then and an expression I'd have to call *feral* replaced her indignation, though admittedly, her eyes were hard to read behind those thick lenses. Exaggerated and blurry, those eyes gave the impression of an oversized, blue-eyed fly or honeybee looking out through a jar of water. And were vaguely familiar, I thought as a random aside. "At least nothing a nice little gal like you would want to hear."

I shook my head wondering what she'd think if she'd been able to see into my thoughts. See that I wanted to hear it all—good, bad, and ugly. "Miss Ivory, I need your help. Please, would you talk to me?"

She sighed. "What about?" Ivory Sternuk would never be confused with anyone's sweet old grandmother. She was tough and sharp, which weren't necessarily bad traits and had probably served her well over the years. Right now though, they were presenting a barrier to me getting even remotely close to her.

"Well, about Miss Alice and also perhaps about the day Jed Jones died?"

"I haven't spoken to Alice Auchinschloss in over fifty years. And why would you want to bring up that ancient history? That's so long ago I barely remember!"

I frowned. "You've forgotten the day you saw a man die?"

Her face warmed but I suspected anger and not embarrassment. "Listen, young lady, did you ever consider that maybe that's something a person would want to forget? Deliberately? It's no fun having to relive that poor boy falling to his death like that over and over. And that's what it was like! Every time I closed my eyes I could see him lying there—his head all crushed in like that... His hair all matted and black with blood. I just thank God I didn't have to carry the image of his face into eternity with me."

Tears filled those glassy eyes, adding to the watery impression so powerfully that I half expected the glasses to fill up and spill over. And she'd transformed from being that strong invincible woman of moments ago into a vulnerable eighty-something-year-old who looked every one of those years.

And I felt bad. Very bad.

I thanked her—sincerely—and apologized, but perhaps she didn't hear me. She'd already turned and was walking away. This time leaning heavily on that stick.

BACK AT THE B&B I made a cup of tea and sat warming my hands around the delicate china cup. My stomach churned as I relived that scene with Ivory, rolling it over in my head. I'd taken that poor woman to the depths of her grief and torment. *How could I have done that?*

If this was sleuthing then I definitely wasn't cut out for it. And yet injustices had been done. Alice Auchinschloss had been murdered. And if her suspicions were correct she was murdered because she knew something about the day Jed died. Or the day Jed was *murdered*. If he'd just died would there be all this fuss and fear? Because the one thing I took from my talk with Ivory—apart from my self-shame—was that she was afraid. It was only there briefly but it was clear in her eyes. She was a strong woman; she'd put on a good show. But I'd bet my supposed inheritance on the fact that she was spooked. About what? The letters? The past? The past being revealed?

If only there was a way to find out what Alice had written in those letters. Pippa Peatree's belief that they were letters wanting to bury that past didn't seem to hold water. Would that have stressed Delvene's grandfather into a heart attack? So, why would Charlene have lied? Pippa seemed to think she took it very well. Or was each letter different?

My head was hurting as I made my way upstairs but I was determined to try to make some sense of all this random information. If I'd compared Charlene's secret baby information to having an extra jigsaw piece and no gaps, this was like having puzzle pieces from several different jigsaws all mixed up in one box.

I took my painkillers and propped myself at the desk—markers and cardboard at the ready. For the next hour I steadily wrote, filling in information under names, dragging back everything my memory had stored. And adding suppositions and hypotheses.

The day had taken its toll and when there was a light knock on the door and I rose too quickly to answer I paid the price. The room spun slowly first and, vision blurred, I groped about trying to find something to anchor me. Then the speed picked up, shadows moved in from the perimeter until there was nothing but black...

"*CLAY!*"

I could hear it all. Hear their concern and worry. Hear their instructions to each other. Hear their plan to call the doctor. I just didn't seem able to respond properly. Not immediately. The fuzziness was fading and I tried to help as Clay and Fiona assisted me onto the bed. The mattress felt like a cloud and, eyes closed, I lay there willing the pain in my head to ease and for the world to return to normal.

Jonah arrived just as they'd settled me, and then he left immediately. The next thing I was aware of was a cool compress on my forehead and someone taking my pulse, then my blood pressure.

I didn't want to open my eyes and have to talk, I wanted to just lie and rest, but I forced myself and tried to sit up. I think it was Jonah's voice I heard first, followed after an infinitesimal pause by the doctor's, both urging me to stay down. I wasn't going to argue. Not even about the little prick in my upper arm, especially when it brought blessed oblivion.

When I woke it was fully dark, obviously very late. A low light burned somewhere in the room casting a soft unobtrusive glow. An explosion of warmth spread through me as I turned to take in the room and connected with the one face I'd begun to rely on in times of crisis. On a sofa chair beside me, Jonah lounged with his mouth slightly open and his head propped by one arm resting on the side of the chair. At his feet sat my pile of cardboard sheets, and his right hand still held a marker.

Wondering what he'd used it for—or if he'd used it—I lay still and watched him. Tiny golden whiskers caught by the light gleamed against his tanned skin. His lashes were dark though, long and dark and lying against a face that looked lined with weariness, even as he rested. And I marveled at how lucky I was to count this man as my friend.

The unease that thought created made me restless and I lifted my eyes again to find myself being just as carefully perused as I'd been perusing him.

"Hey," he whispered. "How are you feeling?"

Warmth rushed through me and I started to push up to deflect attention to that fact. "Rested. Better."

He pointed to the cardboard. "I see you've been busy…"

I shrugged. "It helped pass the time. Did you look? Got anything to add?"

The smile died and he stared at me carefully for long minutes. "Unfortunately I might, though I'm not sure I should be telling you… Are you really feeling okay?"

Curious, I nodded. "I could take on your best bull and win. So?"

He blew out a long sigh. "Charlene didn't die of natural causes."

I stared at him, letting that sink in. "She didn't…" I began to repeat, shock stalling me as I corralled and sorted his words. "Oh… No! Are you saying she was murdered? No!"

So many visceral reactions attacked my body at one time.

In turn I felt nauseous, shaky, chilled, and unbelievably with all that—numb.

"Poisoned," he added, concern in his eyes as he watched me.

"Do they know how? What?"

He sat back in his chair. "Not yet, at least that I know of. All they're saying is that it was ingested, so, obviously it was something she ate."

"Just like Miss Alice..."

My mind was trawling again, trying to make connections. When I realized I was tracing a pattern on the quilt that had been placed over me, I didn't stop; I'd read that repetitive movements like that helped brain function. And boy, did I need help. "Do you think that it's possible this has nothing to do with Miss Alice and maybe to do with Charlene's secret baby?"

He frowned but it was evident he hadn't forgotten the story I'd shared with him. "Big coincidence though, right?" he answered. "I'm sure there's been some over the years, but I can't remember another murder in Airlie Falls. Then suddenly we have two random murders? And why now? Unless it's this secret grandchild...? But why? Revenge for beginning the chain that gave him life?"

"You say 'him'?"

"Figure of speech, though I guess I'm arrogant enough to consider the male of the species as the more likely murderer." He grinned. "I don't apologize for that. I like women to be strong and independent but I also like them to have compassion and gentleness."

His eyes were saying a whole lot more than his words. And as shame once more filled me, I knew I had to put him straight on the compassion and gentleness thing—at least from this gal. "Perhaps this is the time to admit to failing at the last two earlier then."

Just as I began, Fiona arrived with a tray of food, soup left over from the food I'd prepared, plus some oven-fresh rolls and a salad. They both encouraged me to eat the hot soup first and then settled to hear of my encounter with Ivory.

Jonah was shaking his head even before I'd finished. A glance at his mother told me both were sharing the same thoughts. "Honey," he began, "seems you're beating yourself up over nothing. The way I see it Miss Alice and Ivory are two peas in a pod. They both know how to manipulate a situation. Miss Ivory played you this afternoon. She's a wily old cat and she knows how to turn the cards to favor her. And that's what she did."

Fiona nodded. "Did she limp when she walked away? Lean on that stick?"

"Yes…"

They both laughed and then Jonah explained. "She needs that walking stick about as much as I do. But it suits her purpose to use it every once in a while. To get the best seats at the town concert. First in line at the church potluck suppers. To get to the head of a line at the bank or the bakery. To get sympathy and help when there are others who need it more than she does."

Fiona agreed. "We all know what she's like, but she's a member of the community and we let her be. She thinks she's winning when people offer up seats and the like, but it's the ones who know what she's doing and whose manners are far better than hers, who are the real winners. Don't worry about her!"

I thanked them both for their support, but secretly I wasn't convinced Ivory Sternuk had outfoxed me. They hadn't been there. They hadn't seen her face; heard the tremor in her voice and listened to that description. That was real; the stuff of real nightmares.

I settled back and talk turned inevitably to Charlene. Fiona agreed again with Jonah that it was unlikely there were two murderers, but there was only one way to be sure and that was to try to unmask the secret grandchild—whoever that may be.

As if I didn't have enough on my plate…

On top of that I was issued a dire warning from the doctor via Fiona to take it easy for a day or two. When Jonah threatened to take time off work to ensure it happened, I promised to be good. As amazing as spending two whole days with him could be, I was increasingly aware that these people barely knew me and they'd already given up so much.

"By the way," Fiona said as she left the room, "Pippa

Peatree called to make sure you were okay. She was apparently quite impressed by you!"

I smiled. Okay, I could get very used to this small-town life. The pastor's wife was concerned about me. It felt good.

TRUE TO MY word, I rested on Wednesday and was surprised by just how weary I was. By Thursday, though, I was itching to do something. The day before I'd made some lists of the things I could create for my baked goods stall and having imposed upon Jonah to pick up some supplies in return for samples, I was ready to bake.

Fiona faced another busy day in the community and as there was only one of guests at the B&B and they'd checked out early, she was gone before ten as well.

I knew I had to pace myself so decided on just three things—marshmallow raspberry bars, cornflake meringues, and banana pecan loaf. I set the base for the bars in the oven first and set about mashing bananas and chopping pecans. The meringues had a long slow bake time so I wanted those to go in last. The bars needed no more bake time but had to be topped with the jam and marshmallow, so I could do that while the banana loaf was baking.

I was feeling efficient and confident, and though I was a bit weary, I was also exhilarated when everything turned out to perfection, and I was cleaned by one o'clock. Tomorrow at this time we'd be at Delvene's grandfather's funeral and we'd be able to make a nice platter to share for after the service.

I'd just boiled water for tea when a commotion out front sent me scurrying to the entrance. I was imagining a whole gaggle of guests had descended and it was a lovely surprise to see four elderly faces I'd become quickly fond of, ushering themselves inside.

In the chaos of walking frames, walking sticks, oversized handbags, umbrellas, and pump-up cushions I managed to somehow greet them and lead them back to the kitchen. The sun was pouring in, flooding both the kitchen and the patio, but they chose to stay inside and were dragging chairs into position and asking about refreshments before I'd even caught my breath.

"We heard you had an accident," E.T. began.

"Actually we heard you were conked on the head," Lori added.

"By a perverted murderer who stripped you naked and left you for dead." With her fluffy hair, dimples and demeanor, Betsy had reminded me, from the beginning, of Betty White's character Rose, from *The Golden Girls*. Now, as the others shook their heads, I almost laughed out loud at the resemblance today.

"Nothing quite so dramatic, Betsy. But it was disconcerting and I'm so worried about Hank. I'm hoping to get to see him tomorrow. He's still in a coma."

They clucked and nodded over that. "We saw him the day Charlene died, just before he went out to meet you," Lori Sue said.

"Did he tell you anything?"

Martha shrugged. "Well, he said one thing. It was kind of muttered and we've been trying to figure it out since... He said something about *someone not being where they were supposed to be—or maybe someone not being* who *they were supposed to be.* He was mighty anxious to get to see you. Rushed off without eating the refreshments we ordered."

"Double chocolate cake," Betsy added.

Sadly Hank's mutterings meant nothing to me either. Out of context they could mean anything. And considering this was connected to Charlene—could it have something to do with the grandchild? Is that who wasn't who they were supposed to be? But how did that relate to Alice?

E.T. lifted her face, excitement clear for all to see. "Speaking of that cake there are some mighty fine aromas in this kitchen."

As hints went it wasn't subtle, and it jolted me to my feet. "Oh of course! I'm so sorry." I bustled as quickly as hands allowed and got a platter of goodies on the table in time to serve the brewed coffee.

Their appreciation was vocal and excessive. And I tried to hide my surprise at how quickly those desserts were disappearing. I thought of Miss Alice with her diabetes and prayed none of these ladies was ever afflicted. They wouldn't survive without their sugar fix.

Finally sated, Lori Sue sat back in her chair. "But that thing about Hank wasn't all we came to tell you."

"We've been investigating!" Martha announced proudly.

"Wha…" A chill ran through me. "Ladies, you can't do that. Please! I've become really fond of all of you and I can't let you put yourselves in danger! Whoever is behind this is really dangerous!" I touched my head to make the point.

"Eh. Danger schmanger," Lori Sue said with a wave of her hand. "If I'm here before Christmas rolls around again, I'll be ninety. And that's a pretty good life."

"Besides," E.T. added, "we're just doing what old ladies do. Chewing the fat; gossiping. We all do it out there. Relive the past that is—because that's where our hearts and memories are."

At her words my throat tightened. But it relaxed a second later when Betsy said, "And we haven't had this much fun for twenty years!"

Looking across at their shining faces, sparkling eyes, and hopeful expressions, I smiled back. I couldn't deny them. But I'd watch out for them and pray for them. "Okay, gumshoe squad, spill!"

They didn't waste time. One by one they offered their lines, like they'd rehearsed, which of course they hadn't.

"It's Charlene's baby's daddy."

"He's one of the boys on the picnic that day."

"Her own daddy wasn't happy and sent her away!"

"But when she got back—minus her baby—that rat had impregnated someone else and gone and married her—the new gal, that is!"

Two emotions swamped me. Disappointment and relief. I doubted this information had any relevance to Miss Alice's murder or the death of Jed Jones, and I hid that disappointment from them but I was also relieved because surely this topic held far less danger for them. However all they saw and heard was my profuse gratitude and praise for their ingenuity. And I was truly sincere—they'd gone out of their way to help me.

Satisfied they had done well, we took a walk through Fiona's meandering garden and then it was time for them to collect the sample bags I'd made for them and take their leave.

"Now here's my cell number," Lori Sue said, offering a card with spidery numbers scrawled across it. I must have reacted or perhaps she was waiting for me to react because she followed with, "Now don't go looking surprised. I can operate a DVD player, too!" she said proudly. Holding up the phone she added, "Jonah gave it to me. Taught me to use it too. Bless him."

The warmth I'd come to expect at either the sight of him or mention of him again swirled through me, and I pretended dedicated focus on loading Lori Sue's number into my cell. Only after I'd scrawled my own number on her card and pushed it back, did I dare look up. And collided with four beaming, knowing faces.

And then I had no chance of hiding from it. My face must have rivaled the color of Brenda Kinnead's ruby beet relish.

Thankfully, other than their twittering giggles they said nothing. And I was able to make my goodbyes with a small amount of dignity, at least.

"How are you getting back? I could drive you! I should have thought of that!"

"No need," E.T. explained. "Lori Sue drove us."

"We work as a team you know," Betsy added.

Martha nodded. "Lori Sue's a good driver but sometimes she doesn't see everything, so we look out as well. Never had an accident yet!"

Inwardly I groaned and watched them pile into Lori Sue's ancient Ford. And again I prayed—this time for their safe deliverance! As she slowly—very slowly—pulled away from the curb, the rear window descended and E.T.'s face appeared. "Chocolate. We'd like something with chocolate next time!" And with a wave they were gone.

Chocolate. I was grinning as I went back to clear away the kitchen mess but somehow that word was determined to hang around. Why was it tickling my mind? It didn't seem to be bothering me in a baking context. So, *what?* The neat display of boxed chocolate-coated candy I'd noted a few days back wriggled in there, too. I kept thinking it was important but I didn't know why.

Chapter Eleven

MY EXPERIENCE WITH funerals, beside Miss Alice's, had been limited to my grandmother and the grandmother of a friend. The latter two couldn't have been more different. My grandmother's funeral had been arranged by my quirky parents and began like a rock concert and disintegrated into a protest that supported the right to bear arms. Considering my parents were stalwart pacifists this probably had more to do with the recreational drugs and alcohol their guests had provided. Seething, I'd watched it all from the sidelines, grateful I wasn't bearing arms or I may have caused a few injuries that day.

The other was just as alien to me. Warm, loving, and focused on family.

I suspected the funeral of Forster Jacobz would be like the second one.

We filed into the same church where just last week, I'd sat alone, waiting for mourners who didn't arrive. Jonah's hand was warm on my arm as he directed me to follow his parents into a row about halfway down. As I'd come to expect, the whole town had turned out, even the Fab Four who waved excitedly from the other side of the center aisle.

Jonah looked good in his suit, and despite him being a man of few words, his silent perusal of my own outfit had boosted my confidence. Even without words he'd been very eloquent: radiating respectful appreciation—with emphasis on appreciation.

After adopting the Airlie Falls uniform of jeans and boots it was nice to dress up. My clothes had arrived thanks to Jess and I'd thanked her over and over for including such a clever selection. Other than a ball, I could hold my head up at any function. Today, my pale lavender skirt may have been a teeny bit short by local standards, but with its matching cropped tailored jacket and the white lacy camisole, I felt feminine and yet respectful.

The church was filling and Jonah squeezed up tight beside me to make room for others, and I couldn't help but make a comparison to Miss Alice's funeral. Mourners weren't the only difference. Hers had been accompanied by taped music; today Pippa Peatree played the organ—and did it brilliantly. I wondered why she hadn't bothered to do that for Alice?

The newspaper editor Midge Moylan walked in, demure in gray. Her eyes were still red-rimmed from the fire and I wondered if she had an allergy or if... No. This was smoke burn not gasoline fume burn. Wasn't it?

Merline and her family arrived. Merline looked drawn and older than the last time I'd seen her. How hard must it be to know you've got to do this for your sister in just a few days' time? I so wanted to talk with her, but looking at her now I knew I couldn't intrude. Brenda and Sheriff Kinnead settled in beside Merline.

I sat up straighter when Chuck and Chrystal King arrived, fascinated by the older man with them. Straight-backed, no stick, thick white hair, and skin that gleamed in the low lighting and spoke to his Spanish heritage. Chavez King may have been in his mideighties but he could have passed for fifteen years younger. And he would have had no trouble getting about to murder little old ladies.

Finally the family arrived—generations of Jacobzes from babes in arms and children to the great-grandmother, Joy, matriarch herself—and took their places up front beside the coffin. Delvene looked pale and her head hung low. And my heart hurt for them.

As expected the service focused on the man himself, his love of family, and theirs for him. It was beautiful and moving. Delvene had been fortunate to have had him as a grandfather. He was painted as a gentle, loving man. It didn't fit the profile I had in my mind as a cold-blooded murderer.

Hymns I wasn't familiar with floated around me, allowing my mind time to wander. What would make a gentle man commit murder?

I realized with a start that the answer was right there in front of me. Family. A man so devoted to his family would certainly need to protect them. How far he'd go, however, was the question.

AFTER THE BURIAL, we gathered in the church hall where refreshments had been laid out. I noted the Fab Four dived on what I had sent along, and I couldn't help but feel proud. They might be little piggies but they were connoisseur piggies.

When they gravitated over to me I asked them about the pastor, Peter Peatree. "It's struck me that we never hear of him much. I mean, I know he'd be busy…"

E.T. sidled in close, checked to see who was listening and lowered her voice when she spoke. My groan was silent. If anyone had been watching they'd have known she's was about to share a secret. I worried for these ladies—they were anything but discreet. "Well, scuttlebutt has it that he may be up to no good, but it's just gossip, you hear. Apparently he's in Dallas and Austin a lot." She tapped her nose. "Some say it's women."

"Yes and that poor Pippa is left doing all that pastoral care by herself while he's out whacking the—"

"Betsy!" Lori Sue exclaimed. "Potty talk!"

Betsy's eyes grew wild. "I was about to say whacking the Bible at those city women! Saving them!"

E.T. rolled her eyes.

Meanwhile I struggled for composure. Laughing out loud at a funeral wasn't advised or polite behavior. But these ladies were making that very difficult. I hauled in air and tried to inject sanity to the conversation. "He could just be in the city on church business. These days caring for a congregation is like running a business. I bet there are lots of t's to be crossed and i's to be dotted. He's probably got a lot of meetings to attend."

Martha sniffed. "At least our version is interesting."

My laughter built again, and again I struggled to push it back. They were correct on one level though, it did seem to be Pippa who ran the church—but probably all pastors' wives took on all the community work. I'd never belonged to a small pastoral group like this before—so I could only guess.

The girls chatted for a bit longer then wandered off to peruse the food table once more and catch up with old acquaintances.

Alone again, I grabbed a cool drink, and stood back to watch. I was learning there was much to be gained by simply watching people—in the investigative sense. The Kings were interesting. Chavez seemed to be in a disagreeable mood, snapping at everything Chrystal offered him. Perhaps it rubbed off because when Midge passed by, the look Chrystal gave her was pure poison.

I noted a meaningful look pass between Chavez and Ivory Sternuk and I wondered what that was about. It was interesting that Ivory wasn't with her sister. In fact she seemed to give Brenda and the Sheriff a wide berth. I frowned over Brenda, though—she looked even more unwell and exhausted.

I stiffened when another older woman, elegant in her own way, but in clothes that had seen better days, entered the hall. She moved through the crowd, greeting most. She seemed to know everybody, and while the Airlie Falls Code of Conduct ensured she was greeted in return, I did see surprise on a few faces. A younger woman, maybe in her early forties, walked beside her.

Excitement fluttered in my chest.

Haven Jones and her daughter Miss Barbara Jones.

There was uncertainty in the older woman's eyes, but the daughter's eyes exuded polite ice—something I wouldn't have thought possible until now. And I saw the bitterness behind that polite mask that the Fab Four had spoken of. Again I thought that obviously Haven and Barbara would be the natural choice as perpetrators if revenge was the motive. But was it? After all this time?

Unless it was triggered by John Thatcher's passing? Somehow that actually made sense—unlike so many other things that had come to light.

My heart was still beating too fast but now from nerves as I decided it was time to tackle Haven Jones. She was one group away from me in the crowded room and I waited, hoping the sight of me wouldn't send her bolting.

She was shuffling along toward me and only looked up at

the last minute. Right into my eyes. Hers reflected her fear. Her daughter's? Unconcealed hatred.

That almost sent *me* scurrying. It was a powerful—if confusing—message. I ignored her and focused on her mother. "Miz Jones? We haven't met—I'm Rosie Hart. I saw you at Miss Alice's a few times lately but we didn't get to speak."

Her eyes grew rounder, and rows of sweat beaded on her upper lip. "*Alice who*, dear? I have no idea what you're talking about."

I hadn't expected an outright lie. "Alice Auchinschloss. And I'm pretty sure you were there. Once trying to peer through the scrub to see the house and another the day someone tried to burn down the farmhouse. If it can be proved that person thought Jonah Fencott and I were in the house, then that counts as attempted murder."

Haven visibly sagged. This woman had guilt written all over her.

Naturally though, her daughter jumped to her defense. "Excuse me?" The shrill voice beside me was dripping with disbelief and outrage. But even so, I recognized it. The voice on the phone. "Are you accusing my mother of attempted murder? This is ridiculous! And we don't even know this Alice person, so why would my mother be trying to see her?"

I turned to Haven. "You don't know the woman your brother was in love with?"

She scoffed. "Oh that's rubbish! Nothing more than a

teenage crush. If it had been real he would have stayed with her."

"That's right!" Barbara added spitefully. "It wasn't our fault she locked herself away all those years!"

"So you're admitting you do know her?"

Haven straightened, her eyes searching frantically for an escape route. "I don't have to stand here and listen to this!"

Despite her bravado I could see Haven's fear growing and I began to worry I'd pushed her too far. But then again if she really was guilty—and she was high on my list—then that could be a good thing. Barbara spluttered but I cut her off.

"And I'm assuming it was you who called to speak to Alice just a few days before she died."

Her eyes darted uncertainly to her mother who was unable to contain her shock. "Like I already said, this is ridiculous! Come on, Mother, we're leaving."

I watched them leave, frustration building because I had no reason to detain them and no proof they'd done anything. Yes, there was motive, payback for her brothers, but it was weak and I figured it wouldn't hold up in court.

The Fab Four gathered again, forming a semicircle in front of me, and barraging me with questions.

I answered the best I could but my mind was bubbling. A scene over in the far corner captured my attention and I tilted my head in that direction—toward Merline where she was deep in conversation with Midge Moylan. She was another I'd like to know more about. If suspicion fell on strangers in town, then surely that included Midge who'd only been a resident for a short while. "I'd like to be a fly on the wall over there." The moment the words left my mouth I was sorry—these gals didn't need any more encouragement. But thankfully before any of the four could act, the conversation ended and Midge moved away.

And so did my gumshoe gang. Plates were being replenished and once more they'd spied fresh pickings, but I wasn't alone for long. Bearing a smile I was unable to ignore or not respond to, Jonah held me in his gaze until he was beside me. Clay right behind him.

"You okay? Sorry we've not been here. Miz Peatree needed some muscle and Dad here nominated me."

Clay laughed. "Only seconds before you volunteered. Admit it."

I loved watching this family camaraderie. Loved being a part of it even more.

I was also glad Pippa Peatree had a task that kept her busy. Since we met properly at Delvene's she'd turned the full force of her pastoral responsibility on me. I appreciated it but I was beginning to feel swamped.

Clay and Jonah grazed from their plates, and we stood watching the parade of people until a man I'd never seen stopped and shook hands with both my companions.

Jonah turned to me, introducing me to Clive Angelo. "He's the local mailman, and trust me—he's got a pretty big run!"

Clive eyed me curiously. "Rosie Hart? You're the one who inherited Miss Alice's place?"

I nodded, wondering when I'd stop being embarrassed by that question or observation.

He nodded as well. "Such a shame that place has been let go the way it has. It was once a beautiful property. Every time I drive by I wonder what will happen to it. Maybe I'm wrong but it looked like it got to be downright unsafe!"

Jonah agreed, recounting the story of the arched entrance sign.

"That's what I mean," Clive continued. "Just the other day when I was passing and saw Miss Ivory out there I almost stopped to make sure she was okay! With that walking stick and that rough pathway..."

That got my full attention. "Miss Ivory was out there? When?"

He stroked his chin. "Not long ago. Can't say exactly when. I know I was running real late and I'm shamed to say that's why I didn't stop. Let me think..." He continued stroking. "Only a couple of days before Miss Alice passed, I think."

I simply stared, trying to make sense of this. Ivory said she hadn't spoken to Miss Alice in over fifty years.

Clive shook his head. "As a matter of fact I started to wonder what was happening out there! There's never anyone there but you, but there was Ivory one day and then the next day there was another car there. Late in the day, early evening it was. I couldn't make it out properly, but I knew I'd seen it before so it was a local! Looked like Miss Alice had suddenly become real social!" His laughter was innocent and warm, oblivious to the excited turmoil he'd created with this short exchange.

One look at Jonah though, told me that he knew exactly what I was feeling.

Well, maybe not exactly. One of those thoughts focused on Haven Jones. Had she actually gone to see Miss Alice when I wasn't there? Oh! A thought hit me. Could John Thatcher have told his sister something in his dying days? Had he given Miss Alice something that Haven wanted back? And so she'd ransacked the place?

THAT NIGHT I had a lot to add to my lists. That was great. Unfortunately I still couldn't make sense of it all, so that wasn't so great. The positive was that I was starting to feel like I was doing something—even though in truth I probably wasn't getting anywhere.

My suspect list was healthy—the motivation list, not so. I let my eyes run down the names. Haven Jones. Barbara Jones. Chavez King, based on the fact he was one of the seven out there at the picnic that day. His family—Chrystal and Chuck based on Chrystal's snaky behavior at the farm on fire day. Ivory Sternuk—same as Chavez, plus she'd been at Miss Alice's and had lied about it. Bobby Don seemed a very weak addition. So, too, did Dan Casey, but I couldn't discount the fact that I'd seen his truck, clearly marked with the general store name, parked furtively (or so it seemed) near the farm on the day of the fire. Equally weak was Midge Moylan's place on the list. But, like me, she *was* a stranger by Airlie Falls standards.

I needed to begin eliminating some people. Those last on the list would be my first priority.

Over the weekend Fiona insisted we start on the little house. And I had to admit it was huge fun and the most amazing distraction. I hated admitting to fear, but at night it plagued me—wondering what would happen if we couldn't discover who really murdered Miss Alice—and so at times sleep was elusive. This could be what I'd needed. Fiona was thrilled that true to his word, Hank had released money first thing last Monday—right before we were attacked.

I had mixed feelings. It still wasn't sitting easily, especially with the poor man still lying in that hospital bed oblivious of life itself. Fiona saw it from a different perspective. Literally waving away my discomfort, she said, "This is one thing he won't have to worry about when he recovers. See? We're doing him a favor, honey!"

She was very persuasive—just as I'd been warned. Her sense of style was impeccable and I could see the house coming to life in her hands. She listened when I answered her questions about what I liked and how I liked to live, favorite colors and styles, and didn't choose one thing without getting my approval first. As we shopped for new and vintage and assessed what we could use from Miss Alice's, I was aware of the support I'd had all the way through and was glad I added myself to the list of people volunteering to sit with Hank. It felt like giving something back.

Jonah had some catch-up work to do, so I only saw him at night at the B&B. Fiona loved that he was calling in every night and I tried not to get excited by what that meant.

At dinner I asked about Dan Casey and his wife Vicki. "I heard that Miss Alice caused Dan's family a load of heartache and hardship. Is it possible he could have anything to do with her murder?"

The response was shock that it should be considered but they were patient with me, especially when they heard why I was asking.

"Leave it with me," Fiona said firmly. "I'll get to the bottom of it. I know they're about to celebrate their twenty-fifth wedding anniversary next month, and the town is pitching in with a party, so I'll use that as an excuse to start up some conversations."

I would rather have done the dirty work myself, but obviously Fiona would get answers that I probably wouldn't. And if they were all correct about Dan, then I'd be happy to have the proof to remove him from the list. It wasn't like his was the only suspect vehicle in the vicinity that day.

I was also busy fielding calls and texts from Lori Sue and the girls. Even when there was nothing to report, they made sure I knew. One message though bothered me. Apparently Ivory had been out at Riverbend the day Charlene died. The girls didn't know why or who she'd been to see, but they knew she'd been there.

It didn't seem like coincidence to me that Ivory should be in close proximity to both women just before they died. Was I wrong about Haven or her daughter? My instincts— such as they were—were telling me that Haven was guilty of something, but I wasn't sure just what that was. And I also wasn't sure what I should do with the information. Would Sheriff Kinnead listen to me?

I got my answer the next day. Charlene Madison's funeral day: The day my total funeral experience increased to five. That was an increase of one hundred and fifty percent in just under two weeks. At this rate there'd be no one left in this town within the year!

Except that the focal person was different, the funeral was almost an exact rerun of Friday. An interesting fact was watching Merline and Midge Moylan comfort each other. I'd noticed them being chummy last week so obviously they were close friends—close enough for Midge to be sad over Charlene's passing.

I'd also paid special attention to the Revered Peatree, but he seemed to be just a very ordinary pastor of a small community. He seemed to know everyone and I didn't note any slimy behavior or undue attention to women despite the Fab Four's theories. Pippa was again confident, in control—and motherly even though, relatively speaking, she was not much older than me. Ten years, maybe?

Of course the entire town had turned out again for the service—which meant Jonah and Clay were once more packing away the extra seating laid out to accompany the big crowd. Afterwards, at the wake, Fiona had again positioned herself at the coffee station, helping everyone with their hot beverages.

Pippa Peatree had cornered me directly after the service asking if I would mind donating to a church bake sale the following weekend. "Everyone's oohing after your baking, Rosie. I know there'd be a rush for your donations and we'd have an opportunity to add to our roof restoration fund," she'd said. "Would you mind if I call on you this week to chat about it?"

I was actually delighted. Not only that people appreciated my cakes, but also that I was being included in village life. It was a really nice feeling and it gave me the push I needed to take advantage of the fact that the major players were all here in one place at Charlene's funeral.

Sheriff Kinnead was first. During refreshment time I took a deep breath and asked him if I could have a word. The first thing I noticed though was that he looked weary, bone weary. And worried. The gravity of this situation had not been lost on me—especially that I was not only a victim but also a suspect—but for the first time I saw it through his eyes. Someone on his turf was killing old ladies and he had to find them and stop them. I guess I'd look weary and worried, too, if I had that responsibility hanging on my shoulders—as well as a wife who was looking more unwell by the second.

The second thing I noticed was that he wasn't overly happy about my request.

"I hope you're not poking your nose in things that don't concern you, Miss Hart." *Miss Hart*? I'd hoped we'd moved on to Rosie, so that didn't make me feel any more confident.

"Surely you can't blame me, Sheriff Kinnead. I'm guessing despite Charlene's murder and the fact that I was knocked out I'm still a suspect?"

He shuffled from foot to foot, and eyed the door—and I had a feeling he couldn't wait to tear off that suit and bolo tie and get back on the trail of the killer. "Seems to me that we have no proof that those other two events are connected to Miss Alice's death. So, yes, in the case of Alice Auchinschloss, you're still a suspect."

"Your only suspect?"

His shoulders slumped. "Look, I'll admit that the case is flimsy but you have to agree you have the strongest motive."

"Then I'm sorry," I told him, straightening my back and hoping he'd see I meant business, "until I'm cleared, I'm going to keep digging."

He straightened as well. "I could order you to cease."

"You have no jurisdiction over my free time, Sheriff," I said, more gently now, "and I'll try to be as unobtrusive as possible, but I have to keep trying."

He sighed. "I guess there's nothing I can do then except to tell you to be careful. Even if you did murder Miss Alice…" He held up a large weathered hand as I bristled at that comment. "Now hang on a minute, don't go bustin' a vessel. I said 'if' you murdered Alice Auchinschloss; the fact remains there's still someone else out there determined to cause trouble. So take care." He paused then and added sheepishly, "And if you do happen to come across anything of interest, I'd be grateful to be included in that conversation."

After his big speech it was almost a complete about-turn. A green light! "Well, about that," I began in a low voice, "it has come to my attention that Ivory Sternuk visited both Miss Alice and Miss Charlene right before they died. You could check with Riverbend and also with your mailman, Clive."

He frowned as he took that in. "Well thank you, I will certainly check that out. The thing is, Ivory Sternuk has a habit of dropping in on people unannounced. Usually at mealtimes and usually wrangling herself an invite. You wouldn't think she and my wife came from the same parents. The woman must not be able to boil an egg!"

Or she's just plain mean and manipulative, I thought

ungraciously. I said nothing more though, just watched him.

"Okay, all right. As I said, I'll look into it but I'm not sure it'll go anywhere."

"And I'd check on Haven Jones and her daughter. She's been hanging about Miss Alice's farm—even on the day of the fire."

His raised his eyebrows. "Okay. Thank you. I said I'd look into it all and I will."

I guess it was all I could ask. Before he turned away though, on impulse I reached out to touch his arm. "Sheriff, I have something else to say or well, at least to ask. And I'll fully appreciate it if you answer in the negative, but it's about your wife, Miz Kinnead?"

His eyes widened. "You think she's the murderer?"

"Oh no! No, not at all. No, it's just that…" I searched for the right words and while those that arrived were barely adequate they did the job. "It's just that I've noticed she seems tired, and maybe she doesn't look so well. And it's just that I like to cook and bake and—"

"So, I've heard and I must compliment you. There's quite a buzz goin' around about the desserts you've been serving up around the community lately."

I flushed, momentarily blown off course. "Oh, um—good gracious—well that's really nice. Thank you. But"—I swallowed and dived in—"would you have any objection to me offering to help Miz Kinnead with her load? I don't want to intrude on your privacy but I can see how busy she is at the markets and how popular her preserves are, and I also can't help but notice she's struggling."

He eyed me silently for long seconds. And just in that nanosecond before he turned away to search for his wife, I thought I saw those eyes moisten. When he turned back his nose had turned a deeper shade of red and indeed his eyes looked different.

Swallowing deeply he finally answered. "The Fencotts are good people. I've never known them to make bad judgment calls before this. Now I'm not saying you're off the hook, but I think that deep down you're a good person, Rosie Hart. And your offer is neighborly and appreciated. I'll ask Miz Kinnead and if she's in agreement, I have no objections." He then held up that same large hand. "But heed this, I love that woman more than I love the air I need to breathe. If anything happened to her…"

My own eyes filled up. "Not on my watch, Sheriff."

He nodded. "Then thank you. We'll get back to you. Have a good day now—and stay safe."

That conversation buoyed me and I headed over to Chavez King. I knew his type before I was within three yards of him. He watched me walk toward him, speculation in his eyes and the kind of glint that leaves most women cold. He was a heartless womanizer and I doubted age had slowed him down.

Where I'd seen him to be tetchy and mean to his daughter-in-law earlier, he was now all sweetness and charm. The kind that has to find an excuse to touch and whose words would have caused a major oil slip if they'd reached the floor.

I was aware of those knowing eyes, olive skin—not nearly as unmarred and smooth up close as it was from a distance—and strong white teeth that appeared wolfish in his cruel mouth. "It's not like me to miss the arrival of another beautiful woman in town. Allow me to introduce myself, Chavez King at your service!"

The words were accompanied by not just an extended hand to shake but another around my back that was slipping lower even as we stood there.

Forcing a smile, I moved ever so slightly to derail the direction his arm and hand were traveling. Barely had I done that when Chrystal swooped, hovering, asking Chavez what he needed and what she could do for him. She was almost simpering.

"Chrystal—can you see I'm engaged in a conversation with this delightful young woman? Please leave me be."

Her face flushed and she moved away, but the looks she was sending me were almost lethal. Poisoned words had nothing on poisoned looks from Chrystal King. "Your daughter-in-law seems devoted."

"To my money," he muttered bitterly. "Plain women seem to crave wealth and power. It's the only way they'll ever be noticed. Not that a honey-pie like you has to worry about that," he finished smoothly.

Shock and outrage at such utter disrespect for Chrystal

vied with humiliation that I was allowing this man to address me as though I was a commodity. But I stood and endured, hoping the sacrifice would pay off. Pasting on a smile that I hoped betrayed my urge to vomit, I thanked him. And crossed my fingers.

"Actually, I've been hoping to talk with you," I said sweetly.

His answering expression told me he knew I'd fallen under his spell. And the urge to purge grew stronger. His arm once more enfolded me. "Why don't we step outside, it's more private."

And so the fly steps into the spider's web…

Chapter Twelve

OUTSIDE WE FOUND a bench under a shade tree, more because he needed to sit, I suspected. I led right in. "Mister King…"

"Chavez."

"Chavez," I began again. "I'm in a right pickle and I hope you can help me?"

He clasped my hand, bringing himself closer and I almost gagged at the combination of overpowering aftershave and mothballs. "Anything…"

"Well, it's about the day Jed Jones died. You were there, right? And I'm wondering if you could tell me what you remember."

Some of the warmth left his eyes and his gaze was more assessing. "Why?"

I feigned a tear. "Because I've been accused of Miss Alice Auchinschloss's murder! And I didn't do it! And I think it's somehow connected to that day. She left me a clue…" *This was probably dangerous I thought belatedly.* "But I don't know where to start."

His smile was much cooler now. "Pretty little thing like

you a murderer? Never." He loosened his grip on my hand, and I saw right through his own feigned nonchalance. "You say there's a clue? About that day?"

I shrugged. "I shouldn't have said anything," I answered in a whisper. "Sheriff Kinnead will be angry. But I feel I can trust you." *Oh get that bucket, fast.*

"Of course you can, sweet thing. Can you tell me more?" *No way in heck…*

"Well, perhaps if you tell me first, we could work it out together?"

His eyes narrowed and I saw the cruelty of the man just under the surface, but he recovered quickly. "Well, let me see." He lifted his shoulders as though there was nothing new to offer. "We were all there as usual." A lecherous grin appeared, adding to that wolfishness. "Alice and John Thatcher were off being naughty." The grin faded. "The rest of us were just doing what we did. Chatting. Throwing pebbles in the stream. Smoking. The girls were probably getting luncheon ready. They always provided a delicious spread."

"And then?"

He sighed. "And then we heard Ivory scream and we turned to see that Jed had fallen."

"Ivory screamed first? Not Jed?"

He looked annoyed. "Isn't that what I said?"

I nodded. "So, Jed fell. Tripped on a rock?"

"Yes, tragic," he answered, recovering. "Stepped backward poor boy. Friendships were ruined that day. As well as my best flannel trousers! My mother was furious. I finally got another pair. Amazing quality, soft to the touch. That was quite a bonus, let me tell you." The lecherous smile returned. "Many a young lady was persuaded to stroke that fabric." He paused. "You're blushing, darlin'. Thought bein' a city gal you'd be more worldly than that. Still, that can be a bonus sometimes too…"

Not blushing. Burning with rage.

"Did you suspect any foul play, Chavez?" I asked trying to bring him back to task.

His own face began a slow burn. Those eyes narrowed again. "Now why would you ask that? 'Course there wasn't! The boy tripped! He was a half-wit, you know? Didn't take much. To this day I don't understand why John Thatcher took it so hard; was a blessing the way I saw it. That boy was always hanging around asking awkward questions and gettin' in the way of… Well you know what it's like when boys and girls get to be alone don't ya', honey? Well, a third wheel like that isn't always welcome if you get my drift." He leaned in closer, that mouth moving near to mine.

I scooted back along the bench, hoping I'd avoided splinters from the rough wood. I'd gotten more than his drift. His hands followed me and again I moved away. I'd never developed a stronger dislike for anybody so quickly. Ever. And I couldn't hide it one more moment. I knew I was burning my bridges when I pointedly pushed his hands off me and jumped to my feet, putting as much distance between us as I could. Looking at him coldly, I answered. "I think I do. And I wish I could say it's been a pleasure, Mister King. Sadly it was possibly the most repulsive fifteen minutes of my life."

His responding expression was priceless.

If God was fair Chavez King would turn out to be the murderer.

Inwardly I groaned. And I'd just gone and made an enemy of someone I needed to investigate. *Nice going, kid.*

As I turned to leave I saw Jonah coming out into the church garden. I knew by the way his face cleared that he'd been looking for me. After being in the clutches of Chavez King, he was like life-giving nectar to a dying woman. And completely without care as to what message I sent him, I ran to Jonah.

As we prepared to leave, I made a mental note to catch up with Merline—and maybe Midge—as soon as was respectfully polite. Though Merline gave me the opportunity I needed when she reminded me to drop into the salon one day, as we paid our last respects. What I needed now was quiet to assess if I'd made any progress, and while on the surface I thought not, there was a little tickle bothering me. An idea that I might have learned something important. I just wished I knew what it was.

IT WAS LATE by the time we'd cleared away and returned to the B&B. Even later by the time Jonah had left for the night. Fiona had gently bullied us into a game of Scrabble that was the most hilarious game experience I'd ever had. Clay and Jonah both cheated outrageously, leaving Fiona and I both frustrated and exhausted from laughing. So, apart from talking things over briefly with Jonah, and mentally moving Chavez King to the top of my suspect list, I'd had little time to actually go through my notes.

Overnight though, a few things solidified in my mind and I woke with a new purpose and answers I hoped to be correct. Though not necessarily helpful to my case.

I sent off a quick text to the Fab Four asking for any information on Ivory and Chavez. Even the thought of that man was still making my skin crawl. The girls were still bombarding me with messages, mostly about things that were largely unhelpful. Giving them direction would hopefully give their communications purpose.

The plan for the day didn't include much sleuthing—unfortunately—but the fun it promised made up for that. Amazingly, despite the things that had happened at Miss Alice's, the thought of being out at the little house hadn't fazed me, and I was spending the day out there, unloading the items we'd purchased and carried home, and awaiting deliveries of bigger items.

Fiona had loaned me her truck—which was filled with treasures from our shopping excursions, and one of those items—which she'd organized without a blink—was a large whiteboard. And before doing anything else, I set it up in what would be the study downstairs and began filling out my lists and notes.

I'd almost completed that when there was a call from the open front door and Jonah wandered in carrying a cooler, which I soon learned was filled with a container of soup, fresh rolls, sandwich fixings, and drinks. His other hand held a lead attached to a giant dog.

"Meet Tiny," he said—and didn't even smile saying it.

"Hi, Tiny, glad to meet you," I answered obediently.

"Let her smell you, Rosie. Pet her."

"What's going on?" I loved dogs and had never actually had one, so I was thrilled at this opportunity—if a teeny bit awed by Tiny's size. But I was also a bit wary of Jonah's attitude. He seemed so serious.

Tiny on the other hand was gorgeous. Loving and playful. She danced around and jumped up on me—reaching me face-to-face—desperate to lick me wherever she could. Laughing, I pushed her back, rubbing her ears and head as I did. "Gorgeous girl!" I said, waiting for his reply.

"Rosie honey, I want Tiny to stay with you while you're out here. Every time you're out here. Okay? It's just for safety."

I smiled. "What will she do? Lick an attacker to death? Drown them in sloppy kisses?"

His eyebrows went way up. "Probably eat them."

I frowned and he went on to explain.

"She's a beautiful dog, darlin', but she's a trained farm dog. I get the odd big cat or coyote around at calving time, and she's trained to chase them off." He handed me the lead. "If someone comes she'll come straight to your side. If it's all good, just scratch her head or pet her somehow. But if you're worried, snap your fingers and she'll be ready. She'll give warning. She'll growl first. That's usually enough for most people. Takes a bit more with wild animals…"

My head was reeling. "Are you serious? What if I wanted her to stop?"

"Dead serious. If you want her to stop, just call her name and say 'heel.' Tiny, heel," he demonstrated. "She'll do it."

It was amazing to witness Tiny's obedience—and intelligence. She moved to sit upright at his feet. Alert and ready. "Wow…" It was all I could say.

He couldn't stay—and made it clear he wished that to be just the opposite—and I set about emptying the truck. I'd wanted to get the notes done first so, one) I could ensure I got everything down before I forgot it, and two) I could mull over those notes as I worked. Of course having Tiny at my heel with every step made that a little more difficult than I'd expected but I loved her being there.

Brand-new boxes of flatware, glassware, dishes, and pots were put in the kitchen ready for washing and stacking. Loads of baking ware and so many appliances and utensils my head could barely cope! Excitement burbled in my stomach at the thought of making use of all those amazing new toys.

Similarly linens and towels found their way to a walk-in linen closet upstairs and when the washing machine arrived and was connected, I'd get those done as well. Cushions, décor items, and all those things were stacked in a spare room awaiting the bigger items that would hold them.

One of the things we'd taken from the old house was a pair of old rockers that Fiona had organized to be delivered over the weekend. After a couple of hours, I pulled one out into the cool of the deep front veranda, piled on a few cushions and sat back, the cooler and Tiny at my feet as I dived into the fare Jonah had provided, ensuring Tiny had plenty as well as a bowl of water.

The food was not only delicious but it was also plentiful, and sharing it proved to be a good icebreaker when an unexpected guest arrived.

Midge Moylan handed me a fashionably wrapped bag of exotic coffee blends with a warm smile and shaking hands. "I hope you don't mind... I mean, this isn't a house-warming gift or anything. It's just a gift."

I thanked her and invited her to share my meal. The second rocker was pulled out and when I went to get more plates, she asked if she could look around. "It's such a beautiful house!"

In that moment I had completely forgotten about the whiteboard in the makeshift study and of course that's where

I found her.

"Very organized," she said matter-of-factly.

I nodded. "Thank you."

"I see my name there. Am I a suspect?"

Tiny moved close to me and I rubbed her head. "I don't think so, Midge, but I do think you're the answer to one of my puzzles. You're Charlene's granddaughter, right?"

Her shoulders sagged and she closed her eyes, seeming to gather herself before she spoke. "I didn't even get to tell her. I'd been searching for her, knew the origins were here in Airlie Falls—which was why I came here to take over the paper. I finally worked it out. I visited her twice—on the pretext of doing a story on the town. Just trying to get to know her. I didn't want to shock her; wanted to ease her in slowly. But I missed my opportunity." She turned to me. "I didn't murder her—I was hoping to get to know her. My other grandmothers—adopted and genetic—have both passed. I was hoping I'd found the missing one."

Tears filled her eyes and then fell in big plops down the front of her white shirt. It was instinctive to hug her and she hugged back. When we returned to the rockers and our food, and Tiny was settled, I asked if she had any ideas about her grandfather. The look of distaste that came over her face told me what I'd guessed.

"I'm so sorry. He's awful, isn't he?"

She nodded tearfully. "Chavez King is a chauvinist and a bully."

"Does he know? About you?"

"I don't know," she replied, "and honestly I have no intention of building a relationship with that man. I was trying not to let this cloud my opinion—until I met him of course and he solidified my opinion all by himself, but according to Merline, family rumor had it that the union between him and my grandmother wasn't consensual."

She nodded at my gasp. I was hoping she was wrong for Charlene's sake and yet based solely on my own encounter, feared she was right.

"But as to whether he knows about me?" she continued. "During the course of my investigation I know a letter was sent to him advising him that someone had requested access to the files. Not that it was granted. But anyway, perhaps he knows, or perhaps he didn't see the letter. He's made no mention and if the lewd comments he's made have been made knowing I'm his granddaughter, I'd be even more horrified. Some of them are quite disgusting."

I knew what she meant. Again I was amazed at how alike Midge and I were physically—it was a bit eerie, really. It struck me that maybe we were his type?

I changed the subject. "I saw you with Merline—you seemed close."

"She's been everything I'd hoped for in an aunt. Great-aunt," she corrected. "It was Merline I first contacted. She seemed so approachable. She encouraged me all the way. She's been amazing."

After we'd eaten Midge made a timid suggestion. Her head tilted toward the house. "I guess you're trying to discover the identity of the killer so you can clear your name?"

I nodded. I'd avoided the local paper—which wasn't hard to do given it was a weekly only edition. I wasn't sure how much coverage the murders had been given—nor how much *I'd* been given for that matter. I had a sudden feeling that the Fencotts and son had wielded their influence to keep Midge away from me.

"Look," she said, "you've been kind to me. Others might have thrown me out—being a reporter and given your situation. I like you and I'd like to help you. I used to be an investigative journalist. A good one. I promise I won't publish anything you don't approve, but I'd like to go through your findings to see if I can make sense of anything. I don't know these people really well, but I know them slightly better than you do."

I sat and watched her, thinking as I stroked Tiny's head. Thousands would call me a fool, but I trusted her. Sharing my lists and information was a risk—but sometimes risks have to be taken.

I held out my hand. "Deal."

She smiled. "Great! Let's celebrate with some of that iced tea!"

I RETURNED TO the B&B with Tiny, tired and dirty but satisfied. It was late and I'd intended just grabbing a snack after my shower, feeding Tiny, and crashing. But when I came back downstairs wearing nothing but a pair of cotton pj pants and a T-shirt, Clay, Fiona, and Jonah were sitting at the kitchen table.

I went to apologize for my attire but as their faces met mine one by one, I knew there was bad news. I slumped onto the vacant chair. "Hank?" I asked quietly. "Please say it isn't Hank."

The parents turned to Jonah who sighed. "No, honey. Hank's holding his own. But we've had another one. It's Midge Moylan. She was poisoned. She's in the hospital—touch and go."

"No! That's impossible!" All faces again turned to me. "Impossible! She shared my lunch today, Jonah! The lunch you brought out!"

Silence greeted me. And disbelief that this had happened. I saw it in their eyes. But not one ounce of accusation.

Clay roused himself first. "Rosie, I think we'd better call Frank—Sheriff Kinnead. He's gonna be tracing her movements and no doubt he'll discover she was with you, so best we get in first. Do you have any objections to that?"

Objections to having to face the Sheriff again and be questioned about attempted murder? Thousands. Trillions. But I simply said, "No." Because it made good sense.

I'd barely changed into clean jeans and a soft, lemon

long-sleeved T when the Sheriff and Bobby Don both arrived. The latter wasn't looking happy and I figured he'd been told to pick up his game and make sure his facts were correct in future. That would also explain the notebook and pen he had at the ready before we'd even greeted each other.

"Miss Hart, we meet again," the Sheriff began. "Now why is it that every time we have some kind of foul play here in Airlie Falls you're at the center of it?"

I wanted to point out that I had nothing to do with Charlene's death at all, but wisdom overruled indignation.

"She's tryin' to do the right thing here, Frank," Clay reminded him.

"That's right," Jonah added. "Rosie didn't even know about Midge until we told her just half an hour ago."

The Sheriff turned to Jonah. "So she says…" Once more he held up a hand to ward off any onslaught of objection. "All righty, all righty… I will say I do appreciate you saving me time by coming forward. We've been trying to trace her whereabouts and not having much luck." That was accompanied by a pointed look at Bobby Don who bent his head and started scribbling madly—though given there'd been nothing to record yet, it could even have been his grocery list for all we knew.

"So," Frank continued, settling into the sofa chair Fiona offered and stretching his legs out in front. "From the beginning. Tell me what happened this afternoon."

I did, leaving out nothing. Except my whiteboard. And

the fact she'd had the opportunity to peruse it and knew who my suspects were. And the fact that we'd agreed to work together. What purpose would that serve other than to make him mad?

"Why do you think she came to see you?"

I shrugged. "I'm not sure. Curiosity? She is a journalist and I'm a suspect in a murder case." I added a pointed look in his direction with that last bit. "But I think she got a surprise. We had things in common—both from the city—and we both came from families that weren't typical. Dysfunctional really. We got along and when she left I felt I'd made a new friend."

"Okay," he said slowly. "Now the food. You say you both ate the same thing?"

"I purchased that at a café in Easterville," Jonah said, jumping the queue on my question. "I was coming through from checking on my boys and stopped at a place we've been to before. They loan out coolers for picnickers and I got it and the food and went straight to Rosie."

The Sheriff's mouth pulled into a straight line. "I'll ask again, Miss Hart. Did you both eat the same thing?"

Sending a silent apology to Jonah for the Sheriff's brush-off, I took a moment to think. "We both had soup. I had chicken salad and she had bratwurst. But Tiny ate some of everything and she didn't get sick!"

The Sheriff shot Jonah a quick glance. "Tiny—as in your dog Tiny?"

Jonah nodded but the Sheriff wasn't convinced this was a good argument. "Dogs eat disgusting stuff that would make us pretty sick and it don't bother them, so I'm not sure this counts."

"But poison is different surely," Fiona argued as she placed a loaded tray of hot drinks and food on a coffee table. "A healthy grown woman is fighting for her life—that's a hefty dose of poison. That would drop a dog as well, I'm sure of it."

The Sheriff shrugged, took refreshments, checked on times, went over the story again and directed Bobby Don to collect samples of all the remaining food in the cooler. Then he and Bobby Don stood to leave. Other than *thank you* for the snacks, I didn't think B.D. had said a single word.

Frank had one last comment and it was directed at me. "I should warn you that you'll probably be tellin' this story to the big guys from Dallas soon. In two weeks Airlie Falls has seen more crime than it has in its entire history. Two murders, an attempted murder, the fire and two physical attacks—and I'm getting nowhere." He sighed and I really felt for him—despite the fact that he'd lock me up if he got a bit more evidence against me. He had the look of a defeated man. "If it's the same person and I'm praying it is and that we haven't got two loonies on the loose—then that amounts to a serial killer in our midst. So, those federal fellas will probably be down and I'm guessing they'll want to go over everything with you again."

ANOTHER RESTLESS NIGHT followed and I woke feeling off-center. I had completely disregarded Charlene's secret pregnancy because I was convinced it had nothing to do with either Miss Alice's murder or Jed Jones's death. And yet, what other reason could there be to attack Midge?

Dressing quickly I made my day's plan. I'd shoot out to see the Fab Four straight after I'd eaten and then head back out to the house to await the delivery of the fridge and washer-dryer combo. Later in the day I had to be at the hospital to take my turn sitting with Hank—and also have a chance to check in on Midge who was still unconscious as well.

THE GIRLS WERE excited to see me, especially as I brought some double chocolate brownie bars with me. The only problem was that I had to wait for them to eat, and then fuss over Tiny, who sat in the garden with us, before they could tell me what they'd learned. Sadly though, this would be the last time. Now that there'd been another attack I was even more fearful for them. I shouldn't have asked them about Ivory and Chavez; it was way too dangerous for them to keep snooping into others' lives. Like last time, they'd argue, but I'd be firm.

E.T. licked her fingers. "I can't look at chocolate any more without thinking about poor Charlene."

"I know," Martha agreed, her tongue sliding around her lips like a missile seeking a target—that target being any missed chocolate crumbs.

I wanted to say that it obviously hadn't stopped them eating it though, when Lori Sue jumped in—as usual—to explain. "Poor Charlene was diabetic but oh how she loved her cakes and candy."

I understood that from watching the Fab Four in action. They were like vacuums when it came to anything sugary.

"That's how the killer tricked her," Lori Sue continued. "Tempted her with chocolate." She leaned forward conspiratorially. "Doc Mitchum wasn't supposed to tell us but he did. The poison Charlene ingested was in the contraband chocolate she ate!"

I shook my head and willed my frustration down. They were old and they meant well—but they'd called me a dozen times with trivia—or to tell they had nothing new, yet they'd omitted something that was possibly vitally important!

I held their gazes. "Miss Alice was a diabetic too. And she loved chocolate…"

"Ooh," Betsy said clapping her hands. "Have we done good? Have we found a clue?"

"I'm not sure but I'm very grateful for that information." And now if only Sheriff Kinnead would tell me how Miss Alice took her poison… Yeah and he might also explain how pigs fly.

"Okay, ladies—here we go!" Lori Sue had a notebook that she held with outstretched arms so as to read it. I imagine if I told her to get her glasses prescription updated she'd tell me she was fine. "Now," she began, "Ivory Sternuk."

"Money troubles?" I asked.

E.T. almost choked, spraying cake crumbs all over us. "If money problems means having too much then that's what she's got!"

"But she practically lets the town feed her! I thought she had no money!"

"No, no dear," Martha explained. "After John Thatcher took himself out of society, Ivory was heartbroken for a time. Then she went to work in Austin and met a very wealthy man. He was older and had made money in oil. As oil fortunes go, it was moderate but still a fortune to most people. Well, they got themselves engaged and two weeks before the wedding, he up and got run down by a bus!"

"Stepped off the curb, folk say," Betsy said. "They said he was so preoccupied with marrying Ivory that he plum forgot where he was and walked right into the bus."

"So, let me get this straight," I said, "Ivory inherited some money from him?"

"All of it," Lori Sue corrected. "The woman's a millionaire. By Texas standards we'd say that word has a lower case *m*, but a millionaire just the same. There were a lot of legal arguments from his sisters and brothers but the will held up and Ivory got the lot."

I thought of the woman with the cheap track pants who mooched dinners from people—and it didn't add up. "Do we know who inherits after she's gone?"

"Maybe an orphaned cats' home?" Betsy suggested. "She's as batty as a bullfrog in a drought, she's got no children, and she doesn't associate with her only sibling— Brenda Kinnead. So could be that cats' home for all we know!"

So that's what I'd seen at the funeral. "She doesn't speak to her family?" I prompted.

"Some family tiff that goes way back. Anyways, Brenda and Ivory's parents were both very unwell people who needed a lot of expensive care. Brenda and Frank had boys they were trying to put through college and were also trying to pay the medical expenses for the parents. Apparently Ivory—with all that money—refused to help out with the expenses of the parents and so Frank and Brenda borrowed big to make ends meet. That's why Brenda works so hard at that stall of hers. They got debts they're still payin' down."

Goodness. How different life looks when you see it from the inside. Poor Miz Kinnead. I prayed that things worked out so I could help ease her load.

"So," I said moving on, aware of time, "how about Chavez?"

"Well," Betsy began, "apart from being the biggest creep

who ever walked the earth we don't have much. He's as rich as God, too, but I bet a lot of it wasn't made legally."

"Who inherits there, then?"

"Chuck and Chrystal. Chavez has treated them like servants most of their married life. Throws them crumbs. Chuck's nice enough—but he's a weak man. Won't stand up to his daddy."

I rolled this around in my head. "Hmmnn, I suppose you heard that Midge Moylan is the secret granddaughter of Charlene? Well, keep this to yourselves but Chavez is the granddaddy. I'm thinking Chrystal wouldn't like to think that inheritance could slip though her fingers, right?"

The gasps from the four before me were tinged with the delicious aura of both discovery and the forbidden.

"So, she could have killed Charlene to stop her talking!" Lori Sue exclaimed.

E.T. clapped her gnarled hands. "And then tried to knock off Midge to get her out of the way!"

Lori Sue almost jumped out of her seat. "Ohhh, Rosie darlin'—you're onto something!"

I wanted to smile, but there was the small matter of proof. Sure there was motive—but proof? And how did this connect to Miss Alice? Could this be it? Could I have solved the mystery? But then, I also couldn't get Haven Jones out of my head. I didn't have as strong a motive for her, but there were way too many questions to eliminate her yet. "Listen, I can't thank you enough, but we need to keep this to ourselves and you must promise me you'll do that. Okay? This could be dangerous for all of us. And you've also got to promise to stop snooping—well at least until we've solved this. Okay?"

Of course they promised but would they? *Could they?* They were very old ladies who were sometimes forgetful. Less than most their age—but still…

All the way out to the little house I berated myself for saying too much to them. If anything happened—to any of us—I had only myself to blame.

Taking courage from my findings so far, I called the Sheriff and amazingly got straight through.

"Miss Hart? What can I do for you?"

His tone didn't exude enthusiasm and wasn't the most friendly of greetings and I tried not to be put off by that. "Sheriff? I learned today that Charlene was poisoned with chocolate—that is, the poison was in the chocolate. Doc wasn't supposed to tell the Riverbend girls, but he did." I thought I heard a smothered curse as I paused to draw breath. "And so I'm wondering if Miss Alice's murderer used the same M.O.?"

He snorted. "I can't tell you that!"

"Is that a yes?"

"No, it's not—at least…" He was struggling, stumbling over his words.

I gripped the steering wheel harder. "I promise you no one else will hear it from me but—"

His sigh cut me off. "This is ridiculous." His voice sounded so tired. "My chief suspect is calling to ask about the murder method." The rasping of a hand rubbed across day-old whiskers filled the momentary silence as I waited him out. "All right, Rosie—Miss Hart—let this be my parting gift to you. Yes, the poison was in the chocolate, and if you did it, you know that. And if you didn't do it…" I could imagine the shrug that accompanied those words. "Now, I'm finishing this conversation and I'll deny we ever had it. The next person to speak to you about this might well be brandishing a federal badge. You have a good day now."

Chocolates, I thought as I drove on. I should have guessed. She was a fussy eater, Miss Alice, but chocolate was her Achilles' heel. Her weak spot. She wouldn't have even had to speak to anyone. They could knock and leave it on the stoop. And she'd have been helpless to ignore them—or her craving.

Tears filled my eyes as I made my way to the place she'd called home all her days. Life was so cruel sometimes.

Chapter Thirteen

A T THE HOUSE I was surprised to see the delivery people had already been. The refrigerator was in place and turned on. Taped to it was a note from Jonah saying he'd stopped by with food again and happened to be there when the truck arrived. He advised that for a while the cooler would be colder than the fridge, so he left the food in that. There was a P.S. that he'd try to call back later.

"We'll keep our fingers crossed, Tiny. Okay?"

I was sure she nodded, and I know she was as excited at the prospect as I was.

The refrigerator was gorgeous. Stainless steel and gleaming in the late morning sunlight streaming in through the many windows. I had my hand on the handle—ready to peek inside when sense overcame curiosity. Opening it now would be counterproductive. I'd let it chill for a few more hours and then check it out.

Most of my tasks were upstairs, so after filling in my whiteboard and updating all the information, I slipped upstairs to start work. The house was in such perfect shape— but we did decide the bathrooms could stand a makeover and eventually the kitchen as well. I'd decided to start stripping the main bathroom upstairs to ready for the upgrade.

It was hard and dirty work, but strangely therapeutic. After this morning's revelations I had so much to think about. So much to plan and the physical work helped. Finding proof wouldn't be easy. What if I went to Sheriff Kinnead again? Maybe he had information that when tied to mine would create a clearer picture? But then, what if he or clumsy Bobby Don bungled it? Put the murderer on alert? Then any proof would be lost completely!

The more I thought about this, the more it made sense that one of the women on my list was the murderer. It was obviously a woman's crime. Poison usually is. Add that to the fact that whoever attacked Hank and I didn't quite have the guts to carry that to the end. Poison but not physical violence? Sounded like the way a woman would think.

So, Chrystal King? Haven Jones? Barbara Jones? Ivory Sternuk? All had earned their place, some to lesser or greater extent. Surprisingly my lists pointed to Chrystal, even though she hadn't been at the top of my list. I needed to give that a lot more thought.

So how did I get the proof I'd need to clinch the deal?

And so I demolished dated tile work and continued to stretch my brain. During one break to chug on some mineral water, I thought I heard something or someone and relief flooded through me. Jonah? Had I subconsciously been waiting for his return? Hoping? "We're up here!" I called.

Tiny's ears had picked up and a low growl began in her throat. "It's okay, Tiny, I think it's our Jonah! It's all good." I swung my arm over her neck, soothing her, waiting for the inevitable pounding of boots on the hardwood stairs.

When it didn't come, I felt my own hackles rise. With Tiny right beside me I went to the top of the stairs and looked down. "Is anybody there?"

There was no answer and so I started down, keeping the dog right with me, ready to give her the signal if needed. But downstairs was empty. We checked every room on both sides of the house—even the pantry and larder—and then circled back to the main living areas.

The one thing I noted was that the cooler looked as though it had been moved. My eyes then went to the refrigerator. Jonah's note was gone. Had he been here? Creeping over I opened the door—and there sat a pint container of soup. Was that it? Had he not been able to make us hear so he just moved the soup and left? Had he returned especially with the soup and then been in too much of a rush to stay?

Disappointment rumbled through me. Heavy and careless of hurting. He couldn't spare just a moment to say hello?

I rubbed Tiny's head and gave her a snack from the cooler, finding my own appetite had deserted me. Besides, it was time to leave for the hospital, so the food could wait. I piled it all into the refrigerator until tomorrow, locked up and headed back to my car to drop Tiny back at the B&B.

THE SMALL HOSPITAL in Haden that serviced Airlie Falls and surrounds was modest but clean and efficient. I'd certainly had no complaints and I felt certain they'd do their best for Hank and Midge. Hank's room supported that belief. These days, hospitals aren't quiet or peaceful places but Hank's room belied that. It was cool and dim and calm. His favorite country CD played on low volume in the background and a pile of his favorite western novels sat on the bedside table.

I'd stopped by to check on Midge. Of course they wouldn't let me see her, but I was able to ascertain that she was stable, at least. That left me in good time to relieve Hank's grandniece who was rushing to collect her school-aged children.

As directed, I talked to him and read to him. I took the opportunity to thank him for his kindness and support. I told him what we'd been doing out at the house. And I even talked over my suppositions.

I was still hurt over Jonah's decision not to speak when he came to the house, but I was also still looking forward to talking all this through with him—to let his quick brain pick holes in my theory as he'd done before. But by the time a neighbor of Hank's relieved me and took his turn, I'd realized I wasn't even going to be able to do that.

Two texts arrived that left me hanging loose for the evening. There were no guests booked at the B&B, so Clay and Fiona were heading down to Austin to have dinner and the night with their other son, Ben, who'd scored a rare night off from the big hospital where he interned.

Jonah's was more rushed. His crew had struck a big problem and they were going to have to work through the night to shore up a potential disaster.

It was a funny feeling suddenly having my supporters—or wingmen—not there. I was lost and realizing how much of an outsider I still was here in Airlie Falls. It was true what the Sheriff had said. I seemed to be at the center of all this mayhem. More by chance than anything else, but beautiful people had been hurt—even lay dead—and although I had nothing to do with it, I felt guilty. Maybe I shouldn't stay here after this was over. *If* it was ever over.

And then there was Jonah. Could I stay if he didn't feel anything for me? Could I torture myself like that? I had more pride than to moon over someone and make him feel uncomfortable every time he saw me. And this was his home. I'd have to leave.

Maybe the decision had been made.

Slowly making my way back to the B&B, the place I had begun to think of as 'home,' was a sobering experience this time around. Realizing I hadn't eaten much all day, I cooked up some crispy bacon and spicy scrambled egg, and added some salad and toast. It filled the empty spots and once I'd cleaned up there seemed little left but to tend to Tiny and head off to bed.

The doorbell rang late, and for just a moment I forgot I was the only person in the house. Once that thought solidified, I lay still wondering what to do. If it was business, like customers for the B&B, would I know how to book them in? Would it be safe?

Selfishly I'd just decided to ignore it when it rang again, and continued ringing. Heart pounding I jumped up. My room looked out over the back garden so I couldn't see anything through the windows. I dragged on a pair of jeans and slowly made my way downstairs, my eyes on the door and the opaque glass panel. The outer light was on and I could see the outline of a woman and she seemed to be alone.

Was someone in trouble? Someone who needed Fiona or Clay? Taking in a deep breath and hoping for the best I opened the door, surprised—and a bit wary—to see Haven Jones standing there. One of my chief suspects was right there on the doorstep. Late at night.

And I was alone.

Well, almost… A furry head nudged me, rubbed against my hand. Reminding me she was there for me.

Still, my first response was instinctive—I stepped back away from the door. Obviously my face told a story because her hands came out, empty and pleading. "Please, Rosie, I need to talk with you."

Glancing around behind her, I shook my head. "It's late, Miz Jones, and I was already in bed. Maybe we could wait until tomorrow?"

Picking up my tone, Tiny stiffened. I felt her stillness, and I patted her head to soothe her.

Haven ran a hand through hair that was more disheveled than I'd seen it before. Her thin coat hung loose and crumpled. That didn't raise my confidence. "Please, dear. I just need to explain. I can't sleep. I can't think…"

My lips were suddenly very dry. "Explain about what? Why you murdered Miss Alice?"

Her face creased up. "No, you must believe me, I didn't murder her! I wanted to apologize to her!"

What?

It seemed incongruous but her anguish appeared genuine and I was so torn. Closing my eyes, I struggled for answers and when none came I threw caution to the wind and gave in. Opening the door wider, I invited Haven Jones into the house.

I took comfort in the fact that Tiny didn't growl or show any response other than wariness. And the fact she stuck to my side; so close she almost tripped me up.

Haven moved slowly, deliberately—and I realized at once that she was cold. Frozen. Had she been waiting out there trying to find the courage to speak to me?

Concern was my own primary response from that point. I led her to the kitchen where I heated water for tea. Instead of seating her at the table I guided her to a small sofa in the cozy glassed-in nook and placed an afghan across her knees. She grabbed it and pulled it up over the front of herself, leaning heavily into the cushions with a resigned sigh, while Tiny settled at her feet.

Haven's hands shook as she took the tea, and I actually gripped my own cup tighter—for the same reason. When she said nothing I had to prompt her.

She sighed again. Heavily, as though words were an effort. Finally her mouth moved and then the words poured forth. "I'm sorry for coming here, Rosie." She paused again. "Sorry for so, so many things." She rubbed one hand across her brow. "I've made such a mess of things. Made such a mess of my life."

"I'm sur—"

She cut me off. "Let me speak while I can. You see, I blamed Alice for everything bad that happened to my family. It made sense," she said, almost begging me to agree. "If John Thatcher hadn't been so taken with her he wouldn't have been with that group of useless time-wasters. And if he hadn't been off with her that day, he would have been looking out for Jethro—Jed." Her voice dropped. "And he wouldn't have died."

"Your family really suffered."

She nodded. "That doesn't excuse what I did." She paused again, taking sips of her tea. "You see, I got so caught up in my anger I let it consume me. I began drinking—and

I'm ashamed of myself for it. But, well, during those periods I tried to get my revenge."

"Oh dear…"

Again she nodded. "I was so cruel… I caused so much harm. The town hated Alice, and I made sure she knew it. That's why she treated them the way she did…"

"Miz Jones? Ma'am? I don't understand…"

Her eyes searched the ceiling for help. "All those complaints to the authorities? They were me. I did it when I was drunk. I pretended to be her. And then I'd write her anonymous letters and tell her how much she was hated." Her head was low now, but that didn't hide the tears that flowed so freely. "I'm so ashamed. Jo… John Thatcher truly loved her until the day he died. He blamed no one but himself. He shouldn't have blamed himself, but at least he was more fair and gracious than I ever was."

"I spoke to him just before he died," she continued. "We really talked. He told me how good Alice was with Jed. How she really cared for my brother—cared for both of them. But he was eaten up with guilt and knew she deserved more than to be with someone who'd given up on life."

My own tears were falling along with hers. "I don't know what to say…"

She shook her head. "There's nothing you can say, and I don't expect forgiveness, but I do need people to know that Alice was just a brokenhearted woman." She looked me straight in the eye. "I didn't kill her. All I wanted to do was apologize to her."

She sat there for a few minutes and then pushed to her feet. "I've said my piece; I need to go."

"Miz Jones, are you sure you're able to get back home or wherever you're staying? We can call Barbara. I know Fiona would be happy to let you stay here."

She straightened. "Thank you, but no."

As she stood, I reached to comfort her. She was taller and bigger than me but somehow she folded into me, suddenly appearing to be small and vulnerable. It wasn't my place to give her forgiveness but I could offer comfort. And I hoped, somehow, Miss Alice had been listening.

As Tiny and I showed her back to the door, something occurred to me. "Miz Jones, why did your daughter call and try to speak to Miss Alice?"

I felt the tension in her as I spoke, felt her pull back from me. She kept her head down and focused on the door, picking up speed.

"Miz Jones? Ma'am?"

Again she ignored me. For a second I considered not opening the door, but I couldn't do it. And as we reached it, she was through it and into the night before I could ask once more.

Confused, I watched until she was out of sight. Why open up about all the rest and shut down when I mentioned her daughter? Was Barbara guilty? Did Haven know that? I believed her story, but maybe the reason for the confession at this point was to deflect attention from themselves as suspects? Particularly deflect attention from Barbara? There was obviously more to tell, but Haven was keeping the rest to herself.

IT TOOK A long time for me to settle enough to try and sleep. My mind jumped from one thing to another. Haven Jones's revelation had been both shocking and, in a way, a relief. Hoping my instincts were correct, I removed her from my suspect list. But that weird reaction to my question about her daughter pushed Barbara ever closer to the top.

When I finally slept, once more the night was a restless one—my dreams were as scrambled as the eggs I'd eaten, and featured a lot of Barbara Jones and Chrystal King—and each was coming at me with a sharp implement.

And morning offered no bright distraction. Fiona and Clay wouldn't be back until later that day and Jonah was still on the job. Only one thing was clear. This afternoon I'd try to grab some time with Sheriff Kinnead. I was going to put my case to him and pray he did the right thing—and that he worked it out.

In the meantime—for Hank and Fiona—I'd head back out to the house and finish demolishing that bathroom ready for the contractors. I could do that much for them.

AS ALWAYS, THE little house was swathed in sunlight. Whoever ended up living here would be very lucky indeed. The kitchen certainly could do with being opened up to the rest of the living areas but it was a brilliant country kitchen. A new oven to replace the old one was arriving today. Despite it never having been used, Jonah had declared the old one unsafe after so many years and so it was being updated. A double oven no less. Imagine being able to bake at twice the usual rate!

Fiona called as I was dreaming of such a luxury and I appreciated the news she shared. Dan Casey was off the hook. That day he'd been doing what he'd been doing with all his spare time of late—sneaking off to complete a secret project he was creating for Vicki for their upcoming anniversary. That day he'd been foraging for particular wildflower seeds he needed for his gift.

Relief flooded through me that we were eliminating suspects, and I felt I was moving into the day in a much more hopeful frame of mind. But while the work I'd begun occupied my hands, my mind was free to drift—and that hopeful mood soon shifted. Doubts and questions ate away at me, and in no time both my decisions—about whether to stay here in Airlie Falls and talking to the Sheriff—were again weighing heavily.

Determined not to let it all overwhelm me, I worked diligently for the next few hours. Tiny had taken up guard in the hall outside the door with her paws over her ears to block out the noise. The girls from Riverbend had called several times even though I had begged them to leave it be now. I actually stopped taking the calls hoping to dissuade them.

Then they started texting. One text at least. "*Recs widg recuwivry.*"

I smiled. It made no sense and I imagined arthritic fingers trying to juggle tiny keys. I'd call them later. I remembered games I'd played deciphering texts like these and studied it for a second frowning at the jumble of letters. Yes, later, I'd call them.

A text also came from Jonah telling me they were finished and that he was going to catch a few zzz's and then come round to give me some help. My heart skipped; I hadn't expected to see him today, and grinning like a loon, I sent back one warning him I had a lot to tell him—in particular that I felt close to solving this mystery.

It came at a time when I thought we should take a break and wandered down to rummage in the fridge. Beside me Tiny was trying to push her nose past me and make her own selections when she suddenly froze, ears pricked and stared at the front door. Hand on the open fridge door, I froze as well, staring in the same direction she was staring.

Her growl broke the silence, low and menacing. Swallowing deeply I pondered my options. Go and check it out or lock myself in and call for backup? I was partway to the front door when Tiny suddenly spun and uttered the most blood-curdling bark at something to the side of me.

Shaking I turned to see Chrystal King coming out of the study. Her face was white, her eyes burning. "What did she tell you?"

I backed up, momentarily forgetting the command to give to Tiny. Chrystal kept moving in on me. Her voice was manic, crazed like her eyes. "I don't care about your lists and games, I just want to know what she told you! I'm not having someone waltz in and take it all from us now! Do you hear! We've given our lives to that man!"

"Chrystal, please…"

"I just want to know what she said!" It was a demand now. A cold demand.

My brain started working. Tiny was still beside me, her teeth bared. Shaking, I snapped my fingers, terrified when they were sweating so much that nothing happened. I swiped my hands down my jeans. "Tiny, are you ready?" I stammered.

Again I clicked my fingers together—hoping to hear that decisive click. When I did, Tiny leapt into the air and Chrystal screamed, backing up to the door. My heart was pounding—I couldn't watch. No! Tiny would tear her apart!

"No, Tiny! Heel!"

Like magic the big dog stopped mid leap and shuffled to my side, never taking her eyes off Chrystal who had backed up to the door, still screaming, and fled out over the porch and kept going.

Oh my God. Trembling I fell to my knees on the floor. I should chase her! I should go after her! The thought made sense but my body wouldn't cooperate. *Quick. Get out of here!* Thoughts and orders kept coming fast now and I tried to get back to my feet, but before I was even halfway the door opened again and I screamed the scream of my life.

"Rosie! Rosie dear! What's wrong? Are you hurt?" Hands were holding me, helping me. Tiny was beside herself not knowing exactly who to eat. I called her down, dragging in deep breaths, and getting myself back under control.

Finally I looked up into the concerned eyes of Pippa Peatree. Relief washed through me. I pulled myself up and onto a chair, eagerly accepting the bottle of water Pippa pressed into my hands.

She was still talking. "What's wrong, dear? Are you okay? I just stopped by about the church bake sale. Remember? I said I'd call…"

I nodded. Working my mouth to find my own words. "This isn't a good time, Pippa. I have to get to Sheriff Kinnead. Now."

"Is something wrong?"

I looked up into her eyes. "Pippa, I think I know who murdered Miss Alice and Charlene—and who tried to murder Midge. I have to get to him now!"

"Oh my good gracious!" Her hand went to her mouth. "But you can't drive in this state! You've had a shock! I'll take you!"

"No, really, I'm okay. I'll just get my keys."

She stood, assuming her best pastor's wife stance. "I insist! It's my duty to make sure you're safe. Now, get your bag."

To be honest, it was better than being alone. I grabbed my bag and Tiny's lead. Pippa looked at the dog and frowned.

I jumped to make a case. "She's clean and well behaved, I promise."

Pippa's face twisted into a silent apology. "I'm sure she is—but it's—it's Peter. He's allergic and I…" She shrugged.

"Oh… Then I'll just take my car."

"Nonsense! We'll only be half an hour. She'll be okay here until you get back. Let's go!"

Caught up, I let her lock Tiny inside, and I tried to remind myself that *not* driving was the most sensible thing to do and that we'd be back soon. And tried to block out the sounds of Tiny's whimpers and scratching at the door.

We'd been on the road only a few minutes and my breathing was coming back under control. My vision was clearing and I took in one more deep breath and looked around. I needed to get all my facts in order. I needed to be able to tell a coherent story if I expected to be taken seriously. Perhaps if I had a pen…

I flicked my head around to the back seat and then suddenly everything slowed down. My brain functions slowed, searching. Comprehending. And then just like an internal switch was flicked, my vision sharpened. And finally my memory clarified…

I didn't mean to gasp.

That was my undoing.

Chapter Fourteen

W HEN PIPPA TURNED to me, her face was different. Hard. Her eyes flat and cold. Those blue, blue eyes. So like Ivory's. *Now* I got the resemblance. Way too late.

"Worked it out, have you?" Her voice was low and lazy. Very different to the fussing Pippa Peatree, perfect pastor's wife. "Took you long enough. I've been watching you since Miss Alice's funeral. You saw it then."

Disappointment flooded through me. It was true. It had all been there. I'd just not realized. That day in the general store it had almost come back. The boxes of chocolate candy. I'd seen them before. Stacked. But it made no sense and I couldn't remember where. Boxes just like the one on the back seat of Pippa's car.

Now I knew.

The day of Miss Alice's funeral when I delivered the desserts. I'd looked over Pippa's shoulder to see if there were preparations made and there hadn't been. But I remembered thinking there was obviously some sort of celebration—or maybe even some sort of commiseration gift? Because there were two boxes of the candy. King-sized. One opened. It's rich purple satin ribbons hanging loose. The other sparkled invitingly in its cello wrapping.

It meant nothing. The one unusual thing being there were two boxes. Oh and the hypodermic sitting beside the open box... I guess it could have meant anything.

Unless you knew that Charlene Madison, chronic diabetic, had been tempted with poisoned chocolate. Just like Alice Auchinschloss.

Oh my Lord. I wanted to smack myself soundly. It had been there. Right there in my head the whole time. I'd held the answer...

Especially when it hadn't been the only clue. "You dropped the purple ribbon," I said, my own voice flat. "I picked it up in the cleanup."

She didn't care. Barely heard me. She tilted her head toward the back seat. "These ones were a gift for you. The others loved them so I was hoping it would be third time lucky." A frown of annoyance appeared. "Should have been four of course. I really messed up there..." I had to strain to hear that last part because it was more of a mutter than shared speech.

Mine wasn't much better. It was like I couldn't stop echoing the thoughts swirling in my head. "I can't believe I chased Chrystal away. I can't believe I got it so wrong."

"Chrystal? I almost laughed out loud when you had your little hysteria attack." She didn't even try to conceal her enjoyment this time. "I saw her leave. She didn't see me, and

I was so glad when I realized what I'd walked into." She snorted. "All Chrystal's worried about is sharing Chavez's fortune. He's treated them like dirt all these years and she figures she's owed. She'll fight that Midge all the way—and my money would be on Chrystal."

When she turned to look across at me again, the benevolent parson's wife smile was in place once more. "Surprised at what I know? Oh, Rosie... Everybody trusts the pastor's wife. Don't you know that? Everybody needs to unload their secrets. Well, that's what we're there for, isn't it?"

This time the laugh was more of a twitter. I let her continue—still in that sickly sweet tone. "You didn't eat the soup I left for you, Rosie," she scolded, "so I had to try again..."

Oh my heavens. My hands began to shake and I squeezed them tight against me. The soup I'd thought Jonah had left. Similar soup probably left for Midge. I shook my head. I would have eaten that soup except that I was sad Jonah hadn't bothered to say hello. A petulant sulking attack had saved my life.

My heart began to thunder; my brain working overtime trying to figure out a plan. She was driving too fast for me to jump. Culverts lined the edge of the road and played host to a tangle of wild blackberry and lantana brambles. They'd tear me apart. I glanced out again. Pippa would do worse.

But maybe I had more of a chance with Pippa. Maybe I could reason...

And if not? Only one thing occurred to me and I had no idea if it would work. As discreetly as I could I slipped my hand into my bag.

Then I had to keep her talking. And pray she didn't suspect.

"Miss Alice was diabetic too. You tempted her as well, didn't you? These old dears love their sugar."

Pippa laughed. And pressed harder to the accelerator. "She was so easy. Stupid cow. Wanting to drag up all that business from years ago!"

"But why? Why kill her? Why kill any of them?"

"Because she was going to expose it all! Silly old goat couldn't leave the past where it belonged. Who cared whether that boy died by accident or murder? Hasn't she heard of forgiveness?"

Now there was irony.

I could play along here. "Well, I agree that the past is past. What could be so terrible that it could make any difference now?"

"Well, exactly. That's right…" Her tone was confused, like she hadn't expected me to agree. "And I told Ivory that. Told her no one would care, but then I found out there's no statute of limitations on murder cases! They never expire. Did you know that?" Exasperation oozed from her. "Have you ever heard anything so stupid?!"

"No. Never!" Deep breath. I had to go for it. "So Ivory told you she murdered Jed Jones?"

Pippa laughed that sweet pastor's wife giggle. "Poor Ivory. She's my older cousin you know? More like an aunt. I'm named for her. Pamela Ivory Porter. Everyone just called me Pip. Then, 'course when I married Peter Peatree, well it was just a hoot that I was still Pip! Pip and then Pippa. It just stuck."

"So Ivory told you…?"

Irritated now she spat, "You're mighty curious!" Then faster than the sun can disappear behind a cloud she smiled again. "But you know, it's kinda fun bein' able to chat like this. Ivory guessed that I was responsible of course, and I wanted to share, but old ladies forget themselves sometimes."

My patience was at breaking point.

"Oh well, you're not goin' to be able to tell anyone so…" she continued. "Okay, so Ivory came to us just after we took up residence here. It was all getting to her, poor love, and she just needed a kind shoulder. Pete said he felt like one of those Catholic priests hearing confession! What a hoot!"

"Must have been," I muttered, hoping she missed the sarcasm.

"So, she told us how she'd had to get rid of young Jed so John Thatcher would drop Miss Alice and be with her. She was absolutely crazy about John Thatcher. Ivory figured J.T. was only with Miss Alice because she was so fond of his brother Jed, and that he figured she'd help him care for Jed as their folks got older. Though Ivory didn't really believe that was true affection either from Alice. The way she saw it, she was pretty sure Alice was just pretending to care for Jed so J.T. would like her. Anyways, Ivory convinced herself that John Thatcher only felt gratitude, not real love."

I wanted to tell Pippa just how wrong Ivory had been but I had to stay on track. "But that doesn't make sense. The others claimed they saw Jed fall. Why risk perjuring themselves if there'd been a trial? Did Ivory have some kind of hold on them?"

Pippa shrugged. "I don't know and I don't rightly care. I just know Ivory walloped him on the back of the head with a rock."

My own head suddenly felt like it was inside the workings of one of those game shows where alarms ring, bells clang, horns roar, lights flash and balloons and streamers fall from the ceiling. Except I'd won the booby prize. I'd had all the clues. And only now I knew what they meant and where they fit. Too much, too late.

Jed's injuries were to the back of the head. Chavez said he'd tripped backward, the Fab Four girls heard he'd tripped backward—supporting the facts that his injuries were indeed to the back of his head. But that would leave him face up, right? And what had Ivory said? That she was glad she *hadn't had to take the image of his face into eternity with her.*

I shook my head. Jed was hit from behind. And fell face forward. That was the only way Ivory could have missed seeing his face. And she'd basically admitted that to me herself...

She or the group turned him, set the scene before Miss Alice and John Thatcher returned—and the authorities arrived. But again... why? Was their friendship with Ivory so loyal and so precious?

I thought of self-serving Chavez King. I doubted he'd do anything to help anybody but himself. And that meant... The second round of bells and streamers fell. The words Hank had said to the girls as he was leaving to come meet with me echoed in my head. They couldn't remember exactly but said it was something like: *Someone not who they say they were or where they were supposed to be...*

"They weren't there!" That's what Charlene had told Hank.

Startled, she spun to me. "What?"

"They weren't there! Charlene, Chavez, and Forster. They weren't there! They lied to protect themselves. But what could be so damning that they couldn't admit where they were?"

"I dunno, honey, but I guess that's one problem you're never going to solve."

Idiotically that burned me as much as my current predicament. That's human nature for you. Still, I had more pressing issues. I turned slightly to face her. "That's your plan, Pippa? To kill me?" We'd turned off the main road minutes back but I knew this shortcut back road. "Out here on Albertson's Road? You'll never get away with it!"

I saw her still as I said those words and knew I'd gone

too far. Turning she narrowed her eyes. "Please hand me your phone, Rosie."

No way. She couldn't launch at me without running us off into the deep ditches either side of the road, so I quickly buzzed down my window and dropped my phone into the scrub.

Her smile was still sweet. "It won't help you, you know. They'll never find it, even if you were recording me. And by the time they find you, it'll be way too late."

She pulled onto a side road that disintegrated into a track, changing into four-wheel drive as she maneuvered a steep ditch and headed into a deeply wooded area. Pulling to a stop she ordered me out of the car. I was about to argue when I saw the gun pointed at my chest.

I hadn't figured on that one.

"You can't do it, Pippa," I taunted, praying I was doing the right thing as I slowly moved out of the car. "You don't have the stomach for physical violence. Your style is quiet and clean. No blood."

"Keep quiet, you know nothing!" But I noted she paled.

"You couldn't finish off Hank and I when you hit us. What were you looking for out there anyway?"

"Proof! You stupid girl! Miss Alice wrote to Ivory tellin' her she had the proof that she'd killed Jed Jones and if Ivory didn't admit it she'd go to the Sheriff. Told poor Ivory that it'd look better for her if she handed herself in and that she was doin' Ivory a favor by giving her that chance."

I grinned. "But Miss Alice sent the same letter to them all. All four of the survivors from that day!"

"Yes," she bristled, "well I found that out too late, didn't I?" Her indignation built again. "But it still went and stirred things up! There was Charlene telling things to Hank! I had to stop them!"

I shook my head. "But I still don't understand why!"

She rolled her eyes. "The money! Ivory's money! You really are slow aren't you?" Her sigh was deep and dramatic, and I feared she'd clam up but thankfully she continued. "After she 'confessed' to Pete she came over all paranoid, like we'd turn her in or something. So, she took us off to the lawyers and made a will and left everything to us! All that money!"

"I still don't understand…"

"Ugh! So stupid," she scoffed. "Can't you see that if there was an investigation now—even all these years later— that all that money could have got eaten up in lawyer's fees? It could take years and tie up her estate! Even if she died in the middle of it all, the money wouldn't be free to come to us!"

Unbelievable. "And money's that important?"

"You know, honey, here's something to take to that grave with you. Kinda funny really. You see Peter and I have a little problem. It's how we met—at Gamblers' Anonymous! Isn't that a hoot! Ivory didn't know. No one knew. And we've only got a limited time before someone wants to check the balance of that infernal roof restoration fund. Though I'm pretty sure Ivory will help us out there... Especially now." She raised her eyebrows. "Though it's a right shame you won't be contributing to our bake sale. I was serious when I said your desserts would make a difference."

Her face suddenly hardened. "Now I've really enjoyed this. More than you could know, and it's a tragedy because I think you and I could have been friends—but I'm due at the women's guild meeting in an hour, so I'm gonna have to ask you to turn around."

I drew in a shaky breath. I was out of ploys. "No way, Pippa. If you're going to shoot me you can do it facing me."

Fear filled her eyes. "No, you'll turn now or I'll... I'll..."

"Shoot me?" I offered.

"Turn around!" she screamed, and fired a shot into the air.

"No." And I took a step forward. And prayed like I'd never prayed.

She stepped back, still screeching at me, but I kept moving forward. My legs were jello, my heart pounding, my whole body shaking. But I forced myself to move; to maintain eye contact. Thoughts jumped like popping corn. She could snap at any moment. I could push her too far. When did I stop? What would I do then?

But maybe my prayers were being heard because suddenly, like in slow motion, I saw those eyes widen, saw her tilt back and then her whole body fell backward. Arms flailed, the gun waved wildly and legs lifted off the ground.

And I pounced. Grabbing the gun arm and twisting. She kicked and punched but I held her firm, kept her pinned under me.

Until strong arms lifted me from behind, while at the same time boots and dark uniform trousers filled my vision at the front.

The arms came with a voice. A beautiful, deep-timbred voice that rocked through me. "It's okay, sweetheart. I've got you. And Frank's got her. It's over."

Chapter Fifteen

I TURNED AND let myself be held by those strong arms, held tight. All the while, his whispered words and his hands soothed. Soft kisses rained over my brow and I pressed harder into his warmth.

And eventually the shaking eased.

"It's really over?"

He nodded; I felt the movement against me. "Yes, darlin'. It's done. It's finally over. And now *we* can begin… That is if…"

For the first time I lifted my eyes to his. "I think you need to explain."

He hauled in air. "Aw hell, this wasn't supposed to be the time or place—but I was just so damned scared when I knew she had you."

My own breathing had stopped completely. "I'm glad, but could you get to the good part?"

He grinned, the cheekiest, heart-stopping grin. "Good part? You and I. That is if you think you'd like to see where it would go? Where *we* could go…"

I'd never seen Jonah look uncertain. I'd seen him con-

cerned, angry, contemplative, interested, and gentle and
kind. And always certain of himself. I'd never seen uncertain.

"Us? Really? I mean... really?" My tongue felt awkward
and clumsy. "I, well, I wasn't sure..."

"Hell, honey, I'm not sure how you missed that! Though
I've been trying so hard not to give you anything else to have
to worry about. I've been riding poor Frank to get this thing
wrapped up so I could tell you that I think you're pretty
special—and I consider it a very lucky day that archway
almost fell on my truck. A very lucky day."

Nothing could have stopped my smile. Nothing. "So do
I. And I hope I'm going to be grateful for Miss Alice's
inattention to her property for a long time to come."

A *harrumphing* to our left reluctantly pulled us out of our
world for two. Bobby Don was dragging a reluctant Pippa to
the police truck, and Frank Kinnead stood waiting for our
attention. "Sorry to interrupt you two, but we've got some
talking to do, Miss Rosie."

I nodded. "We sure have. She did it. She admitted to it
all."

"We know." He nodded as though confirming his words.
"We heard a lot of it. That was pretty brave of you to call
Jonah and leave the phone on. Gave us the opportunity to
track you as well."

My heart clutched again at the memory. "It was all I had.
If that didn't work then there was nothing left that I could
have done. My fear was that Jonah wouldn't hear the

phone." A chill rippled through me. "And then when the cell phone went out the window…"

"Technology is a double-edged sword, Rosie," the Sheriff explained. "It causes problems and offers solutions. You'd given us enough information for us to use it to our advantage. When we lost contact with you, we tracked Pippa's cell."

As Jonah squeezed me tighter, he chuckled. "And I don't know about you having nothing left, it looked like you had the best of her when we arrived. And she must have thirty pounds and four inches on you!"

I shook my head. "Just plain lucky that rock was where it was, and that it tripped her right over, I guess." I gave him a little punch on the arm. "And never underestimate the power of fear. I was fighting for my life, working with pure adrenaline."

"Yeah well, remind me not to get on your bad side, sweetheart. I can see that I might come off second best!"

The Sheriff wasn't so caught up in our fun. "You know that was a big risk, taunting her like that, don't you? I pray you're never in that situation again—she could have snapped at any time. I'm figuring she's unhinged. You can never apply logic to people like that."

"I kind of knew that, but I couldn't just stand there and let her shoot me without trying. If I'd tried to run, she'd have my back; I'd have been playing into her hands." I sighed. "And I was just plain mad with her, as well. I'd misjudged the people of Airlie Falls. Because, up close, for the most part, all I've ever seen is kindness and caring for their community and their neighbors. These people deserve to be served by good pastoral caregivers. Better people than the Peatrees!"

"Well, amen to that, Rosie," the Sheriff said quietly. "And I doubt you'll believe this, but despite all this business, I was going to tell you today that Miz Kinnead would be honored to accept your help. We talked it over, and we agreed."

I couldn't help it. I gave him a hug. "Thank you, please tell her I'll drop by tomorrow to have a chat. And, Sheriff?" I said, looking up into the big man's face. "I do believe you."

"See, Sheriff? I never get it wrong," Jonah boasted. "I told you she was okay right from that first day."

The Sheriff rolled his eyes, but he was grinning as he turned to head to the truck. Jonah and I both laughed, arms around each other, as we turned to follow. Poor Bobby Don was standing outside the locked police truck trying to convince Pippa Peatree she should stop yelling at him.

The poor Sheriff had stopped, watching the scene and scratching his head.

It was a good thing Bobby Don made great chili.

We left them to it and raced back to rescue Tiny. I owed that girl an apology, and a big thank-you steak.

IT WAS A whole four more days before we had any more answers. Four days where Fiona couldn't take the smile off her face each time her gaze landed on Jonah and I together. Clay was nearly as bad and despite the fact that Jonah and I were just officially starting out down this new road, I swear they were planning the wedding.

My fear of disappointing them warred with my joy at being so fully accepted, and while I'd do everything I could to protect them, I figured I couldn't be responsible for their hopes, and decided to just let go and enjoy this amazing, blissful journey.

Plans for my new home were ramped up and the future was brighter than I'd ever known it.

Investigation-wise, the big guns from the city had taken over and were wrapping it up, and Sheriff Kinnead had only tidbits to share.

The final revelation came from Hank four days on from the day Pippa tried to kill me. He was finally awake and we were all in his room. Of course he was thinner and paler but his eyes were bright and lively. The Sheriff, Fiona, Clay, Jonah, and myself—and Midge in a wheelchair also looking pale but much better—had gathered. Looking at Midge I shuddered to think I could have shared that fate—or worse.

The rest knew the story as much as I could tell them, but there were two holes. "All right, Hank, I can't wait a second longer!" Fiona exclaimed. "Do you know where those other three were when Ivory killed Jed?"

Sitting up in bed, he looked worn and older than before and I couldn't wait to see him back to his strapping best. "As a matter of fact, I do," he began. "That's what Charlene told me—or well, admitted at least. In her words, they were young and impressionable, and probably a bit bored."

I thought of Chavez's words: *chatting, smoking, throwing pebbles into the stream.* Bored.

"Well come on—what were they doing?" Fiona urged again.

"The answer," Hank began again, "lies in the time period. Think about what could be so disgraceful that they would lie about their whereabouts to cover a murder they didn't even commit. So terrible their parents would disown them—that they'd face jail time..."

It was Clay who clicked. His expression was grim. His gaze focused steadily on Hank. "They were Commies? Communists. They were consorting?"

Hank nodded. "There was a heap of secret stuff goin' on even after the war. Charlene says—and I believe her—that she and Forster weren't really into it. They were bored and just went along for a lark. It was Chavez who was the serious one. He was very persuasive and they went along with him. Though, neither of the other two had any real intentions."

I nodded. "Yeah, but try telling that to the CIA back then. No one would have believed them—they'd have been locked up and the key thrown away."

"Worse, I think, especially for Charlene and Forster,

would have been the fear of their family reactions," Clay surmised. "Their fathers were good, salt-of-the-earth, die-hard American men. They'd given to their country and would die for it. Those kids—as they were then—would have been ostracized completely. Left to hang."

"And even to this day, it would have broken their families' hearts to know such a thing," Jonah added softly. "So it's a secret they've kept all these years."

"Two are dead—but will the other two be charged?" I asked. "One's a murderer and at the least, the other perverted the course of justice."

Frank shook his head. "I can't rightly say. It was a long time ago and Chavez and Ivory—the only two survivors—are old. There'll certainly be an investigation, and things will be revealed, and I hope punishments will be meted out, but I can't predict the ultimate outcome. It's possible they both might pass away before it gets to that stage."

"Well, what I can't understand is how Midge got involved? What did Pippa have against her?" Clay asked.

I had a feeling I knew but I let Midge take the stage. "That was my fault, Mayor. When I first came here, I knew no one. Pippa hadn't been here that long either and she befriended me—as a good pastor's wife should, I suppose."

"And you confided in her?" I suggested.

She nodded. "I told her my story—that I was looking for my long-lost grandparents—or at least information about them. She was supportive and it only seemed fair when I discovered the truth that I told her I'd found my grand-mother, Charlene—after all, Pippa was in a position of trust! I trusted her and I thought she'd be excited for me." She tried to stifle an ironic laugh, rather unsuccessfully. "Unfortunately she didn't know I had yet to tell Charlene who I was. Pippa knew I'd been visiting Charlene and she couldn't take the risk that Charlene had told me something. I was collateral damage to some degree. She was just tying up loose ends. Thankfully she failed."

I bent to squeeze her hand, and when she smiled her thanks, I just knew we had a nice future. Friendships were always a blessing.

Standing again, I said, "There was another clue I missed early on. It was right there in my face but the timing was wrong for me. I'd just learned that Miss Alice had forbidden the town to send her off, and more to the point that she'd made me her heir, and I was in a complete daze. My brain was scrambling to put everything together. But, Hank, do you remember we passed Pippa's car as we drove out of the churchyard?"

He frowned.

"Well, we did, and something I saw made me think of the cakes and cookies I'd baked and hoped Pippa could make use of. During the scuffle four days ago, I remembered what that was. Flour. Pippa was covered in flour dust…"

"What does that mean, darlin'?" Fiona asked.

Jonah was nodding his head. "You didn't see all the mess

from the ransacking of Miss Alice's farmhouse, Mom. Pippa had spilled baking goods all over the place. There was sugar and flour from one end of the lower floor to the other. She did it to cover the fact that she'd been searching—tried to make it look like vandals."

I nodded. "It was the only time she could guarantee I wouldn't turn up at the farmhouse unexpectedly. She knew I'd be tied up at the church during the funeral—so she searched the place then. She was returning just as we were leaving—covered in flour dust." I paused. "Which I can see now is also why she wasn't there to play the organ; why they played taped hymns for Miss Alice."

"Goodness me," Fiona said on a sigh. "Murder, Communist sympathizers, a gambling pastor. Who knew quiet little Airlie Falls could hold so many secrets—especially secrets I didn't know!"

When the laughter from that comment died away, Jonah said, "Speaking of secrets, did we ever find out what Barbara Jones wanted when she phoned Alice?"

That was one question I hadn't been able to get a straight answer to, but I'd made an educated guess. "Money, I think. They're both embarrassed about the fact she called and I think Barbara was going to ask for money. Maybe she felt they were owed."

"Do you think she had blackmail on her mind?" Fiona asked.

"I don't know. It's possible, but I've racked my brain and

I can't think of a reason she'd have to blackmail Miss Alice, but then again I don't think Barbara fully understood the situation. And in fact, none of us knew the truth until these past few days."

Hank buzzed his bed into a more comfortable position. "Well, Rosie, I think we have you to thank for that. The guilty people were getting nervous knowing you were poking your nose in to clear your own name. Pushed them to make mistakes…"

Clay cleared his throat. "Seems a good time to announce that I'm going to talk to council and reopen discussions about John Thatcher's donation and request."

Gratitude filled me. I felt I'd gotten to know these long-ago people; know them and care for them. "You're going to reconsider the park?"

He nodded. "Well, I can only suggest—and of course I will use any persuasive powers I have—but with a whole lot of luck, once they've heard the full story…" His voice trailed, letting us fill in the missing words. After a moment, he began again. "I think they'll all go along. The way I see it, this town owes Jethro Jones for not looking deeply enough into his death—well, his murder. Some respect is long overdue."

Everybody in the room brightened at that news and we were still smiling as we made our way back into the sunshine. There we bumped right into Clive the mailman. "Just the person I was looking for!" he said. He dug in his bag and came out with a registered letter. "I need you to sign for this, ma'am. Looks like it's been all over trying to find you!"

It held the return address of the other lawyer Miss Alice had used and was addressed to my apartment there in Dallas. The empty apartment, since Jess was recuperating with her mom.

That had been crossed out and Fiona's address scribbled across it. It must have taken days for Jess's mom to find it, register it—and send it on.

Thanking him, I signed and tore the envelope open. The first page was a note outlining Miss Alice's wishes for me to receive this letter after she'd passed away. As I turned over to the second page, despite being warned, goose bumps prickled my entire body when I saw Miss Alice's spidery handwriting:

Dear Rosie,

If you're reading this then I have already passed, and I hope you have received my gift to you. I know you well enough to know you'll be uncomfortable with it and feel undeserving, so let me explain.

She went on to outline the story of that fateful day all those years ago as we already knew it. There was nothing new and I was surprised at how well we had pieced it all together. Of course, Miss Alice had no knowledge of the fact that the three witnesses hadn't been present—nor any proof that one of them had indeed murdered Jed, just a strong suspicion.

I read on.

I let this bitterness destroy my life and my sister's life. I didn't want anybody to be happy if I couldn't be happy. It was mean and destructive. It was pointless and that past should be buried. I hope I have finally reconciled myself to the fact that I will never have the answers I seek.

And I am finally at peace.

This is due to you. When you came with your smiles and kindness—perhaps blame it on age—but I suddenly realized what I'd lost and missed.

I know I can be grumpy—a lifetime of that is a hard habit to break. But I enjoyed our talks and discussions about books and mysteries. I loved how we solved a few together.

Our discussions about baking took me back to my own childhood and helping my mother in the kitchen and all the dreams I'd had of making a life with someone and doing just what she was doing but with children of my own.

Your youth and ideals reminded me of myself at times, but mostly of my sister who was so bright and kind and intelligent.

I didn't deserve you in my last days but you are a gift I have treasured and am grateful for.

If God is still listening to me, I pray that you find the love that was denied me, that you make a home in one of these houses, and fill it with the children it was meant to shelter and that your home becomes a place to nurture and grow love and new life. It's time this place came back to life and lived in the present, not the past.

God bless you, Rosie Hart,
With my love and gratitude,
Alice Margaret Auchinschloss.

P.S.—I just had a strange feeling about that archway. It seemed important to mention it. Take care with it.

Tears rolled down my face as I read her words. I'd motioned Jonah close so he could read over my shoulder, and his arms circled me, holding me tight.

"She really just wanted me to have the house and everything. There were no conditions—it was just a loving gift. Pure and simple." Gratitude washed through me. And relief. Amazing, precious, wonderful relief. And acceptance.

She'd given me so much more than a home and money. She'd given me a new life. A place to call home and make my own. A place to build friendships and find love.

But then I frowned. "She didn't let it go, though!" I wailed. "Her resentment! Her determination to make them pay! This letter is dated a month ago. She was reconciled then, so what changed her mind?"

Jonah's voice tickled my ear. "Didn't I hear you say something about her having a bad day when you read that article about John Thatcher's last request being denied?"

The internal lightbulb flashed. "Yes, of course! That day! It must have fired her again, enraged her that he'd been hurt again—and distressed that he'd passed away. The love of her life had died and she wanted them to pay for all that pain they'd caused him in life and that, in her opinion, they were still causing him in death. She couldn't help herself. She had to make one last feeble attempt. I just wish she'd told me!"

"You might have talked her out of it. And she respected you. She was probably afraid she wouldn't be able to go through with it if you disapproved."

More tears flowed. "That poor, poor old lady. All along I'd had trouble comparing the woman I'd known to the one everybody else knew. I have to accept we were both right in a funny way."

"But you're also missing one big point," Jonah added gently. When I remained clueless he grinned. "Honey, she won. In the end, justice came her way, and she instigated the whole thing. If she hadn't sent those letters…"

I glared at him. "She'd be alive!"

His smile was as gentle as his tone. "I give you that. But I've got a feeling she'd find that a small price to pay. Which do you think she'd prefer? Something tells me she's mighty happy with the outcome."

He was probably right. Then I squirmed. "But Jonah! Oh my goodness," I muttered. "The archway… Falling like it did. You don't think… I mean, do you think that day that it was like a…"

"An omen? A sign?"

I shrugged.

He smiled, holding me even tighter. "I'll take whatever I can get. 'Sign' works for me." He looked up. "Thanks, Miss Alice—we'll take that as a blessing."

"I'll second that. Now I think we need refreshments to celebrate. Tacos?" I suggested.

He nodded.

"Good!" I added on a shudder. "I want to celebrate surviving my first and last brush with murder! I'm just glad we'll never have to go through that again!"

Footnote: Little did I know…

The End

Don't miss Rosie's next adventure in *Preserving the Evidence*!

Join Tule Publishing's newsletter for more great reads and weekly deals!

Author's Note and Acknowledgements

Welcome to the first installment of the *Hart of Texas Mystery Series*! And thank you for joining us as Rosie Hart begins her new life and adventures in Airlie Falls. There's much excitement ahead—more murders to solve and puzzles for her to unravel—as well as a lot more recipes and delicious goodies for her to discover and share. Some recipes from this story can be found at the end of this book.

Creating this series has been a joy, and one of my favorite author projects—but along the way I've had some help to get her stories polished to the best of my ability and I'm grateful to many people. I am infinitely humbled and grateful to Tule Publishing for loving Rosie and her world as much as I do. The support I've received from the awesome Jane Porter and her team is breathtakingly amazing. In particular, I want to acknowledge super editor and super author, Kelly Hunter, who was the first to go to bat for Rosie and who continues to lead Rosie's Tule cheer squad. Thank you from the bottom of my heart.

I add my most sincere thanks to Nikki Babri, Meghan Farrell and Lee Hyat for working so hard to get this series to print and making it so polished and pretty—and for making me so welcome in joining the Tule family. Helena Newton, freelance editor—thank you so much for your work and for having my back.

Before Tule, though, there were many people who helped me along the way. Author Michelle Douglas—how do I thank you for your friendship, time and patience in talking through plot problems, gentle bullying when needed and for just always being there? And always with a smile. Author and friend Cathryn Hein? A chance across-the-dinner-table comment led me to this point with Tule and I will always be so grateful. Thank you.

To the awesomely talented, awesomely supportive *Newcastle Romance Writers* writing group—you are the best! I can't forget my wonderful Texan content reader, Kristina Birch—your help and advice is priceless.

I've received so much advice and support during this project and my sincere thanks also go to Monique McDonnell, Annie West, Jaye Ford, Shannon Curtis, Paula Roe and Keri Arthur to name just a few. You all, and everyone else who has helped me along the way, are amazing and I will be eternally grateful for your enthusiasm and guidance.

To you the reader: My aim, as always, is for you to forget about life and its chores for a while, make friends with these characters, and have a little bit of fun playing along with me in discovering 'whodunnit'! I always believe a mystery is a puzzle shared with the reader—and it's why I love reading them as much as I love writing them.

Finally, to my family, my husband Robert, my children and grandchildren. Thank you for your continued love and support. It helps so much to know you're there.

Recipes

Like Rosie, I am a home baker. I love to bake simple foods for my family. Over the years I've collected thousands of recipes, mostly passed down from my mother and grandmothers and aunts—and shared by friends and neighbors. I have lots of scraps of paper and several, well-thumbed, handwritten books where I've kept records of those I've been given, tasted or come across over an adult lifetime. Many have been adjusted over the years to suit new products and family preferences, but certainly while several of these recipes have been tweaked by me or my family members, in no way do I profess them to be unique, nor solely my creations. These are simply much-loved, much-shared family favorites. Just as I guess your own recipes to be. They're the best aren't they? Tried and true!

However, if ever I do share a recipe that can be accredited— I assure you that baker or creator will receive full accreditation.

Cornflake Meringues

6 egg whites

2 cups granulated sugar

5 cups cornflakes

Confectioners' sugar

INSTRUCTIONS

These need to be baked slowly a low temperature. Adjust your own oven to suit.

Generally though:

1. Heat oven to 250°F (125°C).
2. Beat egg whites till stiff and able to stand in peaks alone.
3. Add sugar gradually.
4. Blend in cornflakes with a wooden spoon or spatula.
5. Place teaspoonsful on cookie sheet.
6. Bake one hour.
7. Baked meringues will be pale and crisp to touch.

TO SERVE

Dab a generous spoonful of fresh whipped cream on the top of each meringue and then top with a decoratively sliced fresh strawberry. Other berries could be used if strawberries are not available. The slight tartness of the berries is a perfect balance to the sweet meringue. Dust liberally with confectioner's sugar.

This is such a simple dessert or treat that is not only totally delicious, but so elegant.

Banana Pecan Loaf

2 teaspoons lemon juice

1½ regular or 2 small bananas (ripe and mashed)

4½oz (125g) softened butter

4½oz (125g) brown sugar

2 eggs

1 teaspoon baking soda

¼ cup milk

1+2/3 cups (250g) self-rising flour

Pinch salt

1 cup chopped pecans

INSTRUCTIONS

1. Heat oven 350°F (180°C—Gas 4).
2. Prepare a 3½ x 7½ inch loaf tin (9x19cm). Lining recommended.
3. Add lemon juice to mashed bananas.
4. Beat butter and sugar till creamy (in stand mixer if avail).
5. Add eggs. Beat well.
6. Stir bananas into creamed butter mix.
7. Dissolve baking soda in milk.
8. Sift flour with salt.
9. Fold in half flour.
10. Add half milk.

11. Fold in remaining flour and milk and ensure all are mixed through thoroughly.

12. Fold through chopped pecans.

13. Pour into lined loaf tin. Bake 45 minutes or until ready.

TO SERVE

Frost with either your favorite chocolate frosting for a sweeter cake, or with your favorite lemon frosting for a zestier taste. Both are amazing. Your choice.

Peach and Sour Cream Cake

4½oz (125g) butter

1 cup brown sugar

1 large egg

1 tsp vanilla essence

2½ cups self-rising flour, sifted with a pinch of salt

4 cups peeled peach slices—canned or fresh

1 cup sour cream

¼ cup granulated sugar

½ tsp nutmeg

INSTRUCTIONS

1. Heat oven to 350°F (180°C).
2. Prepare 9in (23cm) round cake pan.
3. Beat butter and brown sugar until creamy.
4. Add egg and mix thoroughly.
5. Add vanilla.
6. Fold in sifted flour.
7. Gently fold in peaches and sour cream.
8. Pour mixture into pan.
9. Blend/mix granulated (white) sugar and nutmeg together.
10. Sprinkle this sugar and spice mix over cake batter.
11. Bake approximately one hour.
12. Stand to cool in pan.

13. Optional—sprinkle with confectioner's sugar.

14. Best served at room temperature.

TO SERVE

Fresh whipped cream can make this cake even more of a celebration!

A lovely German lady, who lived with us for a while when we were children, would make this on special occasions. These days it's more of an everyday dessert—but no less welcome.

Date and Pecan (or Walnut) Tray Bake

(Rosie chose to use pecans—but my favorite? Walnuts! I think they're perfect with the sweet dates. I've been baking this for over twenty years—and it's still a favorite. And SO easy!)

4½oz (125g) butter

4½oz (125g) brown sugar

1 egg—beaten

½ teaspoon vanilla

¾ cup dates

¾ cup chopped walnuts or pecans

1 cup self rising flour

INSTRUCTIONS

1. Heat oven to 350°F (180°C).
2. Gently melt butter and brown sugar until sugar has blended and dissolved.
3. Cool slightly.
4. Add beaten egg.
5. Add vanilla.
6. Fold in dates and walnuts or pecans.
7. Sift flour and fold through, mixing well to ensure all ingredients are well blended.
8. Place in greased 11 x 7in (28 x 18cm) tray pan.
9. Bake 20 minutes till golden brown.
10. Cool before cutting.

Your home will smell absolutely delicious! Enjoy.

Rosie's Favorite Ginger Cake

¼ pint (150ml) milk

1 teaspoon baking soda

4½oz (125g) butter

4½oz (125g) corn (or golden) syrup

4½oz (125g) molasses (treacle)

3½oz (100g) brown sugar

1 tablespoon orange marmalade

10½oz (300g) self-rising flour

1 teaspoon mixed spice

2 tablespoons ground ginger

Pinch salt

2 eggs (beaten)

METHOD

1. Heat oven 325°F (170°C).

2. Prepare an 8in (20cm) round pan.

3. Mix milk and baking soda, heat until *just* warm.

4. Over gentle heat, mix butter, syrup, molasses, brown sugar and marmalade. Stir until combined and sugar dissolved. Do not allow to boil.

5. Blend flour with spice, ginger and salt. Mix well to ensure evenly combined.

6. Stir in butter/marmalade (etc.) mix and stir through well.

7. Add warmed milk mixture and beat until well blended.

8. Mix eggs into the batter.

9. Pour into prepared pan.

10. Bake for one hour. Check with a fine skewer to test baked properly.

11. Cool in pan for 15 minutes before turning onto a cooling rack.

12. Top with zesty lemon frosting.

My beautiful Mom made this every winter before she passed away. It always warmed our tummies and our souls. Such a welcoming offering to share.

If you enjoyed *A Bittersweet Murder*,
you'll love the next books in…

The Hart of Texas Murder Mystery series

Book 1: *A Bittersweet Murder*

Book 2: *Preserving the Evidence*
Coming in May 2022

Book 3: *Candy-Coated Conspiracy*
Coming in July 2022

Book 4: *Murder Below the Mistletoe*
Coming in October 2022

Available now at your favorite online retailer!

About the Author

Award winning YA & children's author, **Kaz Delaney**, and her alter ego, have currently sold 73 titles between them over a 26 year career.

Her books have won many awards, among them the prestigious **Aurealis Award** for best paranormal **and ARRA** (Australian Romance Readers Association) **awards.** Her novel '*Dead, Actually*' **(Allen & Unwin)** was nominated for a Davitt Award, (*Best crime novel, Sisters In Crime*) in the YA section. Dividing her time between teaching and writing, Kaz formerly tutored Creative Writing for CSU's Enrichment Program as well as teaching and creating courses for the Australian College of Journalism.

Having always had a love of cozy mysteries, Kaz is having so much fun writing her **Hart of Texas Murder Mystery Series for TULE Publishing**, that she worries it's not legal!

With their family grown and gone, Kaz lives with her wonderful husband at beautiful Lake Macquarie, Australia, a place she describes as a strip of land between the ocean and lake. Like Rosie, Kaz loves to bake and grow vegetables and unlike Rosie, manages to make a mess of every crochet task she undertakes.

Thank you for reading

A Bittersweet Murder

If you enjoyed this book, you can find more from all our great authors at TulePublishing.com, or from your favorite online retailer.

TULE
PUBLISHING

CPSIA information can be obtained
at www.ICGtesting.com
Printed in the USA
LVHW100954281022
731812LV00007B/105